Tides of Danger

Tides of Danger

Elizabeth Baldwin Hazelton

CHARLES SCRIBNER'S SONS   NEW YORK

FOR

J. A. J.

CHAPTER ONE

The fierce flames rising from the sugar furnaces cast their red glow onto the wall of the great water
tank, tinting Trin Delgado's white shirt and pants a pale
pink as he climbed the steps to the top. He dropped to his
hands and knees and crept up slowly, hoping that the sentry who stood guard in the watchtower wouldn't spot him
and open fire.

He knew the guards were edgy. All of Mexico was ha-
rassed by robbers, and only last week there had been a
skirmish at the gate of the hacienda between the soldiers
and a roving band of fifty thieves. The soldiers had killed
four of them and driven the others off, but three of their
own number had been wounded, one of them critically.
Now they were in a mood to shoot first and question after-
wards. It was no time to be moving in forbidden areas.

Trin reached the top of the rock wall, flattened his body
out on it and lay motionless. The figure of the sentry, silhouetted against the night sky, seemed to be facing toward
him, as if the man might have glimpsed the white cambric
of his clothes, in motion, and be straining his eyes for a better view.

Trin waited, his heart pounding, until at length the sentry turned away and walked to the opposite side of the
tower. Then he rose to his feet quickly, and ran along the

wall in the darkness. Beneath him, on one side, the reservoir dropped a sheer thirty feet to the ground below; on the other side, the black water, lighted only by the leaping tongues of flame from the sugar chimneys, was nearly five fathoms deep. Guided by the distant firelight, Trin followed the curve of the wall until he reached the far side of the tank, where a clump of great trees cast a welcome patch of shadow.

The sentry was turning back now, but Trin was safe, hidden by the dark shape of spreading branches. He stood a moment, catching his breath after the perilous run, and looked out over the cane-fields of the Hacienda del Cinco Ríos—the Hacienda of the Five Rivers—where the headwaters of five streams rose in the high mountains on the eastern rim of the million-acre farm. But only one of the rivers, cascading down to the shelf-land of Sinaloa on its way to the sea, remained within the boundaries of the estate, and the tank had been built more than one hundred years ago to guarantee ample water for the cane-fields in periods of drought.

Old Tio, in the saddle shop where Trin worked, had told him it was one of the greatest tanks in all of Mexico. Tio was proud because his great grandfather had been one of the peons who worked a full year to build it. Tio's family had worked on the hacienda for generations, and there were hundreds of others like him, whose families had worked the vast acreage of Cinco Ríos for more years than any of them could remember.

But Trinidad Delgado was not one of them. He and his mother and brothers and sisters had been here only five years. They were bound peons now, but before that, when his father had been alive, they had been free, and Trin was determined that somehow they would be free again.

It was because of that free life, when he had lived on the shore of the Bay of Turtles, on the Sea of Cortez, that he was drawn so irresistibly to the water tank. He and his older brother, Cesar, had learned to swim almost before they could walk. By the time he was nine, Trin could dive in two fathoms of water and stay under a full minute to search for pearl oysters. But Trin's father had died that year, and his mother had come to work for Don Gregorio Velazquez, owner of the hacienda, in order to support her children. So the diving had ended.

Trin was fourteen now, and he dreamed of returning someday to the Sea of Cortez. It would take a miracle to get him there, he knew, but sometimes miracles happened. That was why he came to the tank whenever he could, in spite of the danger.

He slipped out of his clothes and let his sturdy, well-muscled body down into the water without a splash. The first cold shock took his breath away, but he pressed the soles of his feet against the stone wall and thrust down steeply under the flame-lit surface. Growing on the bottom were long feathery grasses, some of them tall as young trees, and gliding through the darkness he felt their leafy tips brush along his limbs.

He kicked his way back up to the air and struck out across the tank in long, easy strokes. The water rippled against his skin like cool satin, and he wished his brother Cesar were with him to share the delicious sensation. In the beginning, they had come for these secret swims together, and Cesar had shared in the danger and excitement of the adventure. They had practiced diving down to the tops of the tall grasses, and talked of returning someday to the Sea of Cortez to dive for pearls.

But Cesar was sixteen now, and he considered such talk

stupid. They could never go back, he said; it was impossible. He no longer shared his thoughts with Trin. Instead, he spent all of his free time with Gonzalo Mendez, who was seventeen, and worked with them in the saddle shop.

Trin reached the far side of the reservoir and rested a moment. Perhaps Cesar was right, he thought. Maybe it *was* stupid to practice for something that could never happen. Perhaps when he was sixteen he, too, might be ready to give up the dream—but not yet.

He thrust down into the depths again, determined to go deeper than ever before. Swimming toward the bottom through the pitch-black water, he felt the weight of it press down on him like a giant hand. For the first time, his body moved in among the grasses, and they curled around him like slimy, clinging fingers. He kicked hard to push on through them, but their thick growth took away his momentum, and he was enveloped in a slithering, swaying forest. His ears ached and he swallowed to relieve the pain, but the pressure was cramping his chest, and he felt as if he were smothering in the bottom of a black pit. He kicked again, frantically, and fought his way up in a steep rise.

As he surfaced, gasping, he caught a sound that might have been a man's voice. Had the guard seen him after all and come in search of him? He held his breath and listened, but with water in his ears and his head throbbing, he couldn't be sure of what he heard. There *was* a sound, he was certain of that, but now it was not a voice, it was something else—footsteps, perhaps, on the stone wall? He sucked in air, silently, and then jackknifed under and swam for the patch of shadow.

He came up under the dark pattern of branches and saw two men silhouetted against the sky, running along the wall toward him. His white pants and shirt lay on top of the wall a few feet away, but there was no time to scramble up and grab them. He could only fill his lungs and duck under again.

If he swam out into the firelit reservoir, the guards could pick him off the moment he surfaced, like a sitting duck—if they were guards. Some fleeting impression of the running figures nagged at his mind. From below, outlined against the sky, they had looked tall, but lean, thin. That was it. They hadn't looked as solid as the soldiers, and he couldn't remember seeing anything on their heads.

If they were not guards, who were they? Could it be his brother, Cesar, and Gonzalo Mendez? Gonzalo had once lived at Mazatlan, he was one of the few peons on the hacienda who could handle himself well in the deep tank. On a night as oppressively hot as this, anyone who could swim expertly would want to come to the reservoir—if he dared. And Cesar and Gonzalo would dare. Gonzalo was bold. He would dare almost anything. Someday, thought Trin, he would dare too much, and it would kill him.

Whoever the men were, Trin could not go longer without air. His lungs were throbbing. He clung to the stone wall and let his head break water. The tiny ripple sound went undetected under the bigger sound of Gonzalo's voice.

"*Caramba!*" he was saying. "What are you—a yellow coyote?"

"It's not yellow to want to stay alive!" Cesar's voice was tight with anger. "The money won't do us any good if we're dead!"

"Who's going to be dead?" scoffed Gonzalo. "It will be no more dangerous than coming here!"

"You're loco!" declared Cesar. "We'll be right under the noses of the guards."

Trin recognized the voices, but the conversation was so obviously secret that he didn't dare make himself known. Fortunately they didn't seem to have noticed his clothes.

"They won't be watching us," said Gonzalo. "They're looking for thieves from the *outside*." He chuckled in amusement. "Last week, fifty thieves on the outside got nothing but bullets. But *we*, on the *inside*—what we get will make us rich for life!"

"It could happen that *we* will get nothing but bullets, too," said Cesar.

"Nombre de a Santo!" said Gonzalo angrily. " 'It could happen' you will be a bound peon forever, because you have the heart of a chicken. If you don't want to do it, there are plenty of others who will. Diego Garcia would give his right arm for the chance."

There was a pause. "Well," demanded Gonzalo, "are you with me or not?"

Clinging to the stone wall, his head barely above water, Trin waited, trying to still his breathing in the silence.

"I'm with you!" said Cesar finally.

"Bueno!" said Gonzalo. "You will not be sorry, amigo! Soon we will be living like ricos in the capital city!"

"May you be right," said Cesar.

They were slipping out of their clothes now. If only they would dive in, perhaps he could get away without being discovered.

Suddenly Gonzalo's voice was knife-sharp. "What's this?" he demanded.

Trin guessed that Gonzalo had spotted his pants and shirt, lying on the wall. Now they would know he was here. He pushed under, then jackknifed and swam down and away. Perhaps he could convince them that he'd been on the other side of the tank. He swam hard and fast, trying to get as far away from them as possible. They'd be standing on the wall, now, watching for him to break water—or if they'd heard him go under, they might be right behind him. There'd been no time to suck in an extra supply of air, and he couldn't hold out much longer. The water roared in his ears, and he pushed on in a fast crawl, until at last he had to go up.

As he gasped in air, he heard Gonzalo shout right behind him, and then he was seized and pushed back under. Water filled his mouth and nose, and he fought his way up, choking. As he broke through, Gonzalo hissed in his ear, "You dirty spy!" Strong hands dug into his shoulders and pushed him down into the blackness again.

Trin fought frantically, clawing at the body that held him under, but the hands moved from his shoulders to his throat, and he couldn't break free. The fingers pressed in, choking him, and he went limp.

Suddenly he was seized and pulled up to the air. "Madre de Dios!" exclaimed Cesar. "You're drowning him!"

"Dead lips tell no tales," said Gonzalo grimly, his fingers still on Trin's throat.

"Let him go! He's my brother!"

Gonzalo's fingers loosened, and Cesar, treading water, supported Trin as he sucked in air in sobbing gasps.

"Son of a pig!" said Gonzalo furiously. "I'll teach you to spy on me!"

"Don't touch him!" commanded Cesar sharply. "He wasn't spying—he was swimming." And still cradling Trin in his left arm, he kicked out strongly and stroked with his right, heading for the wall of the tank.

"He was *spying*," muttered Gonzalo, following them.

At the wall, his brother released him, and Trin clung to the rough surface of a rock, still weak from Gonzalo's throttling attack.

"He was right here, listening," declared Gonzalo insistently. "I saw the ripple of the water when he went under. He heard every word we said."

"Is it true?" demanded Cesar. "Did you hear?"

"I couldn't help it!" explained Trin, between gasps. "I thought you were guards. I swam for the shadows, and when I came up, you were talking." He paused to take a deep breath. "By the time I could speak, it was too late. I'd already heard—too much."

"If you tell one word of what you heard," said Gonzalo, "I swear by all the saints, I'll cut out your tongue and feed it to the vultures!"

"He's my brother. He won't tell!" Cesar promised.

"Take an oath!" demanded Gonzalo.

"Take it," Cesar ordered. "Or Gonzalo will keep his."

Trin hesitated. If he were to betray them, there was no doubt that Gonzalo meant to cut out his tongue—or his heart. Yet if he didn't tell, there would be no way to stop them. And if he didn't stop them, his brother might be killed.

"I won't tell if you promise not to go in with Gonzalo," Trin bargained earnestly. "Let him do it alone, whatever it is. Don't go in with him!"

"You see?" said Gonzalo triumphantly. "Now he tries to make deals. You should have let me drown him!"

"There'll be no deals!" declared his brother.

"But you said yourself—you may get shot!"

"That's the worst that could happen. If I want to take the risk, that's my business."

"And to stop you is *my* business!" declared Trin desperately. "You're my brother. I want you alive!"

"I'll *be* alive. You can count on it," promised Cesar.

"Not if you steal! It's *wrong* to steal, Cesar, and sooner or later they'll catch you."

"You don't tell me what's right or wrong!" snapped Cesar angrily. "I decide that. To be a bound peon is wrong! If we succeed—"

"We'll not succeed," Gonzalo cut in bitterly. "Not with this Judas to betray us."

"He'll not betray us. Take an oath, Trin," Cesar commanded, "or I swear I'll cut out your tongue myself."

Trin had never had reason to fear Cesar, but he knew that he couldn't betray his own brother.

"Say it!" ordered Gonzalo. "En el nombre de Dios—"

"I'll say it," said Trin, looking at Cesar, "but only because *you* ask it."

"Bueno!" said his brother. "Then begin!"

"En el nombre de Dios," Trin began slowly, "I swear that I will never tell what I heard."

He had taken an oath, in the name of God, and now—no matter what happened—he could never break it.

CHAPTER TWO

The Hacienda del Cinco Ríos had belonged to the Velazquez family since the days of the Spanish Conquest, and the great house, together with its outbuildings, was constructed like a medieval fortress. The thick stone walls were cornered by watchtowers, and the massive gates of heavy, studded planks were guarded by soldiers.

Outside the fortification the huts of the peon workers and their families clustered together in a small village, with its own plaza and church. Most of the peons lived there, but Trin, Cesar, and Gonzalo, whose mothers were servants in the home of the owner, lived inside the walls and were permitted to pass freely between the house and the village.

The three boys had crept down the stairs of the reservoir and slipped past the stables and corrals without incident, but as they approached the fortress, they were startled by a shout from the sentry in the watchtower above them.

"Stop!" he yelled, aiming his musket at them. "Guards! Seize them!"

As the guards from the gate rushed forward, Trin stood in stunned silence. Had the sentry spotted them in the tank, or were Cesar and Gonzalo already guilty of some theft?

"Wait a minute!" Gonzalo blustered. "He must be loco! We've done nothing!"

"Don't try to lie!" yelled the man in the tower. "From my post I see everything. I saw what you did!"

So he had seen them in the tank! Now they were in for it!

"Then you saw somebody else!" declared Gonzalo boldly.

"Silencio!" ordered the guard who was holding him. "What have they done?"

"That boy in the middle," said the sentry, indicating Trin, "he has the look of guilt. Ask him! He knows I've caught him in the act!"

Trin didn't doubt that he had a look of guilt. Swimming in the reservoir had long been forbidden because of the numerous drownings in the past. Now that he had been caught, he could expect to be severely punished.

A burly soldier with huge, powerful hands spun him around and pinned his arms behind him in an iron grip. "Confess!" he commanded, "or these two hands will break you in half!"

"Let the sentry tell what he knows," said Trin stubbornly.

"Bueno!" said the sentry. "What I know is—these three are thieves!"

"Thieves!" shouted Gonzalo. "You lie!"

"I speak the truth!" insisted the sentry. "I have seen you working at it, in the plaza."

"What have they stolen?" asked one of the guards.

"Mi compañeros," said the sentry, "these sly robbers have stolen the hearts of the three prettiest *muchachas* in the village!"

For an instant the boys stood in confused silence, while

the guards laughed uproariously at their own joke. Gonzalo was the first to recover.

"*Three* muchachas!" He swaggered. "*Hombre*, you sleep at your post! I, myself, cannot count on the fingers of both hands the number of hearts I have stolen!"

"*Caramba!* You are already mucho hombre!" The sentry grinned. "But the other two—they admit nothing!"

"But equal guilt is written on their faces," said the brawny guard who still had hold of Trin. "If they have not stolen hearts, then they have done something else. Better throw them in jail, till we find out what."

"*Vamanos!*" yelled Gonzalo, "before they think up any more jokes!"

"*Sí!*" Cesar responded. "In another minute, they'll be hanging us! Come on, Trin—vamos!"

As the big guard loosened his hold, he ran his hand over Trin's mop of unruly black hair, feeling its wetness. "Better say you stuck your head in the fountain, *chico!*" he advised, with a knowing wink.

The soldiers chuckled good-naturedly as the boys ran through the gate and into the shadows of the deep archway. Trin realized that they had known all along about the swim. Perhaps they had meant their little joke to serve, also, as a warning. Cesar and Gonzalo were laughing nervously, now that it was over, but Trin couldn't join in. Remembering the conversation in the tank, he was too aware that the scene might soon be played out in earnest, with no laughter at the end of it.

The inner courtyard was a great square, enclosed by the buildings of the hacienda. On one side was the *trapiche*— the sugar works; on the other, the storehouse, offices, and workshops of the farm. At the end opposite the gate was the house, with its many spacious, high-ceilinged rooms, and adjoining it, the small, dark quarters of the servants. Ancient oaks, acacias and elms, planted when the hacienda was new, spread their immense branches over the courtyard, and in the center a fountain sparkled in the glow from the chimneys of the sugar furnaces that burned around the clock. The air was fragrant with the smell of sugar syrup as the boys hurried past the boilers to avoid the blast of heat that poured out of the open door.

Their usual objective was the main kitchen of the house, where Gonzalo's mother was employed as one of a dozen cooks, each with her own specialty. Frequently, when the women were still working at the after-dinner chores, there were scraps for hungry lads, but tonight they were too late. The big room was dark and the food locked away.

The boys moved on to the servants' quarters under the portal, where each family was allotted one room with a floor of hard-packed earth and a small barred window. They stopped at the open door of the Delgado room. The flame of a single candle, burning before a tiny wooden figure of the Blessed Virgin, provided the only light, but even in the dimness Trin could see at once that something was wrong.

Ordinarily, at this hour, the smaller children were asleep on their sheepskin pallets, but now they were huddled around his mother, as she sat on the floor holding his eleven-year-old sister, Taresa, within the circle of her arms. As he knelt beside them, he saw that Bonita, who was six, and little Pancho, who was barely five, had been crying. Their enormous black eyes stared up at him from tear-stained faces. Juan, who was eight, was trying hard to be brave, but nine-year-old Soledad was as tearful as her younger brother and sister.

"What is it?" Trin whispered. "What's happened to Taresa? Is she hurt?"

"Only in her heart," his mother answered softly.

But Taresa had heard him, and as she turned, he saw that her fair skin was flushed from weeping. "Oh Trin," she cried, "they're going to sell me!"

"Sell you!" Trin's eyes searched his mother's thin, worn face, and she nodded in confirmation.

"How can they do that?" he demanded angrily. "We're not horses—or cattle! We don't *belong* to them!"

"We are in their debt," said his mother.

"But we are not slaves!" Trin declared. "A debt can be *paid!*"

"How can it be paid, when it grows bigger each month?" There was a touch of bitterness in his mother's tired voice.

Trin knew she was right. There was no way to pay the debt. Señora Delgado earned one peso a month for her services, plus their room and a few scraps of food from the kitchen, but it had never been enough to clothe and feed a family of eight. Each month she had had to borrow from Don Gregorio to meet their needs. For five years the debt had mounted until now it was beyond anything that she could earn. Like all the other peons on the hacienda, they were bound in service to the patron by an ever-increasing debt they couldn't hope to pay.

"Who wants to buy you?" asked Cesar, who, with Gonzalo, had joined the circle.

"Don Fernando," said Taresa tearfully. "He wants me for maid and companion to his granddaughter."

"Don Fernando!" exclaimed Gonzalo. "That old rico could buy the whole of Cinco Ríos with the gold from his mines!"

It was true. Don Fernando was even richer than Don Gregorio. But the money he offered would not be important. He was an old friend of the Velazquez family. He and his granddaughter had been visiting the Hacienda del Cinco Ríos for the past month, and Taresa had been serving as the young señorita's maid during their stay. If Don Fernando wanted to take Taresa home with him, Don Gregorio would not refuse. She would be sent away as a favor to his friend.

"Taresa will have a good life," said Señora Delgado comfortingly. "She will see the great city of Mexico."

"But I don't want to go!" Taresa's dark eyes traveled around the little circle of beloved faces. "I want to stay here, with my family!"

There was nothing Trin could do but join with his mother in building happy fantasies of the exciting life Taresa would live on the rich hacienda and the happy reunions they would all have when she returned with her young mistress for visits to Cinco Ríos.

Comforted, the younger children fell asleep on their pallets on the floor, and Trin's mother went back to the big house for her late-evening duties as the personal servant of the old patrona, Doña Leona, the mother of Don Gregorio. Cesar and Gonzalo were outside, in the shadows under the portal, and Taresa took her chance to speak to Trin alone.

"Trin," she whispered, "please help me! If Don Fernando takes me away to his hacienda, I know I'll never see any of you again."

Trin wanted to protest, but he couldn't lie to his sister. The young señorita had never before come to Cinco Ríos, and would probably never return. He felt the same heartache as Taresa at the thought of their being parted for the rest of their lives. But a stronger feeling was taking hold of him—a great anger that Don Gregorio had a right to separate a family, to treat them like slaves. What Cesar had said was true: it was *wrong* to be a bound peon!

:15

Taresa's voice broke through his thoughts. "If I run away," she was saying, "will you go with me?"

"You can't do that!" Trin insisted.

"But if I was with *you*—"

"I couldn't protect you from hunger and cold. We might die of thirst in the desert, or be attacked by lions and jaguars in the mountains. I could never let you take the risk."

"But I *want* to!" she pleaded.

"No, little sister," said Trin gently. "We wouldn't have a chance. You'd be worn out before we got beyond the borders of Cinco Ríos. The soldiers would catch us—or the police. They'd bring us back, and we'd be in worse trouble than we are now."

Taresa's eyes filled with tears of desperation. "Oh, Trin, what can I do?"

"I'll make a bargain with you, hermanita. If you go without tears, I'll find a way to bring you back."

"How can you?"

"It may take me a while—even a year or two—but you can count on me. I'll bring you back and we'll all be together." Anger made him strong and sure. "Not here—not as bound peons—but home, on the Sea of Cortez—and *free*."

The desperation went out of Taresa's eyes, and her lovely little face was bright with hope. "Oh, Trin, I'll pray for you every day!" She turned and knelt before the tiny figure of the Virgin, and Trin took his place beside her.

"Holy mother," he prayed silently. "Help me to keep my promise."

Cesar and Gonzalo were still sitting under the portal, and Trin could see that they were whispering together. He knew he wouldn't be welcome, but he wanted to talk to his brother. As he approached, the whispering stopped.

"Is there no escape from you?" said Gonzalo, staring up at Trin insolently. "Must you pursue us everywhere?"

Seeing anger flash across Trin's face, Cesar spoke up quickly, before their antagonism could erupt into a fight. "What do you want, Trin?"

"I have a plan," said Trin, "but I'll need you to go in with me."

"Cesar has plans of his own," said Gonzalo.

"You don't speak for my brother," said Trin sharply. "He has a mind of his own."

"So I have," said Cesar, "and it's made up. I'm going in with Gonzalo. No other plan is any good."

"But it won't help Taresa or Mama," said Trin. "Stolen money won't pay our debt. Don Gregorio would know at once that it was stolen, and throw you in jail. You'd end up before the firing squad."

"I don't expect to pay my debt," said Cesar. "What I do, I do for *myself*!"

"Bravo, amigo." said Gonzalo, rising. "Now you talk sense."

Cesar rose with him. "Remember, Trin," he said, "you took an oath. You're my brother. I trust you to keep it."

"And *I* took an oath!" said Gonzalo, with sinister emphasis. "Remember *that*! If your tongue wags, the vultures will eat it."

Trin watched as they slipped away into the shadows, where they could whisper, undisturbed. He had no intention of breaking his oath. He would never repeat to anyone the conversation he had heard in the water tank. He would have to find some other way to prevent Cesar and Gonzalo from carrying out their plans. He had a double reason, now, for trying to stop them: not only did he want to save his brother from the grave dangers involved in committing a theft but he needed Cesar's help for the plans that were beginning to shape in his own mind.

As he faced the problem, one thing was immediately clear: if he was to stop them, he had to know first *what* he was trying to stop. His thoughts went back to the incident in the reservoir. Cesar had given him a clue. "We'll be right under the noses of the guards," he had said. That meant they intended to steal something inside the fortification.

His eyes traveled around the big square of the courtyard. The trapiche? No, the sugar works were out. There would be nothing there to steal. However, their target might be in any one of the buildings on the opposite side. He considered the storehouse. It was full of goods that could be exchanged for money, but in order to steal enough to be worth the risk, Cesar and Gonzalo would have to cart away a sizeable load. "Under the noses of the guards" that would be impossible. He eliminated the storehouse.

The office of the hacienda? Perhaps. Each pay day a huge pile of coppers was brought out of the office and placed on a massive table in the courtyard, where it was doled out to the peons as they passed by, in single file. Those coppers must come from a safe. But even if they could break into the safe, somehow Trin doubted that it was coppers Cesar and his friend were after. Gonzalo, at least, would be likely to have his sights set on bigger game.

There *was* something bigger, right in the shop where the three boys worked: the silver and gold for ornamenting the saddles. Trin's mind turned back to a conversation in the shop, earlier in the day. Cesar and Gonzalo had been cutting the rawhide into strips, and he had been painstakingly braiding them into a reata, under old Tio's supervision. It was old Tio who had discovered that Trin had good hands. Before that, he had been working far back in the hills, as a shepherd boy. But when the sheep were brought in for shearing, Trin had gone to the leather shop to get his torn huaraches repaired. There he had met the white-haired old man whose gentle face was marred by an ugly scar. Old Tio had noticed his long, lean fingers, and the flexible strength of his hands. He had immediately asked the patron to let the boy work in the shop, as his apprentice.

Trin thought the old man must be the finest craftsman in Mexico, but of all the handsome saddles he had made in his lifetime, the one he was making now for Don Gregorio was the most magnificent. And certainly it was the most valuable, since its mountings were of pure gold.

Thinking back, Trin remembered Gonzalo's loud boasting as he watched old Tio cut an intricate design in the fine leather.

"Some day Gonzalo Mendez will ride down the Viga in the capital city on just such a saddle!"

"Then you will have to be a millionaire, mi amigo," Tio had said, "or a robber chief. This saddle, when it is finished, will be worth ten thousand pesos."

"What I'll be is for you to guess!" Gonzalo had said, strutting around the shop. "But I promise you, I shall have it. And stirrups of silver, and a diamond in the handle of my whip."

At the time Trin had thought nothing of Gonzalo's big talk; everyone knew he was a braggart. But now he wondered. Had Cesar and Gonzalo figured out some way to get this very saddle past the guards? Were they planning, somehow, to ride away on one of the patron's own thoroughbreds? Or did they intend to cut off the gold mountings?

Trin saw his mother coming through the gate from the inner patio of the big house and knew that it must be after midnight. Her last duty each evening was to take the old patrona, Doña Leona, to the private chapel for her nightly prayers. After that, Doña Leona went to bed, and Señora Delgado was free to return to her own quarters.

Watching the guard close the gate after his mother had passed through, Trin realized that the gold and silver in the saddle shop was nothing compared to the treasure inside the gate: the jewels of the Velazquez family. Somewhere in the rooms of the great house were the diamonds and pearls, the emeralds and rubies of the patrón and his ladies—his wife, his mother, and his grown daughters. In imagination, he moved from room to room, and suddenly something clicked in his mind.

He had the answer: he knew exactly what Cesar and Gonzalo were planning to steal.

CHAPTER THREE

The house of Don Gregorio had thirty-seven rooms. Trin had seen a few of them, at one time or another, when he had assisted with special chores in preparation for some important occasion. He had been amazed at the high ceilings and the great sense of space within the walls. It seemed to him that *ten* rooms like the one he and his family shared could be placed inside any one of them.

For the first time, he had seen floors of painted brick, covered with thick carpets, and massive, hand-carved furniture made of imported woods. He knew that somewhere behind locked doors, in an ornately carved teakwood cabinet, there was a complete dinner service of solid gold. Such a thing was almost beyond Trin's imagining, but his mother had seen it. And somewhere else in the house—perhaps in one of the huge bedrooms, in a secret place within the four-foot-thick walls—there was a strongbox where the jewels of the master and his ladies were kept hidden.

But in another room there was a great treasure of jewels *not* hidden—a glittering display that Trin himself had seen. These were the jewels of the Madonna, in the private chapel of the Velazquez family.

Few peons on the hacienda had ever been permitted to

enter the chapel, but Trin had seen it only a month ago, when he had helped his mother to prepare for the arrival of the bishop. The experience was as sharply etched in his memory as if it had occurred this very morning. He had been carrying a great porcelain vase full of flowers for the altar, and his mother had swung open the chapel door for him to enter. There before his eyes had been a scene so opulent that it had taken his breath away: the richly gilded altar, lighted by a blaze of candles, the walls covered with draperies of crimson velvet, the paintings of saints and virgins, the deep red carpet, and the altar cloth embroidered in gold and encrusted with emeralds.

But most dazzling of all had been the hand-carved figure of the Blessed Virgin, dressed in a robe of shining blue satin and wearing a diadem of diamonds and pearls. Hundreds of smaller pearls were sewn onto her dress, several large diamond brooches adorned the front of it, and around her neck she wore a rich chain of gold from which was suspended a single great pearl. It was a lustrous pink, shaped like a pear, and Trin thought it must be the largest pearl in the world.

His mother had told him the history of the jewels: how each one had been given to the Virgin by a member of the Velazquez family in gratitude for a prayer that had been answered. The brilliant array of diamonds and pearls represented the answered prayers of many generations of Velazquezes. But most interesting to Trin was the dramatic story of the great pear-shaped pearl, because it had been given to the Virgin by the old patrona, Doña Leona, fifty-three years ago, when Don Gregorio was a baby.

Then, as now, the country to the north of the Hacienda del Cinco Ríos was Yaqui Indian country, and on the terrible day commemorated by the gift of the pearl a large raiding party attacked the fortification. Doña Leona's husband was away at the port of Mazatlan, to the south, and the young wife and her baby son were alone with the servants. The fierce Yaquis greatly outnumbered the defenders, and the Indians broke down the gate and poured into the courtyard.

With every escape cut off, and the blood-curdling yells of the savages ringing through the big house, young Doña Leona prayed to the Blessed Virgin for help. Suddenly, as though the idea had come to her from a divine source, the young wife thought of the secret vault in the thick adobe wall, built to contain jewels and other valuables. The space was small—perhaps too small to hold even a very slim young woman and her baby—but it was her only hope. With the help of Tio, the saddle-maker, who was then a lad of sixteen, she took down the huge oil painting that covered the camouflaged opening to the vault, and slid back the panel. The vault was empty, save for a large jewel case, which she lifted out.

Handing the baby to Tio, she crawled through the small aperture. By kneeling and bending her head forward in a posture of prayer, she had barely enough space left in which to hold her little son. But when Tio handed the baby to her, he began to cry. It was then that Doña Leona had the second inspiration: she asked Tio to open the jewel case and hand her the great pearl. Swiftly, he obeyed, and the young mother put the pearl, hanging on its chain of gold, into the tiny hand of her son. Fascinated, the baby stopped crying, and Tio closed the panel that covered the opening and replaced the painting. Then he ran back to join the defenders of the fortress.

Moments later the Indians ransacked the room in which mother and child were hidden and carried away the case full of jewels. Before the desperate battle was over and the Indians driven off, many of the defenders were killed, and several of the servant girls were taken away as captive slaves. But Doña Leona and the little Don Gregorio were safe. In gratitude, the young mother slipped the gold chain with its lustrous pendant over the head of the sacred figure in the chapel, and in all the years since then, the Virgin had worn the great pearl.

Listening as his mother related the story, it was hard for Trin to realize that the frail, white-haired old lady he knew as Doña Leona was the terrified young mother who had hidden in the vault, and Don Gregorio, the master of the hacienda, was the infant, but Tio's part in the drama was very real. The ugly scar he bore on his cheek was cut that dreadful day by the slashing knife of a Yaqui.

Señora Delgado had warned Trin not to speak of what he had seen in the chapel, and he had confided in only one person—his brother, Cesar. Cesar had sworn he would tell no one, but now Trin was sure he had broken his promise. Thinking back, he remembered that Cesar had asked him many questions about the structure of the chapel, the figure of the Madonna and her jewels, and the hours when Doña Leona went there to pray. Now he understood why. Now all the pieces fitted together, and he had the answer: *Cesar and Gonzalo were planning to rob the Virgin!*

Trin shuddered at the thought. Surely such a deed would bring terrible misfortune to the doer. He would rather that Cesar and his friend were planning to rob the Velazquez vault, or steal the dishes of gold, or the ten-thousand-pesos saddle—*anything* but the jewels of the sacred statue.

More than ever, Trin knew that he must try to prevent the crime. But to do so he would have to anticipate their plans. In his mind, he visualized the chapel. If he, himself, were planning to commit the theft, how would he go about it?

The chapel had two doors. The front door, through which the family entered, opened onto the inner patio of the house—a beautiful garden of rare trees and flowers. But it was under the constant scrutiny of guards on duty day and night at the inner gate.

The second door was at the back of the chapel, behind the altar. It opened onto the great courtyard, near the room of Gonzalo Mendez and his family. Rarely used, it was kept bolted and barred on the inside with a heavy iron rod. Cesar and Gonzalo might hope to make their getaway through the back, but they could enter only through the front door.

How could they hope to reach it, unobserved? Certainly no guard would admit them through the gate to the inner patio unless they had some specific duty to perform, as he had had, in assisting his mother.

Some specific duty! The thought gave him a clue. Soon there would be *another* occasion for special preparation of the chapel: the bishop, who had stopped at Cinco Ríos on his journey north to Alamos, would be returning. Again, he would stay at the hacienda to rest from his trip—and again he would be conducting masses for the family in the private chapel. Trin had a strong feeling that this time Cesar and Gonzalo intended to make sure that it was one of them, and not he, who assisted in the preparations.

He could prevent that, right now, by speaking to his mother. He rose from the shadows and went into their room. The single candle was still burning before the small carved figure in the niche in the wall. By its light he could see that his brothers and sisters were still sleeping, but his mother, kneeling in prayer, was fingering her rosary.

Suddenly he knew that *he* must pray for help—but not before this tiny representation of the Blessed Virgin. He must pray in the chapel, before the beautiful life-size figure, robed in blue satin and crowned with diamonds and pearls. It was she who seemed most real, most able to answer his prayers.

His mother crossed herself and rose from her knees.

"Mamacita," he whispered, "when you prepare the chapel for the return of the bishop, I must be the one to go with you, so that I may kneel before the Virgin and ask her help."

"You may be the one," she promised.

"Then don't forget: no one else is to go—just me!"

Señora Delgado smiled. "I think no one else will be eager for the job," she said.

When his mother had fallen asleep, he moved to the door and sat just inside it. Across the courtyard he could see the dim shapes of his brother and Gonzalo, still huddled together in the shadows. When at length they rose and headed for their separate rooms, Trin hurried to his pallet and stretched out with his eyes closed. His brother came in and lay down on the sheepskin beside him. Trin stirred, as if his coming had roused him.

"Cesar," he whispered, "I wanted to tell you—I know what you said is true. It *is* wrong to be a bound peon, and it's *right* for us to find a way to be free."

"I'm glad you agree," said Cesar. "You find your way, and I'll find mine." He turned his back on Trin and settled down to sleep.

"No, wait!" Trin protested. "Your way, with Gonzalo, is bad! It will bring the vengeance of God down on your head!"

Cesar turned back to him sharply. "Why do you say that?"

"To steal from—" Trin stopped himself, abruptly. He had been about to say "from the Virgin." He couldn't afford to let his brother know that he had guessed their intent.

Cesar's eyes bored into him. "To steal from—whom?" he demanded suspiciously.

"From Don Gregorio—is wicked," said Trin, covering up. "There's a better way! If you'll help me, we can—"

"I told you, I don't want to talk about it," Cesar cut in coldly. "Go to sleep!"

"But Cesar, listen—"

"Go to sleep!" his brother commanded, in a voice deliberately loud.

Their mother woke, startled. "What is it?" she asked, in alarm.

"Nothing, Mama," said Cesar. "Trin was having a nightmare."

If only it *were* just a nightmare, thought Trin. But it was all too real, and Cesar's startled reaction had betrayed him. Trin was sure, now, that he had guessed right, but nonetheless he resolved to stay awake and keep watch over his brother. After the long day's work in the saddle shop, it wasn't easy. His eyelids were as heavy as silver pesos, and he caught himself dropping off into little catnaps, from which he jerked awake. But he kept the vigil till morning.

The next day he shadowed Cesar and Gonzalo constantly, but they made no move toward the chapel. That night a horseman from a hacienda to the north brought word that the bishop would return the following evening.

Tomorrow, then, would be the day when the chapel would be made ready for the mass. Trin knew it would also be the day when Cesar or Gonzalo would try to get inside, to slide back the bolt and remove the iron bar from the back door. If they could accomplish that without being discovered, then they could return in the night to steal the jewels.

Tomorrow, he would see to it that they never reached the chapel. If they as much as got to the door, he would create a commotion that would attract the attention of every guard on duty. He would start a brawl that would land them all in jail, and the chapel door would remain barred.

That was his plan, but Fate intervened. The crucial day proved also to be the time of departure for his sister, Taresa, who was to start the long journey south with Don Fernando and his daughter. The party was to leave at daybreak, with Don Gregorio and his sons riding part way with their guests.

Taresa's little family had gathered at dawn to bid her farewell when, to their amazement, a groom arrived with a horse for Trin. To make their parting easier, Doña Leona had ordered that he be allowed to ride along with the hosts and return with them.

Trin longed to protest, but what excuse could he give that would not incriminate his brother? Besides, Taresa was overjoyed, and to disappoint her would have been cruel. He had no choice. He was trapped. There was not even a moment to whisper a reminder to his mother—or a warning. He could only hope that he would return before dark.

As he rode off, he thought he saw a gleam of triumph in the eyes of his brother.

CHAPTER FOUR

At another time, the ride south would have been an exciting adventure, but on this day it could be nothing but an ordeal. Trin's nerves were taut with strain, and his thoughts were centered on the house of Don Gregorio and what would happen there in his absence.

The sun rose over the blue mountain peaks to the east, and he knew that already Cesar might be in the chapel with his mother. In her innocence, she would allow him to explore it freely, and while she was preoccupied with her duties, he would slip behind the altar and silently unbar the back door. After Señora Delgado and her son left, no one would have reason to go back there, and his deed would be undetected. The bishop would not arrive until late evening, and he would be weary from his journey. Mass would not be said until the next morning. There would be nothing to prevent Cesar and Gonzalo from sneaking in through the back door, after dark, to steal the jewels.

Trin's muscles tensed at the thought. If only he could get back in time to stop them!

Don Gregorio and his sons would ride only to the south-west boundary of Cinco Ríos; then they would turn back, and Don Fernando and his party would go on alone. But the road, which was no more than a wagon track, rose and fell interminably, climbing over ridges to drop into shaded canyons and then rise again to another summit. The sun reached mid-heaven and slanted down toward the distant Sea of Cortez, and still they had not reached the boundary. The miles seemed endless.

At long last, the great boulder that marked the corner of Don Gregorio's holdings loomed up ahead of them. As they reined their horses to a halt, Trin saw that his sister's eyes had filled with tears.

"Taresa," he whispered, "we made a bargain. If you go without tears, I'll come to get you!"

"Oh Trin, how can you?" she asked doubtfully.

"Remember what Papa taught us," he whispered. " 'Querer es poder'—to will is to be able. I *will* to come, and I'll find a way."

The others were saying good-bye, now.

"I can't hold back the tears," said Taresa, sobbing softly.

"Never mind," said Trin, "I'll come in spite of them. Adiós, hermanita! Go with God!"

When Don Fernando and his party had disappeared from view, Don Gregorio and his sons turned their horses to the north. Trin followed them, grateful to be homeward bound, but the hacienda was many hours away, and it was obvious now that they could not reach it before dark.

His mind raced with thoughts of his brother and the jewels. There was little doubt that Cesar and Gonzalo could enter the back door of the chapel, unchallenged, during the night. The glow from the sugar fires didn't penetrate the deep shadows under the portal at that point. With the door unbarred, the boys would be able to reach the Virgin and strip her of her jewels.

But what of their getaway? The theft would be discovered at daybreak and every inch of the fortification searched. They would have to make their escape under cover of night. It was in that escape that their danger lay. With guards on duty at gates and towers, any move they made would be at risk of their lives, and it was his brother's life, not the jewels, that was Trin's concern.

A chill wind cut through his thoughts. The sun was dipping into the distant sea, and a black mass of clouds was gathering over the mountains to the east. The men spurred their horses into a gallop, aware that the first heavy rain of the season could send flash floods roaring down the canyons. Both men and horses could be swept to their deaths in the raging torrents.

The wind drove the clouds seaward till the sky over their heads was black with them. Night fell, and they descended into the canyons in total darkness, grateful to climb out safely before the storm struck. The hacienda was still miles away when there was a flash of lightning, and a great peal of thunder seemed to split the sky. The clouds opened and let their torrents pour down onto the earth, and Trin feared that the men would rein in their horses and take shelter in the lee of a ridge, but they plunged on, heedless of the rain.

At length, a vivid flash revealed the fortress, less than a mile away. As they drew closer, they could see the glow of the sugar fires, nearly blotted out by the storm.

Don Gregorio shouted a command, and the sentries swung wide the gates to let the horsemen enter. The grooms received their exhausted mounts, and Trin raced across the courtyard to the room where he lived. His brothers and sisters were still asleep, but Cesar was not among them. His mother had already been wakened by the thunder.

"Mama, where's Cesar?" asked Trin breathlessly.

:31

"He and Gonzalo went to the village," she told him, without concern. "They planned to stay overnight with their friends."

Were they really in the village? Trin wondered. Or was the visit a ruse to explain their absence to their families? Had they, in fact, already returned while everyone was asleep and slipped into the chapel?

"Who helped you in the chapel while I was gone?" he asked. "Was it Cesar?"

"Yes, but do not worry," his mother said, brightly. "I have spoken to Doña Leona, and as a special favor you will be permitted to go to the chapel tomorrow."

"Mama," Trin went on abruptly, hardly taking in Doña Leona's kindness, "did Cesar *volunteer* to help?"

She nodded, smiling. "He seemed very eager. He said you had told him about the Virgin, and he was anxious to see for himself."

So it *had* worked out just as he had forseen! He couldn't ask any more questions without making her suspicious, but it was obvious that there had been no trouble yet. He could learn no more until his mother had gone back to sleep.

While he changed into dry clothes, he answered her questions about the day's journey, and when she had settled back onto her pallet, he slipped into his serape and went out under the portal. The glow of the sugar fires was so dimmed by the downpour that it was impossible to see. Flattening himself against the wall, he waited for a flash of lightning. When it zigzagged across the sky, he saw that the door to the chapel was closed, and there was no one near it. He wondered if, in the same swift instant of light, the sentries at gates and towers might have seen him. He remained motionless against the wall, waiting, but there was no sound except the splashing of the rain on the cobblestoned courtyard.

The only way he could find out whether the chapel door had been unbarred was to try it. With the gray curtain of rain to shield him from the guards, Trin ran across the courtyard. There was another flash, and he shrank against the wall, ten feet from the chapel door, while the thunder rumbled. Again he waited, listening for the sound of footsteps or voices over the chattering water, but he heard nothing. Apparently the brown of his serape had blended into the brown of the adobe wall, and he had escaped notice.

He edged along the wall until he reached the chapel door, and stretched his hand out for the knob. If the lightning betrayed him now, he could be shot for a thief, but he had to risk it. The pounding of his heart seemed to fill his throat as his hand touched the knob and turned it, slowly. He pushed inward, and the door opened. He saw the faint glimmer of light from the votive candles, and in that instant a woman's scream shrilled above the rain.

Trin stood paralyzed with shock. The guard at the patio gate barked a command, and the sentries at the towers shouted back. He could hear running footsteps and voices coming toward him. Someone pulled the bell rope, and the warning bell clanged. In a moment he would be surrounded.

The woman screamed again, and Trin made a running leap for the giant oak tree nearest him. As he swung up onto the lowest branch, two figures darted out of the chapel, and somewhere in the darkness a shot was fired. Frantically Trin pulled himself up to a higher branch and lay prone upon it. As he strained to see the courtyard below him, a split-second flash of lightning streaked overhead, revealing the two fugitives as they fled toward the ladder that led onto the roof. There was a volley of shots and a sharp cry of pain.

In the confusion that followed, the sentries ran, firing, toward the cry. A man ran out of the servants' quarters carrying a torch, and Trin saw one of the thieves stumble and fall forward. He lay motionless, face down in a pool of water. In his outstretched hand, he held the jewelled diadem of the Blessed Virgin.

The storm quenched the torch, blacking out the scene before Trin could identify the fallen man. Was the dead thief his brother or Gonzalo? The limp figure lying in the rain could have been either of them. Trin felt sick, and a strange weakness came over him. He had to cling to the tree to keep from falling. Beneath him, people were milling about in the courtyard, screaming and shouting. The voice of a sentry rose above the din.

"There's another one somewhere! Don't let him get away!"

An answering voice yelled, "He was heading for the ladder! Block it off and search the roof."

Suddenly Trin realized the danger of his own position. Soon there would be lanterns everywhere, and if he was spotted in the tree, he would certainly be mistaken for a thief. How could he possibly prove that he was not in on the plot?

He stood up on the limb and reached for the branch above him. He was dizzy with the sickness, and his hands shook, but he grasped it and managed to swing himself up. He was high enough now to be above the level of the roof, but the branch arched up parallel to the building, and he knew there would be an open space across which he must jump. He felt his way out and up toward the end of the limb. The roof was off to his left, but how far? In a matter of moments there would be lights in the courtyard to reveal it, but they would also betray him as he jumped. He stared fixedly through the rain, trying to discern the line of the building, and gradually it took shape—a dim outline, some six or eight feet away. To far for him to spring straight out from his cramped position on the branch.

He let himself down till he was hanging by his hands, facing the roof, and felt the limb sag slightly under his weight. Then he swung his body out and back, as from a trapeze. If he failed to get enough momentum to reach the roof, he would crash down into the courtyard to break his neck—or be seized by the guards. He swung again, higher, and the third time, with a mighty push, flung himself out into space.

He sailed through the darkness and felt the edge of the roof under his feet. He teetered on the brink, fighting for balance, and then fell forward. As he lay on the rooftop, gasping for breath, a streak of lightning flared above him, and in that fraction of a second he glimpsed a lean figure disappearing over the far edge of the fortification. One of the fugitives had made it to reach and cross the roof—but which one?

Trin got to his feet and ran after him, but the shadowy figure was already lost to sight in the downpour. He let himself down over the edge and dropped to the ground. Behind him he heard the guards shouting and knew that they had reached the roof. There was no time to consider where to go. He simply ran with all his strength away from the fortress. Somewhere in the storm, someone else was running for his life.

"Holy Mother," Trin prayed, "let it be Cesar!"

CHAPTER FIVE

For the first hour, Trin ran like a hunted animal, his total energies concentrated on the enormous physical effort of flight. Without conscious thought, he headed instinctively for the protection of the foothills, climbing the rugged, rain-swept slope toward a mesa where he had once tended sheep. With the threat of armed men behind him, he plunged on through the darkness, stumbling and falling over outcroppings of rock only to rise and fight his way on up the winding trail.

At length he stopped, gasping and exhausted, in the shelter of a boulder. The storm had abated somewhat, and far below he could see the red glow of the sugar fires. He had heard no further sound of shooting. Apparently the guards had not glimpsed him or the other fugitive through the leaden curtain of rain. He could make out the tiny flame dots of searchers' lanterns moving around the stables and through the village. Every nook and cranny inside the fortress and every peon hut would be thoroughly searched. Don Gregorio would offer a reward for the capture of the thief, dead or alive, and the nearly one thousand poverty-ridden peons on the hacienda would press the hunt relentlessly, in hopes of winning the money. Beginning at daybreak, men on horses, mules and burros would scour the countryside.

How could a fugitive hope to escape their net? The only chance would be to keep ahead of them, all the way up into the high mountains. Perhaps there, in the great legendary barrancas known only to the Indians, he might be safe from Don Gregorio's men—but there were jaguars and bears, lions and wolves in the mountains, and the menace of the Indians themselves. And Trin was unarmed.

His thoughts went to the other fugitive. Had that lean figure who ran across the roof ahead of him been his brother or Gonzalo Mendez? And where was he now? Had he, too, fled to the hills? Was he armed?

No man on foot could keep running endlessly, without rest. He would have to take cover somewhere. There were several caves in the foothills, but they were known to every shepherd on the hacienda. On a night like this, the shepherds themselves might well have taken refuge in them.

Trin started climbing again. It wasn't safe to rest more than a moment. There could be a soldier following him up this very trail. As he stumbled on in the darkness, he searched his memory for a possible hiding place. During his years as a shepherd boy, he had come to know these hills intimately. He knew the caves, the out-jutting ledges of rock, the stands of trees in the canyons that offered protection for man and beast. But this knowledge he shared in common with all the others who had ever tended flocks on Cinco Ríos. If only there were a place known to him, alone.

Perhaps there was. He recalled a crevice between two huge boulders that had once saved his life. He had been climbing down the side of a precipitous ridge, after a heavy rainfall, when he had heard the rumble of a landslide behind him. There had been no time to run from it, so he had flung himself face down in the crevice between the great rocks. Falling stones and clumps of hard earth had lodged in the small opening at the top of the crevice, sealing it off, and he had been safe inside, as the slide roared over him.

When the earth had finally settled, he had found himself in a narrow triangular-shaped cave, with only a chink of daylight showing at one end. With his bare hands, he had dug a hole and wriggled out through it. He had returned to the scene only once since then, on a hike with his brother, Cesar.

Suddenly the cave had new meaning. *Cesar* knew about it. If he were the other fugitive, perhaps he would remember the secret cave, and Trin would find him there. He hurried up the trail with a fresh spurt of energy.

Reaching the mesa, he crossed it and started climbing again. The trail grew steeper, and the tempo of the storm increased. Trin shivered as the chill wind penetrated his wet clothes, but he was grateful for the rain that beat down on him, obliterating his footprints. There would be no tracks for the searchers to follow in the morning.

He topped a ridge and knew by the rocky conformation of its spine that his secret cave was some two hundred feet below him. The landslide had wiped out the trail, and he felt his way cautiously down the steep, muddy descent. At the entrance to the cave, he stopped, fearful of what might lie concealed within its black recess. He was quite sure that no shepherd had taken refuge there—the sheep were on the lower levels at this time of year—but what of the mountain cats? Even the lions and jaguars could easily wriggle through the small passage on their bellies.

While he hesitated, the rain hammered down on him, and his fatigued body shook with cold. Sheer physical misery forced him to take the gamble.

He inched his way through the opening, every sense alert, but no luminous cat eyes met his, no animal scent assailed his nostrils. He pulled his body into the shelter of the cavity and crouched, tense and ready—but nothing happened. There was only total darkness and the sound of the rain outside.

He crawled to the far end of the cave and took off his wet serape. As he leaned back against a mound of earth, his hand encountered the rough texture of hemp. Exploring further, he discovered that it was the end of a rope—a rope buried under the mound. *Someone had been in the cave.*

He dug into the mound and unearthed a cache of supplies, including blankets, hunting knives, and a store of tortillas and frijoles. In the darkness there was no way of identifying any of it, but Trin was sure the stuff belonged to Cesar and Gonzalo. That meant that one of them would be coming to the cave tonight. It was clear now that Gonzalo, too, knew of the hiding place. If he should be the one to come, Trin might have to fight for his life.

He fumbled in the earth for a gun, but found none. Peons were not allowed to own guns, and if Gonzalo had managed to steal one, he probably would have had it on him. He selected a knife, and buried the other. Then he wrapped a dry blanket around his chilled body and ate one tortilla. He was ravenously hungry, but he didn't dare to eat more. If the man who came should be Cesar, they would need the food for their long flight. He made a pillow of the second blanket and leaned back, knife in hand, waiting.

The rain had stopped, and the first gray light of daybreak had begun to show through the entrance to the cave when suddenly it was blocked out by a figure. Trin rose to a crouching position, his muscles tense. The intruder's body filled the small opening, and it was impossible to determine his identity. As he pressed into the cave, he groaned in pain, and for the first time Trin realized that he might be wounded.

"Santa Madre, help me!" he cried, in a sobbing gasp, as

he struggled to pull himself through the passage. With a final wrench, he drew his body into the shelter and collapsed, face down, on the dry earth.

Trin knelt beside the prostrate figure and saw at once that it was his brother. He touched him, and the wounded boy jerked free and tried to grapple with him.

"Cesar—it's me—Trin!"

His brother stopped struggling and stared at him in amazement. "What are you doing here?" he exclaimed.

"I followed you over the roof." There would be a better time, later, for a full explanation.

Cesar sank back with a sigh of relief.

"You're hurt," said Trin. "Let me get that wet serape off you."

"Go easy. I caught a musket ball in my shoulder."

Trin drew the serape off gently and saw the big, dark stain on Cesar's white shirt. Sometime during his flight he had torn off a piece of the white cotton and packed it into the wound but the blood had seeped through. Trin ripped off his own shirt and tore it into long strips.

As he pulled the bloodstained cloth away from the wound, he felt a metal chain around his brother's neck and, following it with his fingers, found the great pendant pearl of the Madonna. Cesar reached up and snatched it away from him.

"Don't touch it!" he gasped, as sharp pain shot through his body from the sudden movement. "I'm warning you. Don't ever try to take it!" He clenched his fist around the pearl and lay back.

"I don't want it," said Trin. "I only want to bandage your wound."

He felt the blood oozing from the bullet hole and pressed the fresh strips of cotton into it. When he had done all he could to tie the packing firmly in place, he spread a blanket on the ground and carefully lifted his brother onto it. Then he wrapped it snugly around his chilled body.

Cesar lay still, his eyes closed. After a few moments, he said, "They got Gonzalo."

"I know," said Trin softly.

"Everything was with us—the bishop's coming, the storm . . . They'd never have seen us, in that downpour—"

"What happened?"

"The old woman came back!"

"What old woman?" asked Trin.

"Doña Leona. Because of her, Gonzalo's dead."

"She must have come back to pray," Trin murmured, thinking aloud.

"She'd already done her praying," said Cesar bitterly. "We waited until after she'd gone to bed. Who'd ever think she'd get up and come back to the chapel in the middle of the night?"

"Probably the thunder woke her, or perhaps . . ." Trin's voice trailed off. Perhaps she'd had a vision, he thought. Perhaps the Blessed Virgin had appeared to her in a dream, to warn her of the robbery. His mother had told him that the old patrona sometimes had prophetic dreams.

"We'd have made it, if it hadn't been for her. All we needed was one more minute, and then she walked in! It was her scream that killed Gonzalo—and gave me this hole in my shoulder!" Cesar exploded angrily. "But I've got her pearl, and she'll never get it back! I'll see to that, if I have to throw it in the river!"

Trin was silent. It was useless to point out what his brother already knew: that Gonzalo had brought on his death, and Cesar his wound, by their own deed. In his grief and frustration, he had to rage against someone, and Doña Leona had been the accidental instrument of their defeat. Cesar had wanted to be free, and if he had chosen the wrong way, it was because he had no faith in any other. It was too late now, to go back.

"Why don't you say it?" asked Cesar, bitterly.

"Say what?"

"That we got what we deserved."

"I wasn't thinking that," said Trin.

"Why not? You tried to stop me. If I'd listened, Gonzalo would be alive, now."

"No," declared Trin firmly. "He'd have gone ahead anyway, with Diego—or somebody else. He didn't really care so much about being free. What he wanted was to be *rich*."

"I wanted that, too, and now I've got it!" Cesar laughed—a hard, mirthless laugh. "A fortune, right here in my hand, if I can stay alive to collect it." He sat up suddenly, painfully. "I've got to get out of here!"

"Now? In daylight?" said Trin, in amazement. "They'll be swarming all over these hills in a couple of hours."

"Verdad! And my footprints are deep in that muddy slope outside, with no rain to wash them away! They'll lead the soldiers right to this cave. My only chance is to keep ahead of them."

"Where will you go?"

"Over the mountains—to Durango."

"Are you loco?" demanded Trin. "You can't get over the mountains with that ball in your shoulder!"

"I can try. If I stay here—termino! They'll shoot me on sight, or drag me down to stand in front of a firing squad. Don Gregorio has no mercy for thieves—least of all for the thief of his mother's pearl."

He pushed the blanket aside and rose, swaying, to his

feet. "I see you found the cache. Roll the stuff up for me, will you, and put it on my back."

"I'll carry it."

"You mean—you'd go *with* me?"

"Do you think I'd let you go alone?" Trin demanded, almost angrily. "You'd better eat something." He handed Cesar the tortillas and knelt down to gather up the equipment that had been buried under the mound.

"I don't want you mixed up in this, chico," said Cesar, gently. "If you go back now, you can tell them you were out searching for me. But if you go on, they'll think you were in on the theft."

"I'm not going back!" declared Trin.

"Then go wherever you want to go—but go *alone*. Don't come with me. I'll only get you in trouble."

"Eat your tortilla," ordered Trin, rolling the things up in a blanket. "There's no time for arguing."

"I mean it, Trin," insisted Cesar. "If they catch you with me, they'll shoot you down for a thief!"

"Then we'd better not let them catch us," said Trin. "Come on—vamanos!"

The trail grew more rocky and precipitous as they climbed higher. The wind dispersed the clouds and the sun blazed down on them with fierce intensity. Cesar would have dropped fainting, on the trail, but Trin drew him on, half carrying him up the rough slopes. Wherever possible, they walked in the rain-made streams and over sharp outcroppings of rock to avoid leaving tracks. Neither of them had ever been this high up in the mountains before, and the thousands of acres of rugged canyons and ridges were completely unknown to them.

As they climbed, they kept a sharp lookout for the

searchers they knew would be scouring the hills below. For the first hours, they saw no one, but by midday the soldiers came into their view, riding along the shoulder of a ridge far beneath them. After that they no longer dared follow the open trail, but cut through the underbrush until they reached a high tableland where pines, oaks, and fir trees offered cover.

Completely spent, Cesar dropped onto the thick grass under the shade of a great pine. They had lost sight of the searchers, in a deep canyon below, and as they lay resting on the cool grass, there was a sudden sound of hooves behind them. Starting up in horror, they saw a herd of deer coming across the open glade, with a large buck in the lead. Spotting the boys, the buck swerved and led the herd down an arroyo and out of sight.

The moment of shock had unnerved the brothers, and after eating sparingly, they moved on. Cesar was exhausted from the long exertion and the loss of blood, and the going was agonizingly slow. At length, they succeeded in crossing the tableland and started up the slopes beyond.

When night fell, they saw the campfire of the searchers in the glade where the deer had crossed and realized that they were gaining on them dangerously. But even in the face of that threat, Trin knew that his brother could not go on without rest. Cesar's body was burning with fever, and his legs were too weak to support him. There had been no water for some hours, and his thirst was acute, but they were forced to make a dry camp.

Trin found a knoll covered with oaks, from which he could watch the fire of the soldiers on the tableland below, and he stood guard while Cesar slept. As the night deepened and the moon rose, he heard a weird cry from the mountain slopes beyond. Cesar stirred in his sleep and mumbled incoherently. When the sound rang out again, it was much closer.

"What's that?" cried Cesar, startled out of his fevered dreams.

"Wolves," said Trin grimly.

Befuddled by sickness and exhaustion, Cesar sank back into his blanket. "Make a fire," he murmured.

"I can't. It would betray us to the searchers."

The third time Trin heard the eerie wolf cry, it was alarmingly near, and he knew he would have to act quickly, before the beasts caught the blood scent of Cesar's wound. Without guns or a campfire, there would be no way to hold them off.

"Wake up!" he said, prodding his brother gently. "The wolves are closing in on us. The only place we'll be safe is up in a tree."

"I won't be able to climb," murmured Cesar foggily.

"I'll get you up, but you've got to help me."

Throwing a blanket over his shoulder, Trin climbed the tallest of the oaks. With a section of rope he fashioned a hammock out of the blanket and swung it between two branches a good twenty feet above the ground. Then he returned to Cesar and tied another section of rope around his waist. He was knotting it firmly when Cesar spoke in a hoarse whisper.

"Look! Out there!"

Trin peered beyond the circle of shadow cast by the branches of the great oak and saw the ghostly forms of the wolf pack moving stealthily toward them up the moon-washed slope. Swiftly he swung up into the tree and flipped the loose end of the rope over one of the branches on which the hammock was fastened, catching it as it dropped down on the other side. Returning to the ground, he tied the rope securely to the trunk. Then, grasping the slack of it in both hands, he used it as a pulley, pitting his own weight and strength against the heavier weight of his brother. With the hemp taut between them, he braced his feet against the solid oak. "Now—start climbing!" he commanded.

Clinging to the rough trunk, Cesar tried to pull his body up as Trin swung himself to the ground in a mighty heave, but the excruciating pain in his shoulder made him cry out in agony, and he slid back to the ground. Once more they tried, and again the pain was unendurable.

Trin scanned the slope. His brother's sharp cry had sent the wolves scuttling back into the shadows, but he could make out their gray shapes, like phantoms, skulking just beyond the stretch of moonlight. Momentarily, their instinctive dread of man would hold them back, but he knew that hunger and the blood lust would soon overcome their fear. When they moved in for the kill, a man could be torn to shreds in a matter of seconds.

He had to get Cesar up beyond their reach, immediately. But how? It was obvious that his brother couldn't bear the pain of lifting himself. If only he could climb with his feet.

"That's it!" said Trin, aloud. "Cesar, can you wrap your arms around the rope and put your feet flat against the tree trunk?"

"I'll try," said Cesar, maneuvering himself into position, while Trin pulled him slightly above the ground.

"Then you're going to *walk* up the tree," declared Trin. "Lean your head and shoulders back as far as you can and press your feet hard against the trunk while I pull. You ready?"

"Sí."

"Bueno! Vamos—pronto!"

With Trin pulling the rope till the veins stood out in his temples, Cesar began his strange horizontal walk. Step after slow step, he moved painfully up the great oak. Twice his feet slipped and he dangled precariously in space, but Trin clung to the rope with desperate hands, anchoring himself by gripping the base of the tree with his legs.

When at last Cesar reached the level of the makeshift hammock, Trin climbed up beside him and eased him into it. Silently the wolves began to close in, slinking across the patch of moonwash and into the circle of tree shadow. Already they had scented the wounded boy, and recognized his weakness. Their fierce eyes burned up at him, phosphorescent green in the darkness, as they prowled and lunged beneath his hammock, their bared fangs and menacing snarls asserting their deadly intent.

From the tableland below, the eerie howls of their brothers were punctuated by gun fire, indicating that the searchers were busy defending their camp from another wolf pack.

Straddling a branch, Trin fitted himself against the trunk of the oak and looped a rope around the tree and his own waist, to avoid falling, in case he dropped off to sleep. For the next few hours he and Cesar were comparatively safe. Out of reach of the wolves, they were, in fact, protected *by* them from the menace of the big mountain cats. No lion or jaguar would be tempted to break through the circle of angry beasts.

But what of tomorrow? There was no longer any chance that they could keep ahead of their pursuers. Cesar was near collapse. Even with the help of a night's rest, he would not be able to go much farther. The fever had parched his body, and he was tortured by thirst. In his troubled sleep, he cried out for "Agua!" Water was his most desperate need—water, and a hiding place. And on this knoll, there was neither.

Trin leaned his head against the tree trunk and closed his eyes. His body was spent with the ordeal of flight, and his throat was sore with dryness. Yet his brother's life depended on his strength—his ability to get him to a place of refuge, before the soldiers could overtake them. To meet that challenge, he needed sleep. Drugged by exhaustion, he drifted off, only vaguely aware of the wolves beneath him.

All night they persisted, howling and pacing, leaping with snapping jaws toward Cesar and then falling back in snarling frustration. But at the first suggestion of light, they slunk away, and their gaunt, ragged forms melted into the color of the mountains.

Already awake, Trin roused his brother, and using the rope again, carefully let him down to the ground. Once more they resumed their difficult trek up the slopes. The wooded knoll gave way to cliffs of sheer rock, and supporting Cesar, Trin fought his way up the trail. Only the knowledge that death rode not far behind them in the muskets of the soldiers kept him going.

Rounding a turn, they came onto a wide mesa covered with grass. From somewhere beyond, they heard the wonderful sound of water. Buoyed up with hope, they crossed the level land and came suddenly to the brink of a barranca—a great gorge that dropped down abruptly in a series of almost perpendicular cliffs to a narrow river bed, thousands of feet below.

The sound of water came from a rushing torrent that plunged down the canyon, racing in foaming rapids around huge boulders and dropping from ledge to ledge in roaring waterfalls. At its nearest point, the river flowed more than fifteen-hundred feet below the brink, down a sheer wall of rock.

Trin knew that to Cesar the sight and sound was pure torture. He had to have water to survive. Yet there was no going back—and no going forward. The mountain was cut in half by the gorge, and the lifesaving water was beyond reach.

CHAPTER SIX

The great barrancas, cutting their deep gashes through the high mountain country, were Indian strongholds. Though Trin had never seen such a barranca as this one, he had heard many strange stories about them. He knew that the sunlight, striking the stone cliffs, made the walls of the canyon so hot that in the depths there was perpetual summer. The heat turned the rains into steam, and tropical plants and birds flourished in the humid atmosphere on the bottom of the gorge.

It was to these mountains and barrancas that the hostile Indians returned after their murderous raids on the haciendas. The beat of their tom-toms and their night chants had been heard, rising from the canyon floors, but no Mexican who had dared to venture into their sanctuaries had ever come out alive. Trin had no desire to penetrate the depths of this barranca. The mere thought sent a shiver of fear down his spine. But he knew that the Indians somehow traveled from the brink to the river thousands of feet below, and that meant there were trails.

Time was short. By now the soldiers could not be far behind. Trin ran along the rim, searching frantically for a means of descent. Following the gorge as it swung in a westward curve, he discovered a path that twisted down the cliff, a wall of stone on one side, and on the other, the abyss. But when he led his brother onto the trail, Cesar swayed dizzily and turned back.

"I can't do it!" he said, shuddering. "My head is swimming, and my legs are like water. I'll go over the edge."

"I know how sick you are," said Trin compassionately, "but we have to go down. I'll put the rope around your waist and tie you to me."

"Then we'd both go over. No, chico, you go alone. Let me stay here."

"With the soldiers right behind us? Are you loco?"

"Let's stop fooling ourselves," said Cesar. "Whether it happens up here—or down there—I'm going to die."

"The fever's got you out of your head!" Trin protested. "There's water down there, and a good chance of finding cover."

"My throat aches for the water, but it won't save me. The death is here—in my shoulder." Cesar's hand shook as he touched the bandage. Underneath, the wound was black and ugly.

"I'll cut it out!" Trin insisted. "As soon as we find a safe place to hide, I'll dig out the musket ball."

"Whether the ball is in or out won't make any difference," said Cesar. "The poison is not in one place. Believe me, little brother, I know. Deep in my body, I know!"

"I don't care what you 'know'," said Trin, almost weeping with desperation. "You can't quit! I won't let you!"

"Please, chico—face the truth! Even if I could last a little longer, you know I can't make it to Durango."

"Who cares about Durango? We can go *home*—to Turtle Bay. I've been thinking about it all the way up the trail. We'll go to Fortino Chavarria. He's our godfather. He'll help us!"

"It's a good thought, but for *you*, not me."

"For us *both*! Somewhere down in the barranca there'll be a place to hide. I'll cut out the musket ball, and you can rest till your fever goes and the wound heals. All we need is to get *down* there! Come on, Cesar," Trin pleaded, "give yourself a chance!"

He started to tie the rope around his brother's waist, but Cesar pushed him away.

"No. I told you—no rope! I'd only pull you down."

"Then come without it—but *come*!" Trin pleaded. "If you face the cliff—if you cling to it and never look down —we'll make it!"

"Bueno. I'll try," said Cesar, "but if I fall, don't grieve, chico. It will only be that death came more quickly."

"You won't fall," said Trin firmly.

The brothers moved down the steep, narrow descent side by side. Dizzy and strengthless, Cesar swayed dangerously, and Trin placed his arm around his back to steady him. Neither of them looked down at the river, more than a thousand feet below. The trail seemed interminably long, and when they came to a sharp turn, Cesar glimpsed the chasm inches from his feet and fell to his knees, sick with vertigo.

"Don't look down!" Trin commanded, holding him firmly by the arm. "Stay where you are, and don't move!"

"I can't make it!" Cesar moaned. "Let go of me, Trin. Let me go over!"

"*I'm not letting go*! If you go over, you take me with you!" said Trin, with grim determination. "We'll rest here awhile."

When they had rested briefly, they went on down the trail, following one perilous switchback after another until at last they came out on a narrow, boulder-strewn shore.

Cesar sank to his knees at the river's edge and dipped his burning face in the water. Trin waited to scan the rim of the barranca, and seeing no one, flung himself down beside his brother. Together, they sucked in great mouthfuls of water, stopping only to splash it in cool, refreshing handfuls over their heads.

When Trin had quenched his thirst, he studied the terrain around him. Beyond the pool where they drank, the river foamed over a ledge to drop in a roaring waterfall to a pool far below, but upstream, above a stretch of boiling rapids, it flowed smooth and deep between its great walls. It was there, where the gorge dropped some fifteen-hundred feet from rim to river, that Trin hoped to find a hiding place. Standing on the brink, he had glimpsed what appeared to be occasional indentations and recesses in the wall of the opposite cliff, at water level. A similar recess at the foot of the cliff on which he had stood would be completely hidden from the rim. If he could find such a place, it might be the perfect answer to their need. But before he could make a search, he had to find temporary cover for Cesar.

He scanned the banks on both sides of the pool. None of the boulders were large enough to guarantee adequate protection from the sharp eyes of soldiers standing on the brink, but behind him, a low shelf of rock jutted out from the side of the gorge. A man could lie in the shadow beneath it and be unseen from above.

Cesar was still beside the pool, gulping the icy water as if he couldn't get enough.

"Don't drink so much all at once," Trin warned him. "It will only make you more sick." He drew him back from the river's edge and helped him to his feet. "I've got a hunch there'll be a hiding place upriver. I'm going to cut through the rapids and swim along the base of the cliff. There's good cover for you right here, while I'm gone."

He helped Cesar to the out-jutting rock and eased him down under it. "If you lie flat against the wall, you can't be seen from the rim. Stay here till I get back, and don't move. I'll hurry."

He started toward the rapids, but his brother called him back. "Before you go, Trin—just one thing: while you're upriver, if you should see the soldiers on the rim or coming down the trail, *stay there!* Don't come back."

"They *won't* come down if you stay out of sight. Chances are they won't even see that path. The approach was solid rock, and we left no tracks."

"But *if* they should," Cesar insisted weakly, "remember —don't come back for me. It wouldn't do any good. You couldn't save me. They'd only get you, too."

"*You* remember—*lie low!*" said Trin. "If I find a place, I'll get you to it."

He scanned the rim again. There was no sign, yet, of Don Gregorio's men. Sticking close to the wall of the gorge, he ran along the narrow stretch of shore until it gave way to the widening rapids. Slipping the pack from his back, he crammed it into a crevice between two rocks. Then still hugging the cliff, he plunged thigh-deep into the raging waters. The stones beneath his feet were slippery, and the strong current pulled at his body, threatening to sweep him from his uncertain foothold and carry him over the falls, but he fought his way upstream toward a ledge of rock that reached across the river to form a natural dam. Behind it, the river flowed smoothly, cliff to cliff. He pulled himself up over the ledge and slipped into the deeper water. Checking the rim, he saw no one.

He struck out upriver, swimming along the base of the

cliff. Just as he had anticipated, there were occasional indentations where the current had eaten into the rock wall, but the water swirled in to fill them. What he needed was a deep recess where the river had deposited enough silt from the mountains to create a solid embankment above the water level.

He found it some two hundred yards upstream—a cavern that cut back into the cliff, with a narrow bank of silt on which they could camp. Here they would be hidden from every vantage point except the river itself.

Stopping only a moment to rest, Trin started downstream. What he needed now was time—time to reach Cesar, time to get him back to the cavern before Don Gregorio's men could reach the barranca.

Swimming with the current, he covered the distance to the dam quickly and came up under the shelter of a shrub that clung to the cliff at water's edge. Separating the foliage slightly, he peered up at the rim. Two horsemen stood on the brink, scanning the river and its banks. Their coming had been inescapable, yet the sight of them sent Trin's heart into a wild hammering.

The men dismounted and examined the ground carefully, then mounting again, rode slowly along the rim toward the west. Had he failed to erase some track? Trin wondered, or was it just chance that led them toward the path he and Cesar had taken? Scarcely breathing, he watched as they inspected every foot of the rocky approach, then, stopping just short of the trail, wheeled and turned back to pursue their search in the opposite direction.

Trin let himself breathe. The moment of greatest danger seemed past. It was obvious that they had found no tracks, and there would be none, where they were now riding. With Cesar hidden and no clue to lead them to the trail, perhaps they would conclude that their quarry, stopped by the barranca, had doubled back and slipped past them somewhere on the mountain.

The men disappeared to the east, and Trin longed to cut through the rapids to join his brother, but it was too soon to risk exposure. He waited nervously, his eyes on the rim, and after a brief interval the soldiers reappeared. They were riding close to the brink now, studying every detail of the river and its boulder-strewn banks. Continuing their scrutiny, they moved directly toward the path, but again, by some miracle, they stopped short of it. Perhaps now they would abandon their inspection of the barranca and turn back, giving him time to get Cesar safely to the cavern.

Suddenly one of the men pointed downstream. In what seemed a flurry of excitement, they spurred their mounts and rode on, as if in search of a trail.

Trin wondered what they could have been pointing at. From their position on the brink, they couldn't possibly see his brother unless . . . The thought pierced his mind like a needle. Could Cesar, half out of his mind with fever and thirst, have gone back to the pool to drink? He pulled himself up higher out of the water to look downstream, but both pool and sheltering ledge were out of sight around a slight bend in the river.

On the rim, the men had discovered the path, but they paused, apparently debating its hazards. No creature except a mountain goat was more sure-footed than a mule accustomed to mountain trails, but even so it was dangerous. Hesitating, they looked at whatever they had spotted below; then they started down.

Stricken with horror, Trin watched as they rode down the trail, making the steep descent much more swiftly than he had been able to do with his wounded brother. When

:56

they faced away from him to wind around the switchback that had sickened Cesar, he found himself plunging through the rapids to the first sheltering boulder. He flung himself down behind it just as the men faced toward him again.

Peering around the rock, he saw his brother drinking beside the pool. So it *had* been Cesar they saw. He *had* left his hiding place! Trin wanted to shout a warning, but it was useless. There was nothing he could do now to save him.

At that moment, Cesar rose from the pool and saw the soldiers riding down on him. Instinctively he ran from them toward the rapids. The men raised their muskets and fired. Cesar staggered into the churning water and went down.

The soldiers reached the ledge and rode into the pool to catch him before the swift current could sweep him over the falls. As they seized his body, one of them spotted the gold chain around his neck and grabbed it. It snapped— and for one awful instant, Trin saw the great pearl as it slipped from the chain to be caught up in the current. The sun touched its gleaming surface as it whirled on the brink, and then it disappeared in the spray of the falls.

The two men shouted at each other, but their words were lost in the roar of the water. They drew Cesar onto the shore and laid him face down at the edge of the pool. A dark red stain spread over his wet shirt where a musket ball had entered his back. One of the men prodded him with his foot. This time the words he spoke carried across to Trin.

"He won't be going anywhere!"

They mounted their mules and headed on down the trail toward the foot of the falls.

When they had disappeared from view, Trin ran down

the shore to his brother. Turning him over gently, he saw that blood was trickling from the corners of his mouth.

"Cesar!" he cried urgently.

Cesar opened his eyes. "Chico!" he whispered. "I told you . . . not to come!"

"It's all right," Trin assured him. "The pearl went over the falls and they've gone down to search for it. They'll be gone a long time."

"Then *go*—while you can!"

"No. I'm staying with you!"

"There's nothing to stay for. You can't . . . help me . . ."

"I can try!"

"No, Trin. I'm dying!" He tried to raise up, and Trin caught him in his arms. "Please—I beg you—go now . . ." His voice trailed off, and he sank back, gasping. After a moment, he murmured, "Jesucristo . . . forgive me . . . my sins." He made an effort to lift his arm in the sign of the cross, and Trin took his wrist and made it for him. Their eyes met, and then Cesar's lids closed slowly, and his head fell forward.

Trin eased him gently to the ground. Kneeling beside him, he prayed, "Holy Father, have mercy on his soul."

CHAPTER SEVEN

Night fell over the barranca, and Trin lay in the black recess of the cavern listening to the soft ripple of the river as it lapped the narrow silt bank beneath him. His depleted body ached for sleep, but his mind was haunted by thoughts of his brother. It seemed unbearable that only a few minutes and a few hundred yards had stood between Cesar and safety. Yet he had been helpless to save him.

Now he was alone in the hiding place for which they had searched, but there was no comfort in his security. His strength on the long flight up the mountain, his courage, had been for Cesar. Without him, he felt drained and hopeless. Only a sunrise ago he had dared to dream that he and his brother could earn their freedom. Tonight Cesar was dead, and the debt had grown beyond all possibility of paying, because now the value of the great pearl would be added to it.

Trin knew it was lost. He had watched from behind the leafy screen of a shrub on the far side of the river as the soldiers returned from the foot of the falls. Their dour faces had told him that the precious jewel had been carried beyond their reach even before they began a search of the pool into which Cesar had fallen. When finally they had resigned themselves to its loss, they had lifted his brother's body onto the back of a mule, tied it in place, and started up the trail. Seeing them go, Trin had wept.

Now again, he was overcome with grief, not only for Cesar's death, but for his suffering through the agonizing days and nights of flight. He might better have fallen beside Gonzalo in the rain, Trin thought; he might better have died then, quickly, rather than go through that long painful cimb, except . . .

Except! Suddenly Trin sat upright. Cesar's flight over the roof and up the mountain had done one thing that was not yet undone: It had brought *him* halfway to freedom!

In his exhaustion and sorrow, he had been thinking how simple it would be to follow his brother's body down the trail. He could stay a reasonable distance behind the soldiers and then return to the hacienda after word got out that Cesar had been found. If he told them that he'd gone to search for his brother, chances were they'd believe him.

At Cinco Ríos he would be safe. He would be bound by a debt that grew greater every year until even his descendants would be born into bondage, but he would never starve. The hacienda soldiers would protect him from the threat of the wilderness—from wild animals, from Indians, even from the spasmodic guerilla attacks of civil war. He would never be free—but he would be *alive*.

Over the muted sound of the rapids, down-river, he heard the deep, hoarse cry of a jaguar. He was alone in a great circle of danger, yet he knew that if he turned back to the safety of Cinco Ríos, Cesar's agony and death would be meaningless. His mother, his brothers and sisters, he, himself, would be forever trapped in bondage. Only Cesar would be gone, leaving their lives unchanged. But if he went forward, then he might make of Cesar's death a bridge to freedom—*if* he had the courage.

For the first time Trin fully understood what his father had tried to teach him years ago—that courage was the price of freedom. To be free, a man must stand alone. He must be willing to face starvation and death. He must take on his own shoulders the responsibility of providing for himself and for those he loved.

Peons were bound because they were afraid to stand alone. His father had stood alone. He had risked death every day of his life as a shark fisherman. He had faced not only the dangers of the great killers but of the sea itself. And he had died fighting the sea, in the terrible hurricane known as *El Cordonazo*, The Lash. But Trin knew that his father would rather have drowned in the Sea of Cortez, a free man, than to have lived as a bound peon on Cinco Ríos.

If his father were here now—if he could ask him which way to go—there would be only one answer. He would know the dangers ahead, yet he would never tell his son to go back into slavery.

The blood-curdling cry of the great cat echoed again through the gorge, and Trin knelt and prayed for the courage to be his father's son. Gradually his tired body sagged forward until at last his head touched the silt bank, and the soft ripple of the river lulled him to sleep.

Night deepened and the moon rose high above the canyon. Far off, an unearthly scream warned the creatures of the forest that the puma was searching out his prey on the high slopes, but Trin was lost in a dream. It seemed to him that he was standing on the shore of the Bay of Turtles under a sky black with clouds, and as he looked beyond to the Sea of Cortez, it, too, was black and menacing. Something was floating on the dark waters, and staring intently, he saw that the sea was covered with oysters. There was a shattering clap of thunder, the clouds opened, and rain fell into the sea in great drops. Strangely, the oysters opened their shells to receive the rain, and on the far horizon the sun burst through the clouds, lighting the drops of water till they glowed like great pearls. Iridescent with the colors of the rainbow, the pearly drops continued to fall into the oysters, and the sun burned brighter and brighter until its golden fire surrounded him, and he felt the heat of it enter his body. Then sea and sky and falling pearls and even the sun itself faded away, but the light remained, filling the cavern. Trin's whole body was suffused with it, and it seemed to him that it came from somewhere within himself.

Trin sat up suddenly, uncertain whether he had been awake or dreaming. He saw that the cavern was indeed lighted, but it was the pale, cool light of the moon, reflected by the river, not the pure golden light of his vision. Yet the strange, beautiful warmth still filled his body, and his fear was gone.

The first faint glimmer of day lightened the sky as Trin swam quietly down-river. His plan was to search for a trail that would take him up the opposite wall of the gorge so that the great chasm might serve as a barrier between himself and the far-reaching acres of Cinco Ríos. Until the soldiers reached the hacienda with his brother's body, the full attention of Don Gregorio and his men would be focused on the pursuit of Cesar, but with that pursuit ended, the patron would be sure to discover that Trin was still missing. He would immediately suspect him of being an accomplice in the crime and order that the hunt be resumed.

Trin knew it was vital to his safety to get up out of the barranca and head north as quickly as possible, but he was irresistibly drawn to the pool at the foot of the falls. The soldiers had not found the great pearl, but that didn't necessarily mean that *he* could not find it. He had to give himself a chance.

There was no one on the rim to challenge his progress as he cut through the rapids and skirted the pool where only yesterday he and Cesar had knelt to quench their thirst. The trail to the lower level twisted away from the river into a deep cleft in the south wall of the gorge. The roar of the falls filled the canyon as Trin descended in a series of switchbacks, but the pool at their base was hidden from view by a tangled mass of bushes and young trees that grew on the wide and fertile banks.

He hesitated before pressing into the thicket. Such a spot would be the perfect watering place for the wild creatures of the wilderness: the deer and the sheep, the silver-tip bear and the cinnamon and black, the spotted lynx and the fox, the big cats. Only last night he had heard the cry of a jaguar.

He drew his knife and moved into the leafy mass. The early morning light filtered down through the trees, but he could hear no sound except the plunging of the waters, and there was nothing to warn him if any creature stirred in the jungle growth around him. He inched his way carefully, watching for any sign of movement, until only a thin curtain of green hung between him and the river.

He pushed the leaves apart with his fingers, and what he saw stopped the breath in his throat. On the opposite bank a huge cat crouched at the water's edge. His distinctive markings—the dark rosettes on the orange-tan coat, each with a black spot in the center, the bold black streaks on his powerful chest—told Trin that this was the jaguar he had heard in the night. As he watched, the beast dipped his muzzle into the pool and came up with a fish.

Suddenly the great cat tensed, as though warned of an alien presence, and his topaz eyes bored into the thicket. Trin waited, motionless, his heart jolting his body. The jaguar was a savage killer if brought to bay or driven by hunger. This one, reduced to fishing in a mountain stream, might well be ravenous. Already he had caught the man-scent. If he decided to attack, Trin knew he wouldn't stand a chance against the immense and terrible power of the beast.

Time stretched out unendurably as the cruel eyes glared out of the malevolent face, seeking the hiding place of the intruder. At length they seemed to penetrate the small opening in the curtain of foliage and fix on Trin, holding his own eyes in their fierce yellow gaze. The big jaws opened as if to suck in, to taste, the scent of the boy, and the long murderous fangs showed white against the red mouth.

Trin's nerves were drawn so taut he felt his body could no longer contain the tension, but must burst in a sudden, violent explosion; yet he held himself rigid, staring back strongly at the pale eyes. It was the jaguar who broke the spell. With an angry lash of his black-ringed tail, he turned and slunk into the tall reeds behind him.

Trin watched his spotted orange coat disappear as the green growth swallowed him and wondered whether the beast's move was really one of retreat or whether he was, in fact, planning to lie in wait until he could creep up silently from behind and pounce on his quarry. Trin shivered at the thought. If the cat crept downstream to where the river narrowed, he could easily cross it and move in soundless stealth through the thicket behind him.

Trin stepped from the enveloping foliage into the open at the water's edge and looked downriver. There was no sign of the jaguar. He moved upstream to the deep, wide pool at the foot of the falls and stripped the pack from his back. There would be a certain degree of peril in diving, with the great cat somewhere near, but to delay was also perilous.

He dove into the clear water and swam the length of the pool, scanning the bottom for the bright gleaming surface of the pearl. When he came up for air, there was still no sign of the jaguar, and he began a methodical search, swimming back and forth across the pool, trying to cover every foot of its rocky bottom. Where the soft silt had settled between the stones, he sifted it with his hands, but still he found nothing. Perhaps the great jewel had been smashed in its long fall and disintegrated, or had been swept down into the rushing rapids below.

The sun was already reaching into the barranca. It was time to abandon the search. As Trin rose to the surface, he saw the jaguar ascending the north wall of the gorge. He watched the tawny killer move up the precipitous trail until he disappeared over the rim. The beast had shown him the way out. Would he be lying in wait for him when he reached the top? It was a chance he had to take.

Downstream, where the canyon narrowed till the rapids filled it wall to wall, he discovered a ledge jutting out above the rushing waters that served as the approach to the trail. He pulled himself up onto it and started climbing. The narrow path hung upon the almost perpendicular face of the wall, but Trin made the hazardous ascent swiftly. A few yards short of the rim, he stopped and drew his knife. The big cat might be crouching just out of sight at the edge of the cliff, ready to pounce on him as he reached the top. He would have little chance to defend himself if the heavy beast crashed down on him without warning. Even a man armed with a pistol could hardly hope to fire at such close range. But the knife might give him a chance to break free of the deadly claws for an instant—long enough to leap over the sheer wall of the gorge. Better to die in a two-thousand foot plunge to the turbulent river below than to be eaten by the killer.

He moved up the trail cautiously, his knife ready, his eyes on the edge of the cliff above him. Yard by nerve-wracking yard he moved closer to the rim until at last he stood upon it. The cat was nowhere to be seen.

Trin paused to scan the tableland on the opposite side of the abyss. There was no one in view. For the present he was safe, but ahead of him the path stretched across a gently rising plateau which offered virtually no cover. Following it, he would be clearly visible to anyone who might appear on the other side, until he reached and climbed the mountain beyond.

He started up the trail at a run, dropping prone in the short grass to get his breath, then running again until, in a series of sprints, he had covered the distance to the shoulder of the mountain. Already hot and thirsty, he lay in the cool grass and scanned the long slope behind him. No one had appeared, yet he had an uncomfortable feeling of a presence, as though someone—or something—was following him. His eyes searched the landscape around him, seeking the spotted orange color of the jaguar or some slight movement in the scattered clumps of scrub, but there was nothing.

He had heard that the puma—the mountain lion—often followed a man for a long distance, as though awaiting an opportunity to attack; yet if the man turned to face him, the animal would usually slink away. He wondered if the jaguar was like the puma. Perhaps the huge cat was stalking him. But if he couldn't see him, how could he hope to face him down?

Trin started up the mountain. The trail rose sharply, snaking its way up the smooth granite slopes toward the jagged peak. As he climbed higher and higher, he had the persistent feeling of being followed, but when he looked back, there was neither man nor beast in sight.

At length he mounted the fantastic granite crag at the summit and felt as if he were on top of the world. All around him rose the mighty peaks of the Sierra Madre range, forming an almost impassable barrier to the great central plateau of Mexico. Miles to the southeast, beyond those immense towers of rock stretching their snow-capped pinnacles ten thousand feet and more into the turquoise sky, was the city of Durango that Cesar had hoped to reach.

Trin turned to the west, where the rugged ranges dropped ridge on ridge to the coastal plain. Below the foothills the land spread its green miles out to the Pacific, shimmering now in the sunlight of early afternoon. Somewhere along that curving shoreline, to the north, was Turtle Bay.

The thought of it gave him new energy, and he began the tortuous descent on the north side of the mountain. A cutting wind rose, and there was no shelter on the granite cliffs. He hurried down the slippery trail, negotiating its perilous zig-zags without fear, until at last the steep slope eased into a level mesa forested with pines. The giant trees broke the wind and the soft carpet of needles comforted his tired feet. But once more he had the strange feeling that he was not alone, that something was pursuing him.

His thoughts returned to the jaguar. If the big cat was

still trailing him, it would soon have its chance to attack. Darkness was no more than an hour away, and there was no safety here in the woods. The pines stood straight and tall rising one hundred feet and more without a limb. But even a tree with branches low enough for him to reach would be useless. He knew that jaguars were expert climbers. In the deep jungles, far to the south, they spent their lives in the trees, rarely ever descending to the ground.

Trin's legs ached with strain from the steep trails, but he raced through the forest, startling white-tailed deer as he ran. His father had told him of a hunter's trick to keep pumas at bay. It might work with a jaguar—*if* he could find what he needed.

It was twilight when he emerged from the woods, carrying in his arms the trunks of seven small saplings which he had cut and stripped of their branches. The trail dipped into a stony hollow, like a wide bowl scooped out between the peaks, and a brook traversed the bottom, disappearing through a crack in the side. Trin knelt by the gurgling water, grateful to soothe his dry throat with a long drink. Then he dropped the pack from his back and drew his knife. Twilight was brief in the mountains, and night was only minutes away. He had to act quickly.

He began by digging seven holes in a circle and placing the saplings in them, like the stakes of a miniature corral. When he had packed the earth around them firmly, he stepped out of his trousers and cut the legs off midway up the thigh. He put on the short pants and tore the remaining cloth into strips. Then he tied the strips to the tops of the saplings, so that they fluttered like white flags in the breeze.

It was dark when he had finished. He drank again from the brook, picked up his pack, and seated himself in the center of the circle to eat a meager ration of dried tortillas. Hunters, his father had said, used streamers on stakes to protect the bodies of deer they had killed; Trin could only hope that the device would protect him as well.

Later the moon would rise to cast its pale light on the little flags, but now the night seemed pitch black. The beast would be held at bay by the white streamers only if he could see them. Trin prayed that the faint rays of light from the night sky would reveal them to him.

The hours before the moonrise seemed endless. Across the open hollow the forest rose toward the sky like a great black wall, and if the jaguar was lurking at its fringe, Trin couldn't see him. Yet his senses had warned him again of a presence. The wind from the peaks was icy, and Trin wrapped himself in the extra serape and lay facing the woods, his eyes searching the night for the phosphorescent eyes of the animal.

When he found them, he was horrified to discover that there was not one pair of eyes, but *two*! Was it the jaguar and his mate? Or were they the eyes of some other mountain beasts—creatures who might not be held off by the fluttering flags?

The four green-lit eyes moved closer, and Trin saw the vague outline of two great bodies prowling in a wide circle around his smaller circle of stakes. The pairs of eyes had separated now, and there was one pair on each side of the circle. Trin tried to follow them, to be ready to confront them, but it was impossible to face both pair at once.

Round and round they prowled on soundless pads, their phosphor eyes burning down on him, and suddenly he realized that their circle was getting smaller and smaller. Slowly but relentlessly, the beasts were closing in.

CHAPTER EIGHT

The moon rose, full and yellow, and the beasts faded back into the shadows at the edge of the forest, intimidated by the sudden brightness of the fluttering streamers. In the brief moment before their shapes dissolved into the darkness, Trin glimpsed their flat heads and low, crouching bodies, and knew that they were, indeed, cats, but he couldn't discern the black stripes and rosettes that were the mark of the jaguar.

For a time he saw only the green fire of their eyes as they paced back and forth; then slowly, almost imperceptibly, they crept forward, leaving the border of shadow to resume their circling. Stealthily, they padded around him, their long tails lashing, but this time the diameter of their circle was wider, and they stayed a respectful distance away from the windblown flags.

The huge cats were in the open moonlight now, but still Trin could not distinguish any black markings on their coats, and it seemed to him that they were leaner, more gaunt than the cat he had encountered by the river. Was it a trick of lighting, he wondered, or were these cats of another breed—pumas, perhaps, leaner and more hunger-driven than the jaguar?

Whichever they were, Trin knew they were killers by instinct, and though his body was drained by the strenuous day on the trail with inadequate rations, he didn't dare to relax, even for a moment. His eyelids dropped, and he fought to keep them open, as his head pivoted from side to side, following the movements of the two huge carnivores. Round and round they crept in ceaseless, silent circles until Trin was hypnotized by the phosphorescent eyes and the endless motion of his own head pivoting after them. His mind lost its focus, and he felt himself floating out beyond the circle of flags, beyond the circling green eyes to the greater circle of peaks, dark against the moonlit sky.

The rising sun touched his face with its first red rays, and he woke to find the two cats gone. Whether they were jaguars or pumas he never knew, but one thing was certain: the hunter's trick had worked. The fluttering streamers had kept them at bay.

He jumped to his feet, grateful to be alive and safe. The world of Cinco Ríos seemed as far away as a half-forgotten dream. Only the great crags, towering above him like a company of giants, were real. Yet, strangely, he did not feel afraid. Somehow, in these days of flight, he had come to terms with danger. Meeting the challenge of each day, each night, had given him a new sense of strength.

In the distance, he spotted a narrow defile that cut between the crags and found that a trail wound through it to ease down onto a broad plateau dotted with scrub oak and piñon pines. Until now he had not dared to slow down his flight by stopping to supplement his rations with fish or game that he might snare, but the piñon nuts were like a gift from heaven. For the first time in days, he ate until he no longer felt hunger.

He was harvesting an extra supply of nuts to carry with

him when he glimpsed two moving figures on the rim of a ridge far to the east. He ducked under the cover of a low-spreading pine and watched as the two figures ran down the shoulder of the ridge and onto the plateau. Without pausing to rest, they continued to run toward him, approaching at an astoundingly swift pace.

Trin knew at once that they couldn't be Mexicans. His own countrymen would never run at such a pace, without rest, in the midday heat. They had to be Indians. He thought of the Tarahumaras, who could run one hundred miles a day. They lived in Chihuahua, just across the northeast border of Sinaloa, and these mountains would be their hunting ground. He had no intention of ending up as one of their trophies if he could help it.

Running in a crouch from the shelter of one low-slung tree to another, he raced for the western edge of the plateau. What lay beyond he couldn't judge: perhaps a gentle descent, perhaps a sheer precipice. But the Indians were behind him—and gaining. They were still a good half-mile away, and as far as he could tell, they had not yet spotted him, but he knew he was no match for men who could outrun a deer.

Even before he reached the rim of the plateau, six crosses, each supported by a heap of stones, warned him that the danger ahead must be almost as great as that from behind. When he had crawled to the brink and looked down, he understood why. Below him, a trail no more than a foot wide cut down the side of a granite precipice at an almost impossible angle. For six, it *had* been impossible. The six cairns commemorated six people who had fallen to their deaths from this trail.

Trin looked behind him. Through the pines and scrub oak that hid him from their view, he glimpsed the Indians, apparently heading straight for the same spot. They were closer now, and he could see the sheen of their naked flesh as the sun lighted their powerful bronze bodies. They wore loincloths instead of pants, and over their shoulders they carried bows and quivers full of arrows.

Trin hesitated. If by any chance the Tarahumaras were friendly, it would be senseless to risk death on this most treacherous of trails—but if they were *not* . . . He could not take the chance.

He let himself down over the lip of the precipice and felt the narrow path take shape beneath his feet. Once again, as he had done at the great barranca with Cesar, he faced the granite cliff and clung to it with both hands, working his way down without looking into the gulf of space below.

At the bottom, the trail debouched into a grassy meadow crossed by a languid stream. A jungle of willows and cottonwoods along the banks offered the only cover, and Trin had barely slipped into their green shadows when the two Indians appeared at the head of the trail.

For a moment they paused, their keen eyes searching the meadow-land below; then they began a descent of the steeply sloping trail, following its perilous twistings and turnings as casually as if they were walking on level ground. When they reached the bottom, they would be sure to spot his tracks, where he had crossed the grassy stretch to the stream, and know that they were fresh.

But here, at least, he could avoid giving them further clues. He strode into the middle of the stream and walked knee-deep along its curving course. On the banks, the tracks of deer and other creatures of the wild told him that this was the perfect hunting ground for the Indian braves. No doubt they planned to lie in wait for the animals who would come at dusk to drink and to feed on the lush grasses. But first, having seen his tracks, they would search for their human quarry.

When the Indians had had time to reach the foot of the granite cliff, he ducked into the heart of the green thicket. In the moist, loamy soil at his feet, he was horrified to see the tracks of the *jabalí*—the wild swine—most dangerous of all creatures of the forest.

Instinctively his eyes sought a tree large enough to climb, but there was nothing in the green saplings around him to offer a refuge. He stood motionless, watching for the slightest sign of movement, listening for the smallest sound. Everything he had ever heard about the wild boars raced through his mind. He knew that they traveled in packs of thirty or forty, and their tusks, sharp as razors, could inflict the most terrible of wounds. When they sighted an enemy, whether it be one or many, they attacked in a body, fighting savagely until the last one was killed. No man, however well armed, could survive the onslaught of their murderous tusks unless he could climb up beyond their reach.

Yards away, one great oak reared up above the saplings, and he pushed slowly, silently, toward it, wondering if at any instant the boars might rush at him out of the thicket. But there was no movement in the grasses, no sound but the soft ripple of the water, and he went on past the tree, gambling on the chance that the swine had left the meadow at daybreak and would not return till dusk. The oak might serve to foil the jabalí, but not the Indians.

The sheltering growth petered out as the stream tumbled down a rocky slope, and Trin found himself in the open. Only a few scattered boulders offered any cover, and he ran down the treacherous incline, skidding and hurtling toward the nearest rock. Below him, the stream twisted across his path like a glistening serpent to drop over a granite ledge and disappear into the shadows of a canyon.

Suddenly the earth slid out from under his feet, and rolling head over heels down the slope, he plunged into the rushing waters. Swept along by the current, he reached out to catch at something—anything—that might save him, but the slippery stones eluded his grasp, and he was swept over the ledge.

Falling with the foaming cataract, he had one terrifying moment to wonder what lay beneath him, and then, blessedly, he was engulfed by the deep, cold waters of a pool. His body rose to the surface, and gasping and half dazed from the impact, he paddled to the bank and pulled himself up into the sheltering border of cottonwoods.

Far above him, the Indians appeared at the top of the rocky slope, stared down into the canyon, and then turned away, more interested in their hunting ground than in a fleeing boy.

After he had rested, Trin followed the cascading stream, knowing it would lead him to the lowlands—and the sea.

When he emerged from the foothills into the low, hot country, Trin traveled by night, hiding during the day from soldiers or police who might be searching for him. The water and fish of the stream, the occasional wild fruits and edible roots growing along its banks, kept him alive during the forty-mile trek from the mine to the coast, but it was the thought of his godfather, Fortino Chavarria, that gave him hope.

There had been others in Turtle Bay who were friends of his father—kind, gentle people who would welcome him, if he were not a fugitive. But by now, Don Gregorio Velasquez would have had time to alert the police. The people in the village would know that he was not only a runaway but suspected of being an accomplice in a crime. To give him shelter would be to risk imprisonment themselves. The rich master of Cinco Ríos might even have offered a reward for his capture, and the villagers were poor. There might be some among them who would be tempted to betray him.

But not Fortino. He would cut off his right arm before he would betray a friend. And Trin was more than friend —he was godchild to Fortino. No matter what the risk, his padrino would take him in.

At daybreak on the third morning, Trin reached the mouth of the river, and stood, at last, on the shore of the Sea of Cortez. His spirits soared at the sight of the sparkling blue waters, and joyous anticipation tempted him to cover the remaining few miles along the coast by daylight. The highway was miles inland, and the lonely, deserted beaches seemed to offer no threat to his safety. Here and there, the rocky strand gave way to cliffs that dropped sheer to the sea, and Trin had to swim around them, stroking steadily northward toward the great lagoon of which Turtle Bay was a covelike indentation.

As he tramped along the last curve of beach that lay between him and the estuary, he sighted a schooner riding at anchor a mile offshore. The narrow entrance to the lagoon was obstructed by many shoals and sandbars, and it was dangerous to bring in a boat of any draft, but he saw that a lone man was rowing a skiff in from the schooner.

He flung himself down behind a sand bank and crawled toward a thicket of mangroves in the tidal borderland on the south shore of the lagoon. The man might be someone he knew—it could even be Fortino, who made his living as a captain on schooners that plied the waters of the gulf. But if it weren't Fortino, Trin couldn't risk being seen by someone else—someone who might betray him.

Hidden by the tangled pattern of stilt roots, he peered out from the mangroves as the skiff approached and was startled to see that the man at the oars was an Indian. His jet-black hair hung to his shoulder blades, and his bronze face, with its strong, sharply defined features, was an impassive mask.

Trin felt a chill of apprehension. If the oarsman was a Yaqui, perhaps the ship was a Yaqui fishing schooner, but why was it anchored here? Could it mean that the Indians had taken over the village at Turtle Bay? For the first time Trin realized that the little settlement he had left five years ago might have been pillaged and his friends murdered by the revolting tribes.

Travelers pausing to rest at Cinco Ríos had frequently brought word of civil war in his home state of Sonora—of Indian uprisings, and savage attacks on haciendas and towns. But there had never been any mention of Turtle Bay. It was so small a village, and so remote, that he had supposed it safe. Perhaps, instead, it was just too insignificant and its destruction too unimportant to be reported by the travelers.

He knew that he ought to wait until dusk to approach the village, but his uncertainty about its fate gnawed at him until he could no longer stand the suspense. The Indian, rowing past him with powerful strokes, had disappeared around a curve half a mile up the lagoon, when Trin waded into the shallows, being careful to avoid the innumerable stingrays with their slashing tail thorns. Crabs scurried into hiding at his approach and scores of birds soared up from the sandbars, betraying his presence by their startled flight, but the schooner was far away, and there was no one to see him as he struck out for the opposite shore.

The tide was with him and he crossed easily, carried along by the flow of water. Turtle Bay was some three miles in from the sea on the northern side of the great lagoon, and Trin chose to swim the distance, hugging the shoreline and its dense forest of mangroves.

Resting for brief intervals, he saw in the clear, unruffled waters all the little creatures he remembered from his childhood play in the shallows: the sharp-spined purple sea urchins and the tiny light green sand dollars, the flat pearly clams and the blue-clawed swimming crabs, the huge stalk-eyed conchs and the big hermit crabs housed in the cast-off conch shells, and almost invisible, the *botete*, the poison fish, lying in their small depressions on the bottom. He wondered if the great sea turtles still floated in the bay, and pressed on, eager for the familiar sight of the enormous creatures. But the tide turned before he could reach his destination, and his body was too weak and tired to fight the strong seaward pull of the current.

He grasped at the arching roots of the mangroves and drew himself up into the thicket. The tangled mass had tapered to a narrow border, and Trin twisted and struggled through the gnarled stilt roots until at last he emerged from the dark labyrinth into an open stretch of sandy flat-land. Beyond it he glimpsed the blue sparkle of a covelike bay with a tortoiseshell island of turtles floating on its warm waters. He was home! Turtle Bay was no more than five hundred yards away.

He crept cautiously across the hot expanse of sand until the whole bay came into view, and he saw the semicircle of adobe houses nestled along the crescent of white beach. His eyes sought out the one that had been his home before his mother had to sell it and go to work at Cinco Ríos. Everything about it looked achingly familiar—the two palms, taller now, that spread their broad leaves over the patio, the great banyan with its grove pillars stretching to the wall of the house next door, the house of Fortino Chavarria. The houses, all of them, were there, intact. But what of the people inside them? Were they his Mexican friends? Or were they Indians?

He lay prone behind a small sand hill and studied the scene for clues. Several dugouts were beached on the white sand, but they were of a type used by both Mexicans and Indians. They told him nothing. He searched the shoreline for the skiff from the schooner and spotted it beyond a clump of palms below Fortino's house.

There were no people in sight, but that was not unusual. This was the time of heat and *siesta*, when his countrymen took refuge in their shaded patios or napped inside the thick-walled houses. If they stirred at all, it would be on the other side, where the homes faced the road and the little village store. It might be that no one would appear on the beach until the men took their boats out for night fishing.

The thought of waiting the interminable hours until dark to find out who was inside the house of Fortino was unbearable to Trin, and without consciously making a decision, he found himself crawling across the sand toward the village. Here and there a sand dune or a clump of bushes gave him shelter, but for the most part he was in the open, visible from the small iron-barred windows, if anyone bothered to look. He could only hope that in the blistering heat of this hour, no one would choose to look out onto the white glare of the flats.

As he came within earshot of the houses, he heard a faint sound of a musical instrument. The lapping of the water on the beach mingled with the music, until it was an unidentifiable jumble that could be either Indian or Mexican. He crawled closer, and realized that the music came not from the house nearest him, but from somewhere farther up the beach. As he inched forward, listening, the distant music became clearer and he recognized the instrument as a guitar—and the melody as Mexican.

Uplifted with joy, he rose to his feet and ran toward the house of Fortino. The sound of hoof-beats approaching along the road jolted him back to caution, and he took shelter in the banyan grove. Just over the wall, the musician burst out with a gay, exuberant song, drowning out the hoof-beats, and Trin couldn't judge whether they had passed by or stopped. If they had stopped, there was danger in them, and he knew he should flee back to the mangrove thicket, but he had reached the wall of Fortino's house. He couldn't turn back without looking over it.

He pulled himself up the trunk-like roots of the banyan and crawled along a branch until he could peer down into the Chavarria patio. The heavenly fragrance of baking bread filled the air, and in the corner beneath him three pots were bubbling over three separate fires in an enormous old stove built of stone and adobe. The tall, willowy girl in full red skirt and white blouse who bent over the pots, and the homely young musician, half-hidden by a huge sombrero, who serenaded her while she stirred and tasted, were strangers to Trin.

His eyes moved to the long porch that fronted onto the patio. In its shade, two men sat at a table shredding turtle meat with their knives. Trin recognized the small, wiry man facing him as Castillo, the village carpenter, but he could see only the back of the other one—a broad-shouldered, lean back that he couldn't identify.

Where were Fortino and his family? Could he have sold his house to Castillo and gone away—or died? Trin's heart sank at the thought. And then, from inside the house, a woman's rich warm voice called out, "Angelina! Look at the bread!"

"*Sí Abuelita!*" answered the tall, willowy girl, and Trin realized with sudden shock that the black-eyed beauty at the stove was no stranger at all. Five years ago, Angelina, eldest granddaughter of Fortino, had been his skinny, ten-year-old playmate.

The voice was that of Hortencia, wife of Fortino, and a moment later she appeared, a plump woman with silver-touched hair piled high on her head and eyes that sparkled.

"Paco!" she ordered crisply. "If you want to eat of the turtle, you'd better stop the singing and help your father and brother with the shredding!"

Paco! Then the musician under the sombrero, and the broad-shouldered young man at the table were the sons of Castillo! Trin knew them both. They had been in their mid-teens when he was nine, and too old to pay much attention to him, but Castillo had been his father's friend, and surely now they would be his.

Before he could put them to the test, a boy's voice, hushed but excited, called "*Abuelo! Abuelo!*" and a slender lad of seven or eight scrambled over the wall on the opposite side, and dropped down into the patio. A small mongrel dog with the long curly coat of a spaniel dashed out of the house, barking and dancing in instant response, and Trin noted happily that it was Pepé, the little pet of the Chavarria grandchildren, who had been equally devoted to him in the days when he was playmate of Angelina and her brothers.

"*Quieto*, Pepé! *Quieto!*" ordered the boy, trying to silence the dog's barking. "Where's Grandfather?"

The urgency in the lad's voice was unmistakable, and his

grandfather emerged from the house—a man not tall, but strongly built, with powerful arms and legs and a great deep chest. The face beneath the thatch of straight gray hair was kind, but the strength was there, too, in the steady eyes and square jaw, the wide, firm mouth under the bristling mustache.

A great joy filled Trin's heart at the sight of Fortino, and he would have called to him, but the words spilling out of the small boy stopped him.

"Grandfather!" the lad was saying, insistently. "The police are coming here!"

"Let them come," said Fortino, in a deep, calm voice. "We have nothing to fear."

"There is *always* something to fear, when the police come!" said Castillo, the carpenter, nervously rising from his chair. "What do they want?"

"They're searching for a thief!" the boy told him. "I heard them talking in the store. His name is Trinidad Delgado, and they think he will come here. If we find him, they will pay us a reward!"

"Trinidad Delgado is our *friend*!" said Fortino firmly.

"But Grandfather," the boy cut in, "they will give us *gold*!"

There was a loud hammering on the outer door of the house, and Trin was startled to see the Indian appear from an inner room.

"It is the police," he said, in a voice as devoid of expression as his face.

Trin could wait no longer. He tried to crawl backwards with a slow, imperceptible motion, but his hands, wet with sweat, slipped on the branch, and as he caught himself, it creaked and swayed low over the heads of the group in the patio. The keen eyes of the Indian spotted him instantly, and the others followed his glance. Even the dog caught the motion and reared up to bark at him in frantic excitement.

For one brief moment Trin stared back at the circle of startled faces, and then he swung down from the branch and fled toward the bay. At water's edge, he took refuge under an overturned dugout. There was no time to risk the long run across the open flatland. In a matter of minutes the whole village would be alerted, and with the promise of gold, almost any of the townsfolk might join the police in their search.

Peering out from under the dugout, he scanned the scene for a hiding place. There could be no safety in any of the houses or in the scattered clumps of trees and bushes. Even if he could reach the mangrove thicket, it, too, might be subject to the scrutiny of the police. The waters of the bay, smooth and crystal clear, offered almost no cover, yet he could think of no other—until, far out, he glimpsed the turtles. If he could swim out to them before the police reached the beach, if he could approach them silently so as not to rouse them from their lethargy, perhaps he could float on the far rim of their circle. At that distance, with only his head above water, he might escape notice in the mass of great floating bodies.

He crawled out from under the boat and saw Pepé bounding toward him. Apparently the little dog had rushed out when the door was opened for the police, and now he barked in wild delight at discovering his quarry. Trin backed quickly into the shelter of the dugout and drew the spaniel with him. A moment before, he might have slipped silently into the bay; now he was trapped by the love of the little pet.

Precious time passed, while Pepé licked his face and

squealed in ecstatic welcome. Holding the dog in his arms, trying to quiet him, Trin's thoughts went back to the circle in the patio—the little boy excited by the promise of gold, the stoic face of the young Indian. Was one of them, even now, sending the police after him? Or would one of the others, one of his friends, betray him?

Desperately, he commanded Pepé to lie down, to stay. And finally, with a pleading whimper, the little animal obeyed. Swiftly, Trin slipped out from under the boat, and with a brief backward look toward the house, slid into the water.

The ebbing tide was carrying the turtles out toward the lagoon, and the swim was a long one. So far, no one had appeared on the beach, but even if the villagers kept silent Trin knew it was only a question of time until the police would press their search beyond the houses to the shore. There would be danger each time he surfaced for air.

He pushed through the water in a fast crawl, swimming close to the bottom until he was well beyond the shallows. When the cramp in his chest forced him to go up, he glanced quickly toward the shore and saw the Indian moving from the banyan grove to the beach. As he ducked under, he realized that his glance had taken in something else: Pepé, whining and barking at the water's edge, was betraying his course to the Indian as clearly as though he could speak the words.

He jackknifed beneath the surface and swam with frantic urgency toward the island of turtles, but there had been no time to fill his lungs, and what little air he had gulped in was quickly spent. When his need drove him up again, he saw that the Indian had launched the skiff, and with the spaniel in the bow, was rowing toward him with powerful strokes.

Instinctively, Trin sucked in air and went under. His mind told him it was useless to go on. His depleted body, already trembling with exhaustion, was no match for the fresh strength of the Indian. But his stubborn will refused to surrender. From some inner core of himself, there seemed to come a final measure of energy, more of spirit than of body, and he pushed forward, reaching with each desperate stroke for the shadow that would tell him he was beneath the floating monsters.

His lungs were bursting, but he held himself under until at last he saw the dark mass above him. Swimming upward cautiously on a long slant, he sought an open space just beyond the huge reptilian bodies, but at that moment the turtles became aware of the approaching skiff. Taking instant flight, they dove down just as Trin thrust upward, forcing him back with the tremendous impact of their weight.

He struggled to make his way up between them, but in their panic, the turtles bit at him with cruel beak-like jaws, driving him back into the murky depths. The cramping pain in his chest became an agony, and he fought for his life, beating at the monsters with his fists, but the blood from his wounds blinded him and he was unable to break through to the life-giving air.

Suddenly something below him seized his legs and pulled him down. Too exhausted to resist, Trin surrendered, and felt powerful arms drawing him into an abyss.

CHAPTER NINE

Trin's father, in his own boyhood, had once come close to drowning in the same Bay of Turtles. He had often told Trin of that strange moment when, suspended between life and death, he had seen visions of people and incidents out of his past—visions so compelling that he never forgot them. It was, he had told him, an experience he had shared in common with many men who had been rescued in the final moment before death could claim them.

Now Trin himself was suspended in that same awful moment. As his limp body was drawn down into the shadowed waters, the agonizing pangs of drowning seemed to recede from his consciousness, and he saw his father's face before him. In that instant, he remembered the story and realized that he, too, might be saved—by the Indian. And then he felt himself floating free of his body. All sense of pain was gone, and he felt weightless.

Gradually, he became aware that he was looking *down* on the surface of the bay. The turtles had made their escape into the depths, but the skiff was riding there, with the dog in it. The head of the Indian broke water, and Trin saw him grasp the gunwale of the skiff with one hand, while with the other arm, he brought to the surface his own drowning body.

Watching as the man struggled to lift his body into the boat, Trin felt as if he were *two* beings: one, the unconscious boy in the arms of the Yaqui—the other, the Trin who was looking down upon the scene.

While his unconscious body remained in suspension between life and death, the dimensions of time and space were strangely altered for Trin, and he found that he could *see* whatever place or persons his mind centered upon. His thoughts shifted to his family at Cinco Ríos, and he saw them as clearly as if he were with them inside the small, dark room that was their home. It was the hour of siesta, and his brothers and sisters were dozing on their pallets while his mother sat beside them, fingering her rosary, her dark eyes swollen and shadowed from much weeping.

The image of his mother faded, and he saw his body lying in the bottom of the skiff, with the Indian working over it. The water had been emptied from the lungs, and Trin was aware that there was a faint heartbeat. He sensed that the two separate parts of himself must become one, in that body, if he was to survive.

There was a slight gasping intake of breath, and he felt himself being drawn back. His heart began to beat more strongly, and he sucked the air into his lungs again, and the two parts of him merged. With the first faint glimmer of consciousness, he felt the weight of his body's weakness, and its pain, and knew he was alive.

For a brief interval, he was miserably sick, and then the sickness passed, and he relaxed into a deep sleep.

He woke slowly, becoming aware of a rhythmic rising and falling motion, before he opened his eyes. There was something familiar about it—a rhythm that reached back into his past. He lay, still half asleep, enjoying the gentle rocking motion until the realization of what it was jolted him wide awake. He sat up, opening his eyes to find that he was in almost total darkness, but the motion was unmistakable. It *had* to be a ship at sea—a ship rising to the swells, then dropping into the troughs of the waves and rising again. He had been out in his father's boat too often to forget the feel of it.

But how had he come from the Bay of Turtles into the dark interior of a ship? His thoughts raced back to the Indian, and he remembered with complete clarity his strange experience at the moment of his near-drowning. He wanted to think about it—to try to understand it—but this was not the time.

He knew that the Yaqui had saved his life. Apparently, for some reason, he had not turned him over to the police. But *why*? It was not like an Indian to pass up the chance of a reward—unless . . .

Unless he knew of a way to get even bigger money! With shock, Trin realized that during his sleep of exhaustion, he could have been shanghaied. A strong boy of fourteen would bring a good price. Perhaps the Indian had sold him into slavery, and he was, even now, bound for some far port in the Orient.

Exploring the darkness around him, he discovered that he was in a low bunk with another bunk above him. He fumbled his way to the companion ladder, climbed it, and peered out onto the deck. The ship was a little fore-and-aft schooner, running before the wind, and there was no one in sight. Trin knew there had to be a man at the helm, but that would be aft of the cabin, out of his line of vision, and the distant murmur of voices coupled with the tempting odor of hot frijoles suggested that the rest of the crew was in the galley.

He crept across the deck and took refuge behind a skiff. On its bow he read the name of the vessel: *La Virazón—The Sea-Breeze*. Crouched in the narrow space between the skiff and the rail, Trin scanned the passing coastline to the east. The hazy blue ridges pitching steeply to a lowland indented with lagoons could be none other than the great Sierra Madre range whose slopes he had so recently descended, and beyond the vast expanse of blue water to the west, the long rugged peninsular of Baja California rose through the mist. Wherever she was bound, the schooner was sailing northward on the Sea of Cortez. Before she could go out into the Pacific, she would have to turn south. It occurred to Trin that if he could find a hiding-place, perhaps somewhere in the hold, he might be able to slip overboard when *La Virazón* put into the next port.

One voice, rising above the others, warned him that someone was coming from the galley. He flattened himself on the deck and peering around the bow of the skiff, saw that the man approaching was the Yaqui. He pulled back and lay motionless, wondering if the Indian had seen him. He held his breath, straining to hear the man's footsteps, but the Yaqui was barefoot and his light soundless tread gave Trin no clues to his whereabouts.

Suddenly the suspense was broken by the clamorous barking of a dog, directly behind him. As he tried to twist around in the narrow space, the animal leapt on his back, flattening him to the deck with its weight. He struggled to rise again, only to find that he was blocked by the straddled bronze legs of the Indian. Flinging off the dog, he slipped between the man's legs and fled the length of the deck, followed by a tumult of barking and shouting as Yaqui and dog raced after him.

At the stern, the long, lean spider of a helmsman lunged

:89

out to seize him, but he wriggled free and shot up into the rigging. Swaying perilously on the ropes, he looked down to find the Indian coming up after him. The man was shouting and gesturing, but the wind, singing through the rigging, and the dog's barking drowned out his words. Trin climbed higher, knowing that the Indian was gaining on him. His only chance of escape, now, was to leap into the sea, and there were miles of wind-whipped waters between him and the shore.

"Don't jump!" This time the words reached him, and Trin looked down to find the Yaqui only a few feet below him.

"You'll end up in the belly of a shark!" the Indian shouted. "Look there!"

Trin followed his gesture and saw a large dorsal fin cutting through the ultramarine blue of the water as the monster cruised parallel to the *Virazón*.

"Better for you to come down and fill your *own* belly, amigo! You must have the hunger of a shark yourself, after sleeping for two days!"

Trin stared at him in amazement. Two days! Could he be telling the truth?

"Do not fear me!" said the Yaqui. "I am Yaño—your friend!"

"Then why did you bring me on this ship?" Trin demanded.

"To hide you from the police! Here, there is no need for running. Look below!" He indicated the deck far beneath them.

Trin looked, and saw three men waving and trying to make themselves heard over the wind and the dog. One of them was his godfather, Fortino Chavarria. The other two were the Castillo brothers, Paco and Raúl. The barking, prancing, whirling blur paused momentarily, and Trin realized that the dog was Pepé.

"You see?" said the Yaqui. "Here, you are safe!"

When he had filled his stomach with three huge portions of hot frijoles and numberless tortillas, Trin sat atop the captain's cabin with Fortino and told him the whole painful story of Cesar and Gonzalo and the great pearl.

"Don Gregorio must believe I was an accomplice," Trin finished, "but I swear to you, Padrino, I have committed no crime—except to run away."

"You were right to run," said Fortino emphatically. "There is a job to be done, and no one but you to do it. You are like me now, mi hijo—the *man* of the family—and we have much the same responsibility. You want to free your family, and I want to *keep* mine free."

Trin knew that Fortino was thinking of the eight grandchildren he had taken in as his own when their parents had died in the fever epidemic. Without him to provide for them, they, too, would be forced into bondage, but while he lived, they would remain free.

"For a man as old as I and a man as young as you," Fortino went on, "it won't be easy, but it might happen we could help each other."

The circle of peaks distinguishing the port of San Fernando de Guaymas loomed ahead. When the schooner approached the guano-whitened island of Pajaro that defended the entrance, Fortino took the wheel. As captain and the most thorough seaman aboard, it was he who would pilot *La Virazón* into the land-locked harbor. Trin took a position on the opposite side and held it with him, getting the feel of the vessel as she responded to the pressures of waves and currents and the helmsman's will.

"If only the schooner was—" Trin broke off abruptly, knowing why his wish was impossible of fulfillment. For as long as he could remember, his godfather had been saving money to buy a schooner of his own. One year he had had almost seven hundred pesos, but that had been the year of the fever epidemic. It was then Trin had learned that it was not only costly to live but to die. One had to pay a high price for the requiem mass and burial in consecrated ground. When Fortino had paid the priest for the burial of his son and daughter-in-law, a big slice of his savings was gone, and a man who had, suddenly, eight grandchildren to feed and clothe could no longer hope to buy a ship.

"You were thinking," said Fortino, "that if La Virazón was mine, we could set our course for the oyster beds of Baja."

Trin nodded.

"Then what would you say if I told you she is?"

Trin stared at his godfather, hardly daring to believe what he had heard. "Padrino! She can't be!"

"But she is, mi hijo!" Fortino's eyes were shining. "Not all mine—but half! My good friend, Pedro Barraza, bought the other half. He's an old sea captain and grandfather like me, Trinidad. Always we have worried about how to make the little ones safe when we are gone. To leave money is not good. Money soon melts away and there is nothing left. But a ship is a good legacy. She earns her way. Put money into a ship, and she will bring money back to you as long as she sails. So for more than a year now, we two old men have been searching for a schooner we could afford to buy—an old vessel, but sturdy, sound of keel and strong-ribbed—"

"And you've just found her?"

"Two weeks ago, in the port of Altata. Between us, we

had all but three hundred pesos of her price, and that we'll be able to pay if we can get to Baja."

"*If?*" asked Trin apprehensively.

"It depends on whether we can get divers," Fortino explained.

"You have *me!*" said Trin. "And what about the Yaqui? Can't he dive?"

"There is no better diver in all of Mexico. Since he was a boy your age, Yaño has gone with the pearlers every summer to the oyster beds. He knows them all."

"Then you have *two* of us, Padrino!"

"Two wouldn't pay the cost of the voyage, mi hijo. A vessel must have fifteen or twenty divers to make any profit. That's why Captain Barraza went on ahead to Guaymas, while I stayed in Altata to ready *La Virazón* for her voyage."

"Will he find them there?"

"If we're lucky! Most of the pearling expeditions are outfitted in Guaymas and the Yaquis gather there for the hiring. The vessels that get to port first get the best of them."

"But you already have Yaño—"

"That's because he's my friend."

Trin stared at his godfather in puzzlement. He knew that most of the divers on pearling vessels were Yaquis. They were strong men and daring, more willing to risk death in the depths than most Mexicans. But they were not *friends*. When the pearling season was over, they went back to their towns on the Yaqui River to join their tribesmen in plots of rebellion. At any time they might return to massacre the very men they had worked for.

"You're thinking of the raids," said Fortino, reading his mind. "It is true that a great many Yaquis are still our enemies, but there are some who are not. Some, like Yaño, never go back to the river towns. They prefer to live among us and become our neighbors."

Trin was skeptical. "I have heard that those who live in our towns give *help* to those who attack us," he said. "They pretend to be our friends, but they work to send food and weapons to the guerillas who hide in the barrancas."

"I don't believe Yaño pretends," said Fortino. "I trust him. I hope you will trust him. Diving in the Sea of Cortez is not like diving in a reservoir, Trin. A man faces death every time he goes down. There will be much you need to learn, and Yaño can teach you."

"Has he ever found a great pearl—like the one I must find for the Virgin?"

Fortino shook his head. "Such luck is not given to many. A man may search a lifetime and never find a great pearl. But Yaño has found some *good* ones. And each summer there is a new chance. From Cabo Palmo all the way up the coast of Baja to San Bruno Bay, two hundred divers— maybe three hundred—will be working from vessels like this. Some one of them will bring up a great pearl. It could be Yaño. It could be *you.*"

Trin understood what his godfather was trying to tell him—that at best, he had a two hundred to one chance.

"If we get to Baja," he said, thinking aloud.

"Sí, my son," said Fortino. "*If!*"

CHAPTER TEN

The sun was setting as Fortino eased the schooner into the safety of the harbor. Across the bay, Trin could see the little town of Guaymas set like a jewel within a ring of bleak red mountains. Above them, a drifting cloud mass took on the cerise hues of sunset, turning the smooth water to flame and casting a warm glow over the flat-roofed adobe buildings that clustered around the church. Moored offshore were three vessels—a schooner and two luggers.

"All pearlers," said Fortino, as he steered the *Virazón* to a good berth. "Good thing the capitán rushed back here ahead of us."

"What if he didn't get here in time?" asked Trin anxiously. "What if the divers were already hired?"

"Then it would be useless for us to go," said Fortino. "Without divers, there would be no hold full of pearl shell and no pearls. But Guaymas is the capitán's home town. If there were any divers to be found, he'd know where to find them."

"How soon will we know?"

"Very soon, my son." Fortino lifted his hand from the helm to point out an adobe structure, apart from the others, on the slope of the hill. "You see that house, Trinidad? The capitán built up there so he could see every ship that entered the harbor, and if I know my old friend, he's on the roof now with his spy-glass, looking for the *Virazón!*"

"Will he recognize her?"

Fortino chuckled. "He'll be out to us in a dinghy before we can drop anchor!"

But when the anchor was down and the sails were furled, Captain Barraza had still not appeared. It was obvious that Fortino was not only disappointed but disturbed. He ordered a boat lowered and signalled Trin to join him. With Yaño at the oars, they headed for the darkening shoreline.

"Maybe the capitán was too busy to come," Trin suggested hopefully.

"Sí. It could be he *did* have trouble getting divers," agreed Fortino. "Maybe he's gone out to the Yaqui huts along the inlets."

The dinghy touched the beach, and they jumped out. Trin and Yaño ran her up high and dry on the sand, and the three of them started up the trail toward the captain's house. As they neared it, Trin saw a dim rectangle of light showing through a small barred window.

"Padrino!" he cried excitedly. "Your friend is home!"

"The light tells us nothing," said Fortino quietly. "The son, Ignacio, and his wife and children also live in the home of the captain. It was for them he went in with me to buy the schooner."

He knocked on the door. When at length it swung open, a dark, hulking figure loomed between them and the dimly lighted background, and Trin had a fleeting impression that it was not a man but a great black bear.

"Buenas noches, Ignacio," said Fortino.

"If you're looking for my father," said a hard, grating voice, "you'll find him in the cementerio!"

Fortino stared at the man in confusion. "Cementerio?"

he repeated. "I don't understand, Ignacio. What are you saying?"

"I'm saying my father is dead!" said Ignacio sharply.

"Mother of God!" murmured Fortino, crossing himself. "Qué Dios lo benedicas!" His body seemed to sag, and Trin put an arm around him in support.

From somewhere behind the hulk, a woman's voice cried, "Por Dios! Let the capitán come in!"

With a grunt, the bear-like figure stepped aside, and Trin saw a young woman with an infant in her arms.

"Lo siento, Capitán Chavarria!" she said apologetically. "My husband was not thinking. Come in, por favor!"

"Gracias, Maria, gracias!" said Fortino, his voice barely audible. With the help of Trin and Yaño, he walked heavily to a chair and sank into it. "Forgive me," he said, "it is the shock. He was my very good friend."

Maria brought a decanter and glass from a cabinet and set them on the table beside Fortino. "It was a shock to us, also," she said gently, as she filled the glass with an amber fluid. "And a sad loss. The capitán was a loving father and grandfather."

The room was lighted by a single lamp, and Trin saw that three small children, a little girl of five or six and two younger boys, had stopped their play to stare at their elders with curious eyes.

"Drink this, Capitán," said Maria, offering the glass to Fortino. "It will make you feel better."

"Gracias, Maria, you are very kind." When he had downed the drink, Fortino asked. "How did it happen?"

"He dropped dead on the street, the day he got back from Altata!" declared Ignacio harshly. "I only wish it had happened before he went!"

The cruel words struck Fortino like a blow, and he

:97

sprang up from the chair, strengthened by anger. "Nombre de Dios!"

"Please, Capitán," pleaded Maria, "do not listen to him. He speaks so because he is upset. He does not mean what he says!"

"Por Dios, I mean every word!" insisted Ignacio, moving toward them, his heavy shoulders hunched, his head thrust forward belligerently. "He should have died before he put his money into that hulk out there in the harbor!"

"God forgive you, Ignacio!" said Fortino. "He did that for *you!*"

"Then he was a fool! What do I want with that old, rotten boat?"

"She's not rotten" declared Fortino, controlling his anger. "She's a sound ship, and she'll earn a good living for you and the family."

"She'll earn me nothing!" said Ignacio. "I'll sell my half as soon as I can find somebody stupid enough to buy it!"

"You will *not* sell, Ignacio," said Fortino firmly, "because I'll not give my consent, and you can't sell without it!"

"You won't stop me, old man!" shouted Ignacio. "Before you persuaded my father to buy that old tub, he had *money* to leave me. It's *money* I want—silver pesos in my hands!"

"And how long will you keep them?" demanded Fortino. "How long will it be before you've thrown them away on gambling and brandy?"

"What I do with them is none of your business!"

"It was your father's business," declared Fortino, "and he made it mine. It was because he knew how silver would slip through your fingers that he bought the schooner, so your wife and your children would not go hungry, so you and they could remain free. I have given him my promise,

:98

Ignacio, and I intend to keep it. You cannot sell without my consent. It is so written in the agreement. You will take your father's place, as he would have wished, and sail with us to Baja."

"And what will you do there, without divers?"

Trin watched Fortino's face as he got the full impact of the man's words. In the tension of their conflict, the question of the divers had been forgotten. This, then, was the answer: there were none. Captain Barraza had died before he could hire them.

"If you have not hired them, then I will," said Fortino, his jaw tight.

"I think you will find, Capitán, that the other pearlers have beaten you to it," said Ignacio, with an insolent smile. "But if there were any Yaquis available, what would you use for money?"

His hard eyes glinted with triumph, and Trin knew that in some way Ignacio Barraza had his godfather cornered.

"I happen to know, Capitán," he went on boldly, "that when my father died, he had *on him* all the money that was to have been advanced to the divers."

"And where is that money, now?" asked Fortino.

"Would you have me bury my father like a beggar, without absolution?" Ignacio demanded self-righteously. "I had to pay it to the priest!"

"You didn't have to pay all of it!" said Fortino.

"The cost of a Christian burial is very high," declared Ignacio defensively.

"It is high," said Fortino quietly, "but not *that* high. What have you done with the rest of it?"

"There was none left. I paid it all to the priest."

"You're lying, Ignacio." Fortino's voice was low and controlled, but the muscles of his jaw stood out in tight knots.

"That money belonged to the partnership, and we will need what was left of it to secure the divers."

"It's gone!" shouted Ignacio, in a rage. "I tell you there will be no divers—and no pearling in Baja! You can let the ship rot in the harbor!"

Listening in helpless anger, Trin clenched his fists, wishing he had the strength to smash the hulking Barraza, as Barraza was smashing his godfather's hopes and his own. Fortino himself had said that it was useless for a ship to cross to Baja without a good number of divers; now it was clear that even if any could be found, his padrino couldn't hire them. Each Yaqui diver demanded a sizeable advance payment, in silver pesos, before he would embark on the voyage—and the pesos were gone. In place of a partner and friend, Fortino now faced a formidable foe.

"And if the ship were to rot in the harbor," Fortino was saying, "how would that benefit you?"

"I'll tell you how!" Barraza roared. "If I can't sell without *your* consent, then you can't sell without *mine*. And when it comes time to pay the three hundred pesos you owe on the schooner, then you can come to me and *beg* for a chance to sell, before they take her away from you!" He strode to the door and swung it open. "You'll *beg*, Capitán —or lose every peso you've put into her! Unless—" His wide mouth twisted in a sneer—"unless you have hidden, somewhere, a chest of gold!"

He started out the door, but something made him pause and turn back. "You haven't introduced me to your friends, Capitán," he said craftily, moving into the room. "You have in him, perhaps, one diver," he said, indicating Yaño, "but the boy—who is he?"

"We are both divers," Yaño cut in quickly. "The boy is a friend of mine. I brought him aboard."

"Hm–m," murmured Barraza thoughtfully. "I would have thought he was Mexican, not Yaqui." His eyes bored into Trin. "What's your name, chico?"

"José—" Yaño tried to cut in again, but Barraza stopped him.

"Let him speak for himself!" he commanded sharply.

Trin stared back at the searching eyes, set too close together in the swarthy face. "My name is, as my friend said, José," he declared evenly.

"José *what?*" demanded Barraza.

"Just José," Yaño cut in. "He has no father."

"Silencio!" shouted Barraza angrily. "Let him answer! Tell me quickly, boy—where did you come aboard? Was it Turtle Bay?"

"Where he came aboard is none of your business!" said Fortino sharply. "The boy is Yaño's friend, and I have hired him as a diver. There will be no more questioning!"

Barraza smiled unpleasantly. "As you say, Capitán Chavvarria!" With a last piercing look at Trin, he went out quietly, closing the door after him.

There was a moment of complete silence, as the eyes of Fortino and Yaño met, while Trin looked from one to the other.

"There is danger in his questions," said Fortino softly.

"Capitán," whispered Maria, moving to them swiftly, "I have heard gossip in the town. It is said that the police search for a peon boy who has run away from a great hacienda. My husband has heard it, too. He has spoken of a reward. It was that he was thinking of, when he asked the questions. I saw it in his eyes."

"I saw it, too, Maria," agreed Fortino. "We must hide the boy."

"We can't hide him here!" protested Maria. "There is no safe place!"

"Come with me, Trin!" offered Yaño. "We'll go to my people."

"No!" protested Trin. "We have told him I am your friend!"

"He's right," said Fortino. "They'll search the Yaqui huts first of all."

"There is one place they will not search," declared Yaño. "It is there I will take him, Capitán."

"You're sure, Yaño?" asked Fortino.

"Capitán, I swear to you. If the boy is not safe where I take him, there is no place where he will be safe."

"Go with him, my son!" commanded Fortino. "And quickly!"

"Wait!" whispered Maria. "Ignacio may still be outside. I will look." She started for the door, but Yaño stopped her.

"No, Señora. I will look!"

"Then go by the back door," she said, indicating the direction. "And walk softly. He may be hiding, and he must not see where you go!"

Yaño disappeared, slipping out soundlessly, as they listened. In the corner, the children were preoccupied with a game of their own.

After a moment, Maria spoke softly. "I'm sorry, Capitán, that to your grief should be added this bad trouble with my husband. I wish there might be something I could do to help."

"You have helped, Maria," said Fortino gently.

"I must tell you about the money," she whispered. "You were right—it didn't all go to the church. But it *is* gone— all of it! As you said, it went for the brandy and the gambling. I tried to stop Ignacio, but I could do nothing."

"Try not to worry, Maria. I will see that you and the children are taken care of," Fortino promised. "There will be a way."

Yaño slipped back into the room as silently as he had left it. "Barraza is gone," he whispered. "I saw him running down the trail to the town."

"He's gone for the police!" said Maria, in distress.

"We'll go the other way—to the inlets," said Yaño. "I'll borrow a Yaqui canoe there to take us to the secret place."

"Then go now, Trinidad!"

Trin's eyes sought Fortino's and held them in urgent questioning. How could he, they asked, trust this Yaqui Indian, this man of a tribe that had so often tortured and murdered his countrymen? How could he know it was safe to go alone in the darkness of night with him, to a secret place known only to his people? Who would there be to find him, to save him, if the Yaquis decided to make him their victim?

"Come, amigo, quickly!" commanded Yaño, moving swiftly to the door.

"Trust him, my son!" whispered Fortino, gripping Trin's shoulders in farewell. "Vaya con Dios!"

Yaño slipped out into the darkness, and Trin followed him.

CHAPTER ELEVEN

The Yaqui moved through the night with cat eyes, his feet swift and sure on the narrow path that cut across a cleft in the hills. Close behind him, Trin was guided only by the dim outline of his figure and the almost imperceptible contrast in the shades of darkness that separated brush from rock and trail. Straining his eyes to their limit, Trin followed the Indian through what seemed like miles of blackness, his mind too intent on the effort to keep pace to think of anything else.

When at length they dipped down to the shore, the slight sheen of reflected starlight on the smooth waters made the going easier, and he was able to observe something of his surroundings. A delicate tracery of foam, curling up onto the sand, marked the lower boundary of a wide beach, and in the darkness of its upper limits the silhouette of a thatched hut was faintly visible. If there were others beyond it, they were enveloped by the night, but Trin guessed that Yaño had reached the settlement of his people.

There was no sound except the restless whispering of the sea, and no light to suggest a village, but this was not surprising, for it was the custom of Indians—and, in fact, of most of the poor people of Mexico—to go to sleep at dusk and rise at daybreak. The Yaqui passed the first hut, running lightly along the beach above the swirling edge of foam. Following him, Trin made out the dark shape of palm trees and knew there would be a cluster of huts beneath them. Dead ahead, a ghostly white form seemed to materialize out of the sand, and Yaño paused beside it. Catching up, Trin saw that it was a dugout canoe.

"This is the canoe of my friend," Yaño whispered. "Wait here!"

He disappeared into the gloom under the palms, and Trin stood alone in the darkness. A vague feeling of uneasiness crept over him, and his mind began to conjure up images of what might happen to an alien intruder if some wakeful Yaqui were to discover him there.

He got into the canoe and lay flat on the bottom. It was double-ended, carved from a single log, and braced inside with struts. Its ghostly appearance came from the hard coat of white plaster with which the Indians covered the wood inside and out, to make it waterproof. Trin had often seen the dugouts in coastal waters when he had been out in his father's fishing boat, and he knew they were seaworthy and fast.

He lay motionless, staring up at the stars as he waited and listened. Suddenly, without even a whisper of sound to warn him, the stars were blotted out by a dark form bending over him. His body tensed, and he held his breath. The figure was broader and heavier than Yaño's and it stared down at him in silence with eyes he could not see. A second figure appeared, and he heard a low chuckle.

"Good!" whispered Yaño. "Mi amigo has already gone to bed."

Relieved, Trin sprang out of the canoe.

"This is Pahsiko," said Yaño, "and he, too, wanted to sleep. I almost got a knife in my belly for waking him."

Trin wondered if the man was really angry, for he made no response. Instead, he lifted one end of the dugout and waited for Yaño to lift the other. Handing the paddles to Trin, Yaño took hold and the two Indians carried the little boat down to the water. A moment later, the Yaqui, still silent, pushed them off, and with Yaño at the bow facing forward, and Trin at the stern, they paddled out into the void of the bay.

The dark outline of land disappeared behind them, and ahead there was nothing but a moving infinity of water. Trin wondered if the Yaqui was setting his course by a star. Certainly there was nothing else in the vast murmuring emptiness to guide him, as he sent the canoe slicing toward its mysterious destination.

Paddling in rhythm with Yaño's long, powerful strokes, Trin felt as if he were moving in a dream. The lonely flight had the quality of a nightmare. Even the silent Indian in the village added a note of menace. How much did he know of where they were going and why? If the police came to the village in search of Yaño and his "friend," could he be trusted?

The serrated mass of an island erased the stars to the south, and Trin wondered if this was to be his hiding place, but the canoe cut past it without slackening speed. A breeze sprang up, slapping the roughened water against the hull, and he felt the sting of salt spray on his skin. Other islands loomed only to melt back into darkness as the dugout passed them.

Suddenly Trin became aware of a hard black shape rising like a great rock out of the sea, directly ahead of them. Still the canoe shot forward on a collision course, and Trin shouted, "Yaño! Look out!"

"Stop paddling and duck down flat!" the Yaqui commanded sharply.

Trin obeyed and with one long, final pull, the Indian followed suit. The dugout glided foward in silence until it slowed to a stop. There was a hollow sound of water washing against rock.

"You can sit up, now," said Yaño, his voice echoing around them.

Trin raised up into total blackness. There was no glimmer of starlight, no slightest sheen on the water. His eyes, now well adjusted to the varying densities of darkness, could see nothing.

"Where are we?" he asked.

"In a cavern. At the entrance, the rock is barely two feet above the water, but inside it rises to thirty."

"How could you find it, in the dark?"

"There is a way, but I can't tell it to you. There are many secrets about the islands in this sea that are known only to my people."

The canoe rolled gently, and Trin judged that the Yaqui was tying her bowline to some projecting rock.

"I've brought you here because you are godson to my friend, the capitán, but this is a place of refuge for the men of my tribe, and I can't let you see beyond the darkness."

"Is it here we will hide—in this cavern?"

"Only *you* will hide!" said Yaño. "I will go back to Guaymas to help the capitán."

The prospect of staying alone in the pitch black silence of the cavern, knowing that at any moment some unfriendly Yaqui might come upon him, was appalling to Trin, but he made no comment.

"How long will you be gone?" he asked, instead.

"A day or two, maybe three. Until it is possible for *La Virazón* to sail."

"How can she sail if there are no divers?"

"I will try to search out divers in the river towns, but if there are none who choose to go, there may still be a way to go without them."

"How?" asked Trin, in surprise.

"There is one who knows a secret that could help us. It was he who found this cavern, and I would not have dared bring you to it except that he is kin to me, many fathers back."

"Who is he?"

"The oldest man in my tribe. The spirits speak to him and make him very wise."

"Will you go to him now?" asked Trin.

"Sí! He is here, on the island above our heads. You will stay with him while I am gone. Come!" The Yaqui slipped into the water beside the canoe. "We have to swim out. Take it slowly and stay close to me."

He pushed off, and Trin fumbled his way over the side and followed the sound of his long easy strokes. They had gone some ten yards when Yaño called back, "Keep under! We go out now!"

Trin jackknifed, and when he rose to the surface he saw that he was beneath the stars again. A few feet away, the sheer black cliffs towered to the sky.

"We'll swim to where the cliffs are lower," said Yaño, appearing beside him. "And we must hurry. If you should see this island by daylight, they will not let you leave it." He struck out to the west, swimming strongly, and his body was quickly swallowed up in the dark, wind-ruffled waters.

Unable to see him, Trin strained to hear the rhythm of

his strokes, but the roar of the sea in his ears drowned out all other sounds. He felt cold and terribly alone in the darkness, and the Yaqui's final words lingered in his mind. ". . . they will not let you leave it." *Alive,* he thought.

He swam frantically, guided by the line of foam at the base of the cliffs, until a cry so sharp that it pierced through the suck and slap of the sea stopped him in mid-stroke. He treaded water, listening, and heard it again, wild and uncanny, rising from the darkness just ahead of him.

An answering call echoed from the cliffs, and this time he recognized it as the strange wolflike cry of the loon. A loud braying "ha ha ha ha!" followed by a shrill "ky rie, ky rie, ky rie!" came out of the dark waters, to be answered by "tuc-a-ree, tuc-tuc a-roo!" from the cliff, and Trin realized that Yaño was communicating with someone on the island in the voices of seabirds.

When the code had been completed, the Yaqui led him to the sheer face of the cliff. Treading water, he gave one final call, the sharp "tee-arr, tee-arr!" of the tern. A deep "keow, keow!" came in answer, and a moment later a heavy rope slithered down from above. At Yaño's command, Trin grasped it and started the long climb, hand over hand. His arms, already tired from hours of paddling the canoe, felt as if they were being wrenched from their sockets, but he mounted the rope grimly, twenty feet, forty, sixty, driven on by fear of the approaching dawn.

As he reached the top, the stars were beginning to pale, and he could make out the dim figures of two men. One of them reached down to seize his arm and pull him to safety, but he did not relax his iron grip, and when Yaño clambered up after him, the Indian challenged him sharply in the Yaqui tongue. There followed what sounded to Trin like a heated argument, and he listened in nervous suspense, aware that with one simple shove the man could send him plunging over the cliff's edge.

The argument ended abruptly as Yaño broke the Indian's grip, and pulled Trin after him up the steep slope of a hill that reached its summit several hundred feet above them. At a point halfway up, they paused for breath, and Trin asked, "What were they saying?"

"They were angry because I brought you here."

"And they wanted to kill me?"

"Sí! They said it was already too light, that you could see the shape of the island and describe it to your countrymen."

"I will never tell anything of what I see. I swear it by the Holy Virgin!"

"I believe that," said Yaño, "but they do not."

"Then why did they let me go?"

"I told them I will let the Old One decide."

Darkness paled into daybreak as they reached the summit and dropped steeply into a miniature valley, made habitable by a natural spring. Several huts nestled in the lush green growth of palms and ferns that marked the oasis, but the hut of the Old One stood above the others on a broad ledge where a spring gushed out from a cleft in the rock to fall into a pool below.

As they approached the two-room bamboo structure, Trin saw that an old woman was making a fire in the open-sided kitchen. Yaño spoke to her briefly in Yaqui, and then drew Trin into the hut. In the gloom of the small room, he could barely make out the bed in the corner, where the lean figure of the old man lay on a bamboo mat, covered with a single blanket.

"He is asleep," whispered Yaño, "and the spirits may be

speaking to him in his dreams. We will wait until he wakens."

"Will he be as angry as the others when he sees me here?" asked Trin.

"He is my great, great grandfather," said Yaño, "and he will listen when I tell him the reasons."

"But will he let me go?"

"If he trusts you. He is a very wise man, and he will read what is in your heart."

"If he really can, then he'll *know* he can trust me. But what about the others? Will they listen to him?"

"In my tribe, the young men respect the wisdom of the old."

Yaño dipped a half-gourd into a large earthen olla, and offered Trin a drink. When they had both drunk deeply of the cool water, they lay on the hard dirt floor, waiting. Trin's body was tired from the long, strenuous night but his nerves prickled with tension and he was unable to relax. The rays of the rising sun filtered through the interwoven bamboo of the walls, and the ancient one stirred on his mat. Trin watched him breathlessly, but he did not waken.

"You are impatient," said Yaño, with an amused smile. "I, too. He sleeps late, for a Yaqui. But he has more than a hundred years to make him weary."

"There are a thousand questions in my mind," said Trin, "but I know I have no right to ask them."

"If they are about this island, I cannot answer them. No Mexican but you has ever set foot on it. To your people, it is like many other islands in this sea—a place of cliffs that cannot be scaled, an eyrie for birds. Only the Yaquis know its secrets. If you were to go back to your people and tell what you have seen here, you would die. Even I could not save you."

"I will not tell," said Trin. "I've given you my promise. But it was not of this island that I was thinking. It was something you said, in the cavern."

"Then ask your question. I will answer, if I can."

"The capitán said it would be useless to go to Baja without fifteen or twenty divers," Trin began, "but *you* said we might be able to go anyway. How can that be?"

"We could go *only* if the Old One will share his secret," said Yaño. "It is like this, amigo: the pearlers all know where to look for the oyster beds. The Bay of La Paz is a good place, and the waters of Canal San Lorenzo and the nearby islands of San José and Espiritu Santo. Loreto is another good place, and the Isla Coronados. If *we* had twenty divers, we would go to Bahia Mulegé and the Isla San Marcos. But no matter which of these places we chose, there would be other ships there, too, with their divers— altogether maybe fifty—maybe one hundred and fifty— even more. And when we found a good bed, the other ships would rush to anchor over it and send down their divers. If we had *twenty* divers, we could bring up a fair share, but with only two . . ."

"They'd come up with ten times as many!" said Trin, getting the point.

"Sí. You are quick," exclaimed Yaño. "With so many divers, the good bed would soon be exhausted, and we would have to move on in search of another. And each time we found one, the same thing would happen over again. Always, we would get only one tenth. *But*—if we could go to an oyster bank that is unknown—in a place apart from the others, where we couldn't be seen—"

"Then we could take our time, and even with only two divers we could bring up all the oysters in the bed!" finished Trin excitedly.

"Excelente! Now you understand as well as I!"

"And that's the Old One's secret!" exclaimed Trin, his mind racing ahead. "He knows of such a place!"

"Sí! If he remembers!"

"You're not sure?"

"It's many years since he has spoken of it," said Yaño. "And he has not seen it since he was my age. I am twenty. He is one hundred and six. It is a very long time."

"Eighty-six years!" said Trin, appalled. "He'll never remember."

"I think he may," said Yaño. "Now that he is so old he remembers the things of long ago better than those that happened yesterday."

"Did he ever tell you about it?"

"Sí, he told me often, when I was a boy."

"Then couldn't *you* find it?" demanded Trin.

"No. He has told me the story of how he came upon it, but not where it is, or how it looks from an approaching ship."

"If he doesn't remember, or if he won't tell us the place, couldn't we search?"

Yaño shook his head. "Have you ever heard of the Placer de le Piedra Negada?" he asked.

"No."

"It is a huge sunken rock on which great numbers of large pearl oysters have been found. Everyone *knows* it is near Loreto and that it may be reached eleven fathoms down. Every year the divers search for it. I, myself, have searched. Yet many, many years go by when no one can find it. If it is so of a rock that is *known*, what of the Old One's secret? It is a tiny black dot somewhere in a great sea—and only he knows the place. We will do well to find it, even if he tells us where to search."

The Old One stirred again and mumbled, and Yaño rose and crossed the hut to kneel by his pallet. He spoke to him in the Yaqui tongue, and the old man opened his eyes. Almost at once he became aware of Trin and raised up on his elbow to stare at him.

While Yaño talked to his great, great grandfather, Trin studied the aged Indian. His straight white hair hung to his shoulder blades, and his wrinkled skin seemed stretched across the strong bones of his face like thin parchment. Everything about his frail, withered body suggested weakness, yet Trin sensed a powerful life force behind the sunken, unfathomable eyes.

He met their gaze steadily, looking away only when the old woman came into the hut with a basket of tortillas and an olla of coffee. Yaño poured the thick black beverage into three earthen cups. Handing one of them to Trin, he said, "I have told him who you are and why I brought you here."

"Is he angry?" Trin whispered.

"He has not said so. While we eat, I will ask him to tell us the story of the secret oyster bank."

"But how will I understand him?" asked Trin.

"He knows your language as well as his own," said Yaño. "When he was a boy, the Jesuits taught him to speak and write in both tongues. For many years he was interpreter for my people."

From a corner of the room Yaño took two rawhide stools and set them beside the old man's bed. "Sit here with me, amigo," he said. "The years have taken away the keenness of the Old One's ears, and he may want to hear you speak."

For a few moments the three of them munched the warm tortillas and sipped the hot, bitter brew in silence, and then Yaño made his request, in Yaqui. The old man's answer was short and firm.

"He says he will not tell the story because you are Mexican and will not believe the way it happened," Yaño translated. "He says only a Yaqui can understand."

"But I *will* believe it! Please, Señor," said Trin, appealing directly to the aged Indian, "if you will tell me the story, I will believe whatever you say—and I will try to understand as if I were Yaño."

The dark, penetrating eyes bored into him. "You cannot understand with the mind of Yaño unless you know of the spirits as Yaño knows of them," said the Old One, in a deep, clear voice.

"He speaks of the beliefs of my people," Yaño explained. "The padres have taught us to worship your God, but we have not forsaken our own."

"Old Tio, on the hacienda, told me the Yaquis make food offerings to the sun and moon," said Trin.

"Sí. It is true. And for us, there are also the sacred deer and the black dwarf of the rainbow—and there are others, many others. But to understand my grandfather's story, you need only to know about the guardian spirits. In our belief, there is always a spirit who guards us from danger and gives us power."

"Is it something like an angel?" asked Trin.

"Sí. It may appear to us as a beautiful person with wings, like the angels of your faith, or it may come in the shape of a coyote or a snake, or a sheep or a dog. Sometimes we see it when we are awake. Sometimes its message comes to us in dreams. Perhaps you have had such a dream and did not understand its meaning."

"When I was in the mountains, I had a strange dream," said Trin, remembering his night in the barranca.

"Tell it to the Old One," said Yaño. "He will understand it."

The aged man was lying back against crude pillows stuffed with raw wool, his intent gaze fixed on Trin.

"I dreamed I was standing on the shore," said Trin, addressing him, "and there were low black clouds in the sky, and under them, the sea was black, too. I saw that there was something floating on the water, but I didn't know what it was. I stared until I could make it out, and I saw that it was oysters. The whole sea was covered with them."

The Old One raised up and leaned forward, listening intently.

"Just then," Trin went on, "there was a loud clap of thunder, and the rain began to fall in big drops. While I was watching it, the oysters opened their shells, and the raindrops fell into them."

The black, sunken eyes of the old man seemed to catch fire, and he whispered something to Yaño, in Yaqui.

"What happened next?" asked Yaño, his own eyes lit with excitement.

"Nothing else happened, except the sun came out and the light of it made the raindrops look like pearls. And then, the sun got brighter and brighter until—" Trin's voice trailed off as, in his memory, he felt again the golden warmth that had enveloped him in the cold and dark of that morning.

"Until?" whispered Yaño.

"Until it seemed to be inside of me," Trin murmured, his mind still back in the barranca, reliving that strange moment of exaltation.

The two Yaquis were silent, and Trin brought his thoughts back to them. The old man was still staring at him, but something had changed. The sharp, searching gaze was gone, and he looked at Trin warmly, as a father might look at his son.

After an instant, Yaño spoke. "Did you know, Trinidad, that in the belief of my people, when a raindrop falls into an oyster, a pearl is formed?"

"No," said Trin. If he had ever heard it, he had forgotten, but it occurred to him that it might have been something Old Tio had mentioned, long ago. "Does the dream have a meaning?" he asked.

The Old One smiled and nodded. "It was a good dream," he said. "Because of it, I will tell you my story."

CHAPTER TWELVE

The ancient Yaqui drained the last bitter drops from his earthen cup; then eased his shriveled body into the softness of the pillows. His head sank back against the horizontal pattern of bamboo, and he closed his eyes.

"Is he going to sleep?" asked Trin anxiously.

"I think he is looking back, in his mind," said Yaño.

There was a long moment of silence before the old man spoke. Then, without opening his eyes, he murmured, "Tears of angels—"

"He is speaking of the raindrops," Yaño whispered.

"Falling—from sky to sea—congealing into pearls—" The words came like a sigh from the wrinkled lips.

There was another long pause, while Trin waited in suspense, wondering if the old Indian could possibly remember back across eighty-six years.

"It was long ago—many lives ago," said the Old One, at last, opening his eyes. "That boy—young and strong like you, Yaño—that boy who dove deep into the sea—he must have been someone else."

"He was *you*, Grandfather," said Yaño. "You had been all summer along the shores of Baja with the pearlers, remember? And your ship had set sail for Guaymas with her hold full of pearl shell—"

"Sí! And many pearls!" said the Old One.

"You were a day out to sea, when the hurricane struck—"

"*El Cordonazo*—the Lash!" The sunken eyes stared into space as the aged Indian fixed his mind on the scene from his past. "It fell on us like a great whip!"

"Sí! You had to flatten down before it!"

"There were war drums in the sky—and long knives of fire—"

"The thunder and lightning—"

"The wind was a devil, beating the ship, and she fled as a child before him," said the old man, reliving the dreadful hour. "A helpless child, running for her life. But he killed her!"

"Sí, Grandfather. He hurled her against the rock face of an island—and you fell into the sea."

"I fell—" He paused, in memory feeling the terrible, raging anger of the sea. "I fell, and the waves buried me."

"You fought your way up, but each time you sucked in air, a mountain of water smashed down on you—remember?"

"No man could live, in that sea."

"You knew you would drown, Grandfather."

"Sí—until *he* came!"

There was a long pause as Yaño waited for the old man to go on.

"He?" whispered Trin. "Who was *he?*"

"Sh! He will tell you," said Yaño.

"I was down, far down in the darkness under the waves," said the Old One, "and it was there he came to me: a great sea-serpent with scales of gold!"

"A sea-serpent!" Trin breathed, in amazement.

"He had a long tail, and a body thick as a man, and I felt

him coil around me and draw me down and down—into the depths."

"You tried to struggle against him, but you were too weak," Yaño reminded the old man.

"Sí, I was too weak, and he drew me down until I felt a strong current pulling toward the island—and *into* it! The serpent loosed his coils and swam with the current, and I was carried after him."

"You were *inside* the rock base of the island, Grandfather, and you said everything was blacker than night," Yaño filled in.

"Sí, except the serpent," agreed the Old One. "Even in the darkness, he was golden. And I knew then he was not a true serpent, but my guardian-spirit. I followed him through the black channel until I was dying for need of air —and then I could not see him. The serpent was gone, and above me was the faint light of day."

The old Indian lapsed into silence, as though spent from reliving, in memory, his desperate struggle for survival.

"When you came to the surface, you saw a narrow beach and swam to it, remember?" said Yaño. "And you dragged yourself up beyond the waves and dropped down on the sand."

"I slept," said the Old One. "All through the day and the night, I slept. And when I woke, the storm was over and I was on the shore of a lake—a small lake inside a ring of cliffs."

"A *lake—inside—*" Trin repeated, trying to get the picture.

"He means that it *appeared* to be a lake," explained Yaño, "but it was really a lagoon of sea water. You see that pottery bowl, Trinidad, the one beneath the olla?"

Trin followed his gesture and saw a small round bowl that caught the slow drip of water from the porous earthen olla above it.

"The rim of that bowl is the ring of high cliffs," said Yaño, "and the water in it is the lagoon."

"Sí!" said Trin, visualizing it. "And if we put that small bowl into a much larger bowl full of water, it would float in the middle like an island. But to get from the water of the big bowl into the water of the little bowl—"

"—the little bowl would have to be cracked!" exclaimed Yaño.

"I see it!" said Trin excitedly. "The black channel was a big crack in the land!"

"Excelente!" said the Old One. "You see it well. It was a big crack—but six fathoms down. In the cliffs *above* the sea, there was no crack at all."

"And no one knew what was inside," said Yaño, "until *you* dove down, Grandfather, to find the crack, again."

"Sí! It was then I found the oyster bed, beneath the water of the lagoon!" said the old man. "Hundreds of oysters—many large and very old—hidden in that secret place!"

"Did you find any pearls?" asked Trin eagerly.

"I did not look. A man may live without pearls," said the old Yaqui, "but not without water to drink. I looked for a way to stay alive."

"He swam out through the crack," said Yaño, "but only the bodies of the dead—and broken parts of the ship— floated on the sea. No man was alive but him, and the shell and pearls were gone—all swept away by the storm."

"Then how did he stay alive?" asked Trin.

"From the broken timbers he made a raft, and with a

piece of torn canvas he set a small sail," Yaño explained. "But he was five days at sea and nearly dead of thirst before he was picked up by a Yaqui fishing boat."

"And he never looked for pearls at all?"

"When he was strong again, it was no longer the season to go, but in the next summer he went with a ship to the island and they found many pearls—and one great one, fit for the crown of a king. But that is another story," whispered Yaño, "and the Old One grows tired. I must ask him, now, how to find the place."

The aged Yaqui was leaning back against the pillows with his eyes closed, and Trin wondered if he had fallen asleep.

"Grandfather," said Yaño gently, "do you remember the location of the island—on the compass?"

The old man opened his eyes. "The location is not important," he said. "The story has been told."

"It is important to my friends, Grandfather. The capitán is without divers, except for me and Trinidad, and he must look for pearls in a place where there will be no other ships."

"No man must look for pearls," said the Old One. "They bring only greed and death. Without them, a man may live many good years."

"We will not be searching out of greed, Grandfather," said Yaño. "The capitán needs pearls and shell to pay for his ship and feed eight grandchildren."

"Sí, Señor," said Trin earnestly, "and I need them to buy the freedom of my mother and five little brothers and sisters. If I don't find pearls, they will be bound peons until they die."

"Not only they, Grandfather, but their children after

them for many generations," said Yaño, "so great is their debt."

"Please, Señor, I beg you—tell us how to find the island so I can make them free!" pleaded Trin.

"To tell you is to condemn you to the evil spirits," said the Old One. "For three summers, I told the secret—and for three summers it brought greed and murder and storms that sank the ships. The island is a place of devils!"

"But the guardian-spirits will go with us, Grandfather!" said Yaño. "Already they have spoken to Trinidad in his dream."

The sunken black eyes stared at Trin thoughtfully. "Sí. They have told him it will be a summer of good pearling, but they have not said what will come *with* the pearls. They have not spoken of the devils."

"Perhaps they have not spoken of them because there will be none," said Yaño. "Do you remember how to find the island, Bisabuelo?"

"It is written down—from long ago," said the Old One. "No one else lives who knows the place, and I shall die before the summer ends—"

"Oh, no, Grandfather!" protested Yaño.

"Sí, my son. I am full of years, and it is good. I shall die soon, and I have sworn to take the evil secret with me."

"Oh please, Señor—give it to us, for the capitán and for my family. It can't be evil, when we go for *them!*"

"Trinidad is right, Grandfather. Tell me the place on the compass, and I will swear to tell it only to Capitán Chavarria and no other!"

The aged Yaqui looked at them with unseeing eyes, his thoughts turned inward, and Trin waited in breathless silence.

"There was one ship that sailed in search of the island and came back safely," the Old One said, at last. "It was the summer after the great earthquake, and they never found an island with a crack in its side. It may be that *you* will not find it because it is no longer there. The earthquake may have closed it up!"

"You are right, Grandfather—it may have. But please, let us search!"

"Sí, my son. For the grandchildren and for the brothers and sisters, I will let you search!"

"Gracias, Señor, gracias!" said Trin gratefully. "Con el favor de Dios, we will find it!"

"And may the guardian-spirits protect you from evil!" said the Old One. "Go now, Yaño, back to your friend, the capitán, and tell him to make ready. When you return, I will give you the degrees on the paper, that he may set his course!"

Just before dawn, two mornings later, Trin and Yaño descended the rope down the face of the cliff and swam into the cavern where Pahsiko waited with his dugout. The Old One had kept his word, and Yaño carried with him the degrees of latitude and longitude set down by the first captain who had gone in search of the island, guided only by the diver's memory of the place.

Within the hour *La Virazón* was to sail from Guaymas harbor, setting her course for the island of San Pedro Nolasco, the great mass of volcanic rock that was to be the point of rendezvous. For men in a dugout, the island was several hours away, and the two Yaquis paddled strongly, in silence. The prospect of the tremendous adventure ahead filled Trin with excitement, and he longed to talk to Yaño, but the presence of the taciturn Pahsiko inhibited him, and he held back the questions that nagged at his mind.

The sky brightened swiftly over the mountains to the east, and the sun rose in a blaze of gold, tinting the breeze-riffled waters with iridescent rainbow hues. In the distance, Trin saw the splashing of a great school of tuna, and later, swordfish played about the dugout, their bodies glittering as they leapt and turned in the morning light.

The sun climbed higher, the morning grew hot, and the mirage so familiar to voyagers on the Sea of Cortez began to alter the shape of the Sonora coastline. Headlands were lopped off into islands, only to melt away entirely in a shimmering haze. Misty blue bays seemed to reach inland, obliterating the shore, and the vague outline of islands rose where there were none, while real islands were lost to view. It would be difficult, Trin thought, to find the Old One's secret place if the mirage created fantasy shapes to confuse them.

The loud barking of seals warned them that they were approaching their rendezvous, though the long, narrow mass of San Pedro Nolasco did not emerge out of the shimmer until they were almost upon it. The sky was filled with hundreds of birds flying to and from their nests on the guano-whitened heights, and countless seals and sea lions raised their voices in protest against the invasion of their precincts, but *La Virazón* was not yet in sight.

The two Yaquis paddled to the southern end of the island and scanned its cliffs for a landing place, but the inaccessible ramparts that furnished a perfect haven for birds offered no welcome to man.

"Can't we just wait in the canoe?" asked Trin.

"No," said Yaño. "Pahsiko must not be seen with us. To

protect you, he has lied to the police." He spotted a rocky projection and paddled toward it. "He will wait in the canoe on the far side of the island until he sees that we are safely aboard ship."

Yaño climbed onto the projecting rock and pulled Trin up after him, while Pahsiko paddled against the surge of water to keep the canoe from being smashed.

"Gracias, Pahsiko!" Trin shouted down to him, but his voice was lost in the barking of the seals, and the impassive Indian turned his craft away and sent it cutting northward.

"It's all right," said Yaño. "He understands."

"So the police did come to his village!" said Trin.

"Sí, they came, and Ignacio Barraza with them. They searched every hut. They even waited till the fishermen returned with their dugouts from the day's fishing to see if you were with them. He must be a powerful man, your patron."

"Don Gregorio? Sí! He is very powerful—and very rich."

"I think he has offered a big reward. He must be very anxious to catch you."

"Do you think anyone in your village told the police anything?"

"No. Only Pahsiko knew, and he lied. It is for that he must hide. If Barraza should be on the ship, now, and see him with us—"

"Barraza!" exclaimed Trin. "But surely he won't be there! He refused to go to Baja when the capitán asked him."

"If he found out *La Virazón* was sailing this morning, and with only two divers aboard, he might suspect there was a *reason*—and change his mind!"

"How could he know there were *any* divers aboard? He won't know we are meeting the ship."

"I wasn't speaking of us. The capitán signed on two Yaquis."

"Where did he find them?"

"They found *him*. They had already signed on another vessel, but they spent their advance of silver pesos on brandy and ended up off somewhere where nobody could find them. When they sobered up and came back to Guaymas, their ship had left without them." Yaño chuckled. "It is not the first time that has happened."

"Are they good divers?" asked Trin.

"I don't know them. They come from Bacum."

The name sent a shiver of dread along Trin's spine. Bacum was one of the Yaqui river towns. Indians from Bacum would not be like Yaño. They were of the hostile breed.

He strained for a sight of the vessel, through the haze, but there was no sign of her. All around him, the wild creatures continued to protest the presence of two aliens in their midst. Outraged sea lions reared up out of the water, propelled by indignant whippings of their tails, and back in a narrow cavern one mammoth bull bellowed his warning as he corralled his large harem of cows.

Overhead, the air was thick with birds in numbers beyond anything Trin had ever seen. Parents flew back and forth incessantly, feeding adolescent chicks that waited in hundreds of nests. Singly and in pairs, the fluffy youngsters waddled on the brink in niche over niche, rising to the crest of the island one thousand feet above the sea.

Yaño watched their death-defying antics with amusement, but Trin's mind was still occupied with menace of Barraza.

"If Barraza is on the ship, he'll turn me over to the police the first time we touch land," he said aloud.

"On the land we touch first, there will be no police."

"But when we return to Guaymas—"

"Sí, he will make trouble," Yaño admitted.

"When the Old One said pearls bring greed and death, he was thinking of men like him," said Trin.

"If he is on the ship—" Yaño paused.

"If he is, what then?" asked Trin anxiously.

"Then we should not go to the island."

"But I *must* go!"

Yaño shielded his eyes and peered through the shimmer of the mirage. Dimly, he could discern the outline of a schooner sailing toward them.

"I think it is *La Virazón*," he said. "Before we worry more, let us see, first, if Barraza is on board."

The vessel hove to at a safe distance from the island and lowered a skiff. As Trin and Yaño swam to meet it, they saw that the two men at the oars were the Yaquis from Bacum. Climbing in over the gunwale, Yaño spoke to them in their native tongue, but they merely grunted in response. Their faces, as they rowed back to the ship, were sullen and inscrutable, and Trin was depressed by a feeling of foreboding.

The skiff neared the schooner, and he strained to identify the figures that stood at the rail. The long, spidery one would be Garcia, who had reached out from the helm to catch him that first day on deck. The short, stubby one had to be Paco Castillo, the musical cook, and the lean muscular young man beside him would be Raúl, his brother.

The Yaquis were pulling in close, now, and joyfully Trin recognized the solid figure that stood a bit apart from the others as his padrino, Fortino Chavarria. His spirits rose. He had identified them all—and none was Barraza. But at that moment, a fifth man appeared beside Fortino, and his huge bearlike shape was unmistakable.

"He is there!" Trin whispered. "Barraza is there!"

"I see him!" whispered Yaño.

"Please, Yaño. Even with him, I must go."

"Sí. For you and the capitán, there is no other way," said Yaño. "We will go, amigo. But evil will go with us."

CHAPTER THIRTEEN

Throughout the centuries, from the days of the Spanish explorers to Trin's own time, men had learned that the Sea of Cortez was one of the most unpredictable bodies of water on earth. In spite of its prevailing calm, tales of seafarers told of wild convulsions of water that boiled up from the depths to rage above the surface like mountainous tidal waves, and giant whirlpools that sucked down ships and men.

Scattered along its seven-hundred-mile length, wrecks piled up on rocks or on uncharted reefs testified to the treachery of the sea, and helmsmen of fishing and trading vessels tried to hug familiar shores as they moved up and down the coasts. But for *La Virazón* there was no choice. To reach her destination, the little schooner had to strike out across the deep and perilous waters.

Watching from atop the fo'c'sle as she cut through the swells, her decks splashed with spray, Trin was acutely aware of the dangers ahead—the hourly menace of wind and tide and current, the death threat from the killers of the deep. But these he had expected—with these, he had an even chance. The threat from the enemy on board was different—personal, perhaps inescapable.

Barraza had greeted his arrival with silence, but in the

hours since, the great hulking figure had seemed to be shadowing him, watching, listening, waiting. Trin longed to talk to his godfather, but it was not until he took his turn at the wheel under Fortino's supervision that he had a chance to be alone with him.

"You are troubled that Ignacio Barraza is aboard," said Fortino, as Trin, intent on steering the vessel, kept his eyes on the compass.

"Sí."

"I, too. Until the last moment, it seemed that we were free of him. We were already out of Guaymas harbor and passing the Pajaro Island light when they stopped us."

"They?"

"The police. He had them there, waiting," explained Fortino. "They came aboard—he with them—and searched the ship."

"For me?"

"For you and Yaño. He thought I would have picked you up somewhere on the way out."

"But he didn't guess how *far* out!"

"He guessed then," said Fortino, "and he tried to tell the police. But Ignacio is not much respected in Guaymas, and they were sick of his false clues. When I told them I knew of no boy who was a thief and had no thought of taking one aboard, they believed me. And they should have. It was the truth!"

"Did *he* believe you?"

"It wasn't the truth he was after," declared the captain. "But when he saw he was beaten, he made a great apology for his 'mistake'!"

"And then they left—and he stayed?"

"He climbed down into their boat with them, but before they cast off, he came back on board. If I could have put him off then, I would have done it for you and Yaño," said Fortino earnestly, "but the schooner is half his!"

"He came back to catch me," Trin said grimly. "When he went down into their boat, he made some plan with them. Maybe he has thought of a way to get me off the ship and take me back in a skiff to Guaymas."

"He alone—against all of us?" protested Fortino. "He is a big man, my son, but not that big!"

"How do we know that he would *be* alone?" asked Trin. "He is a tricky one, and I have seen him talking to the Yaquis and Garcia. They are not your friends, padrino. It may be that he has already made them *his* men. And if he has also a gun—"

Fortino puffed on his pipe a moment in silence. "I suppose that with them—or a gun—it might have been possible this morning," he admitted finally. "But now it is too late. We are too far out to sea."

"Then he will try to find some other way," declared Trin, "because he knows I am Trinidad Delgado—with a reward on my head!"

"He knew that in Guaymas," Fortino agreed, "but then he was thinking only of himself. Now I have given him reason to think of someone else."

"Who?"

"*You*, my son! Today I have told him your story as you told it to me. He knows that you are no thief, that you want only to pay back the debt and make your family free."

"You think knowing that will stop *him?*" demanded Trin, in amazement.

"I think it will, if he has any goodness in him," insisted Fortino. "And I can't believe that in the son of Capitán Barraza there is no goodness."

I *can!* thought Trin, but he kept silent.

:132

"I know your thoughts, my son, but you may be wrong," said Fortino gently. "He has made no move against you."

"But he follows me! He watches—and listens."

"He watches us all. His mind is full of suspicion, and he suspects that *we* may have a plan." Suddenly the captain's voice dropped to a whisper. "He is coming aft now to watch the *compass!* I'll take the wheel, Trinidad, and you go forward. But remember—we will give him a chance to prove that he is not all bad. There is time."

The breeze freshened and drew ahead, and the ship met the challenge, sailing with full canvas close to the wind. Standing in the bow, the salt spray in his face, Trin felt for the first time the exhilaration of the adventure. Fortino was right—there was time. His mind leapt ahead to the secret island, and instinctively, he searched the far horizon.

"With this head wind, it will be days before you sight it—*if* it is there at all!" whispered Paco Castillo, who had emerged from the galley to slip up behind him.

"Then—you know?"

"Sí. The capitán has told me and Raúl because we are old friends, but the others believe we are bound for Baja, and—" he shrugged his shoulders expressively—"who knows? It may be they are right! If we cross the sea without finding an island with a crack in it, Baja is where we will end up."

"You don't believe there is such an island!" said Trin accusingly.

"Have I said I didn't?" asked Paco. "Ever since I crawled naked on the sands of Turtle Bay, I've heard strange stories of this sea. Who am I to say what is true and what is not?"

"If you'd heard the Old One tell his story, you'd believe it."

"*You* believe it—and the capitán, too—because you are

:133

desperate. For both of you, the island *must* be there! Yaño believes it because it is the story of his great, great grandfather, and me—I believe it because I am *stupid!*" He grinned at Trin disarmingly. "But my brother Raúl—he is the smart one, and he doesn't believe it at all."

"Then he will learn that it is bad to be so smart," said Trin, grinning back, "because we who are desperate *and* stupid enough to search, *we* will find the island!"

"If we do, Raúl will not be the only surprised one. Those two back there—" Paco indicated the two Yaqui divers stretched out asleep on the deck aft of them—"I don't trust them any more than the big Grizzly!"

"The big grizzly?"

"Barraza. Is he not as ugly and hostile as a grizzly bear?"

"Sí," agreed Trin grimly. "It is a good name for him."

"All three of them think we're bound for the Bay of Concepción," Paco went on, "and I would bet you a silver peso, if I had it, that Zapo and Insa intend to jump ship as soon as we get there and go over to the big schooner they signed on in the beginning."

"You mean they're just using *La Virazón* to get them there?"

"Exactly. And the Grizzly has his mind on the town of Mulegé!"

"Mulegé is on the bay?"

"Sí. When Barraza climbed down into the boat of the police, I saw them give him papers before they cast off."

"Papers!" said Trin, aghast. "Maybe for arresting me!"

"I had the same thought, amigo. I would bet a hundred pesos the Grizzly means to turn you and Yaño over to the police at Mulegé," declared Paco. "So you can see, my friend, why I am stupid enough to believe in the island—because if it is not there, then two divers will desert and two will go to jail, and there will be nothing for anybody!"

"It will be there!" asserted Trin firmly. "There will be shell and pearls! And those two Yaquis will be diving for *La Virazón*, whether they intend to or not!"

The cry of "All hands, ready about, ahoy!" rang out above the wind, and the two of them sprang to their stations. Trin, who had learned to tack on his father's boat, stood ready to let go the rope committed to him, and on signal, the helmsman put the wheel down.

"Helm's a lee!" shouted the captain, and Raúl answered "Helm's a lee!" Each man carried out his duties of letting go and hauling in, on order, and the ship came about without losing ground. Catching the wind as it shifted across the bow, the sails filled away, and the little schooner gathered headway on her new tack.

For three days she continued to beat to windward, and as she sailed into the dark pre-dawn hours of the fourth, Trin felt an excitement that was almost beyond his containing. If the Old One had given them the correct position of the island, it would be visible off the starboard bow at daybreak. Taking his turn at the wheel, while Paco stood lookout, Trin found it difficult to keep the course, so intent was he on watching for the first light. But before it came, the wind died away and *La Virazón* was becalmed.

Prisoners of dead air, Trin and Paco kept their impatient watch, and as the stars began to pale they were joined by Yaño and the captain, with his binoculars. Day broke, and together they searched the horizon for the dark shape of land rising out of the endless stretch of sea—but there was nothing.

"It's not there!" whispered Paco, appalled.

"Not to our eyes," said Yaño, "but perhaps, in the capitán's glass . . ."

For what seemed an eternity, they waited as Fortino peered through his glass at the ever-brightening scene. At length, Trin could endure the silence no longer. "Padrino?" he whispered urgently.

"No, my son," said Fortino quietly, "even with the glass I see nothing. But the haze is already up."

"Then it could be blotting out the island!"

"Sí. It could be."

The sun rose to blaze down on the blue waters, and the day grew hot. Trin felt his nerves tighten as the hours passed, and knew that the others were plagued by the same question: was the island there, beyond the haze, or was the sea as empty of land as it looked?

In the early afternoon a very light breeze came out of the east, and the schooner got under way again. Though Yaño was at the helm and Raúl on lookout, Trin and Paco stood watch with them, too concerned to go below. They had been scanning the shining expanse of sea for more than an hour when Trin spotted a small dark shape on the horizon, not where the captain had expected the island, but due west.

"Paco, look!" he whispered, nudging him. "Could that be it?"

"Sí! It is there! We have found it!" shouted Paco, exploding with excitement.

"You have found nothing," said Raúl, joining them at the rail. "What you see is a mirage."

"No!" insisted Paco. "It is real!"

"Wait and see!" advised Raúl, coolly.

As they watched, the dark blue patch grew strangely tall, then taller, until finally it rose above the sea and floated in mid-air.

"Now do you believe me?" asked Raúl. "What we search for is an old man's dream of his youth. There is no island with a crack in its side!"

But when the breeze freshened and swept away the haze, they saw an island, solid and unmistakable, rising from the sea exactly where the captain expected it to be.

"Land ho!" shouted Trin jubilantly.

"Land ho!" echoed Paco. "Now, my brother, who is right?"

"So we have raised an island," said Raúl, with a shrug. "What is that, in a sea full of islands? The question is: does it have a *crack* in it?"

CHAPTER FOURTEEN

The sun was setting as *La Virazón* neared the island, and even from the crow's nest it was already too dark to see below the surface. Faced with the danger of submerged pinnacles of rock, the captain had no choice but to drop anchor in the safety of deep water, some three miles offshore. In the bright light of morning, with a man on the masthead to give warning, the schooner would edge in closer, but for the night, both ship and divers would have to wait.

Standing at the rail with Yaño and Paco, Trin surveyed the island. Its cliffs of volcanic rock, rising sheer from the blue-black sea, looked dark and forbidding against the fading sky.

"I wonder if it's true," he murmured, half to himself.

"If what's true?" asked Paco.

"What the Old One said: that the island is a place of devils."

"We have brought our devil with us!" said Yaño grimly.

"Sh! To speak of him is to see him!" whispered Paco. "He's coming this way."

A moment later, a huge hand seized Trin's shoulder in a crushing grip, and spun him around. "Tell me, *José*," said Barraza, with a sneering emphasis on the name he knew to be false, "what do you call this island?"

"It has no name," Trin told him. "The capitán says it does not appear on any chart."

"Yet he has managed to sail to it," said Barraza, with a nasty smile. "Perhaps, like yourself, it has a name you don't choose to tell—a name known only to your Yaqui friends." His small eyes shifted to Yaño.

"I have not seen the island before," said Yaño, meeting his gaze, "and if my people have a name for it, I've never heard it."

"Yet you find it extremely interesting."

"In an infinity of sea, any island is interesting," Yaño replied.

"And when a ship bound for Bahia Concepión sails far off its course to reach it, it is *especially* interesting!"

"It was the wind that took us off our course," said Trin.

"Sí. For nearly four days," said Paco, "we have been beating against a strong head wind."

"I know what the wind has done for four days," said Barraza sharply, "and what it has *not* done!" Turning on his heel abruptly, he walked aft to the captain's cabin and disappeared down the companionway.

"He suspects something," said Yaño, "but he doesn't know *what*. And unless there is a need—unless we *find* what we have come for—we will not tell him of the Old One's story. There is too much greed in him."

Barraza emerged from the cabin, the captain's binoculars in hand, and taking a position at the rail, he slowly scanned the island, studying every rock and crevice until the last light was gone.

The night was damp and cold and there was no moon. Standing anchorwatch while the others slept below, Trin paced the deck alone, yet he had a curious feeling that he was *not* alone—that there was something near him.

Could it be the island? Three miles away, it was lost in blackness, but it filled his mind, pulling at him until he could hardly contain the urge to swim to the base of its dark cliffs and search for its secret. Was it something more than a hidden passage to an oyster bed? he wondered. Was the place really haunted? When he had asked the ancient Yaqui how to find the island, the old man had said "To tell you is to condemn you to the evil spirits." Was the presence he felt a spirit?

The thought sent a shiver through his body, and he wished that the little dog, Pepé, was at his side. But Pepé was asleep with his master, in the captain's cabin.

Pushing the idea aside, he began to whistle a cheerful melody, but the whistle died on his lips as a huge arm locked around his neck from behind. He tried to cry out, but an immense hand clamped over his mouth, cutting off the sound. This was no spirit, but a physical presence, horribly real, and Trin knew that his assailant was the big Grizzly.

"*Now* you will tell me why we have come to this island," growled Barraza, loosening his clamp on Trin's mouth barely enough to let him speak.

"I've told you!" insisted Trin, forcing the muffled words through the thick hand. "It was the wind!"

"You lie!" declared the man, in a hoarse whisper. "It was no accident of wind that brought us here. We have come for a purpose!"

"Then ask the capitán!"

"You know the answer as well as he does. You're *all* in on it. I can feel it. There's *something* about that island,

and you'll tell me what it is, or por Dios, you will not have the breath to speak!"

Barraza tightened his hold on Trin's neck, and the great forearm pressed cruelly into his throat, choking him. He struggled to tear it loose, but the man maintained his grip, this time clamping the smothering hand over his nose as well as his mouth.

"There will be no air for you until you are ready to tell the truth—and without air, a man dies quickly."

The pain in Trin's throat and lungs was agonizing, and he tried to make a sound, but Barraza only increased the pressure, and Trin understood that he was sadistically prolonging the torment until the last possible moment. With a supreme effort, he fought to break free, but the massive arm gripped him in an iron vise.

Suddenly he heard a low growl. Barraza cursed, and Trin realized that Pepé had followed the man out of the captain's cabin and was attacking his legs. Keeping his hold on Trin, Barraza tried to shake the dog off, but Pepé continued to snarl and bite viciously. With the dog's teeth in him, Barraza reached down to grasp the animal, and tearing him loose, flung him skidding down the deck. In that moment his hold loosened, and Trin gasped in air and tried to shout for help, but the brutal forearm choked him off.

The little dog regained his feet and courageously rushed back at his adversary, but this time the big man was ready for him, and with a swinging kick, booted him into the air. Trin heard the dog squeal with pain and waited for the thud of his body on the deck, but there was no sound. With horror, he realized that Barraza had kicked him over the rail. Pepé was in the sea, and even if he hadn't been crippled by the blow, he couldn't possibly survive long, with the heavy current and the sharks that prowled the night waters.

Clawing at the murderous arm, Trin tried again to make a sound in his throat.

"So! Now you are ready!" gloated Barraza, relaxing his hold only enough to let his victim breath.

"Pepé!" gasped Trin.

"You will not speak of the dog," the man muttered, clapping his hand over Trin's mouth. "He is not worth saving. But you will speak of the island—to save *yourself!*"

"Sí—of the island!" agreed Trin, desperately trying to speak through the muffling hand in time to save Pepé. "We have come . . . to search for pearls!"

"Pearls! On that rock? You think I'm fool enough to believe that?"

"The Yaquis . . . believe it!" insisted Trin, forcing out the words. "We go ashore—in the morning—to search for an oyster bed . . ."

"The Yaquis!" exclaimed Barraza, tightening the clamp on Trin's mouth. "*Caramba!* I have been stupid! It is not pearls you would go ashore for, but *Yaqui friends.* That's why you stand watch on a night when no watch is needed!"

"It *is* needed! The anchorage is exposed to wind and a heavy current."

"It's not wind you watch for, but a *signal.* This island is a place of meeting. That's it, isn't it?" demanded Barraza. "You expect an Indian fishing boat to meet you here and take you to a hiding place in the mountains of Baja!"

"No! No!" Trin tried to shout, from behind the barrier.

"You expected to go ashore while I slept, and when I woke, this schooner would have been under way again, without you! But it won't work!" croaked Barraza. "You outwitted me once, but you won't do it *twice.* When that signal comes, you'll be bound and gagged down in the hold!"

"They'll . . . find me."

"They won't even search!" declared Barraza, dragging the struggling boy toward the hatch. "When I've hidden you, I'll call them up and tell them you dove in to save the dog. They'll believe the sharks got both of you!"

He kicked at the hatch, trying to open it with his foot. "You're worth *gold* to me, Trinidad Delgado, and this time I mean to collect it!"

A second kick lifted the cover of the hatch, but as Barraza tried to shove it aside, there was the sound of a thudding blow—a blow so powerful that Trin felt the shock of it in his own body. Knees buckling, the big man swung around to face his foe, and Trin made out the solid figure of Fortino. There was a smashing impact of fist on jaw, and Barraza sank to the deck in a limp heap.

Grasping Trin by the shoulders, the captain demanded, "Are you hurt, chico?"

"No—it is Pepé—"

"What about him?"

"Barraza kicked him overboard!"

"Por Dios! Then it *was* a dog's yelp that woke me! All hands ahoy!" Fortino shouted. "Man overboard!"

But Trin was already racing to the rail. Vaulting it, he dropped into the sea. The cold plunge took his breath away, and he rose to the surface, gasping. In the darkness, he could see nothing, and treading water silently, he stilled his own breathing to listen for the small sound of a dog paddling. But if there was any sound, it was drowned out by the suck and slap of water against the hull of the ship.

"Pepé! Pepé!" he called. "Answer me, chico! Speak!"

There was no answering bark or whimper, and Trin let

the current carry him as it would have carried the dog. Swimming soundlessly, he moved along the length of the schooner, reaching out with each stroke in search of the small, furry body, but his probing fingers found only the empty water.

On the deck of the ship, there was a jumble of voices as men hurried to light torches and lower a skiff, while Trin, following the pull of the heavy current, swam away from them into the darkness of the open sea. Something moved along his thigh, but as he stretched out his hand to grasp it, it slithered swiftly away. A fish! A large one, by the feel of it. It might have been a shark! he thought, sudden fear tensing his body. In these black waters, dropping to fathomless depths beneath him, there would be no pectoral fin visible to warn him that a killer was approaching.

Urgently, he called again, "Pepé! Pepé!" and from somewhere behind him answering voices shouted "Ahoy! Ahoy!" A faint glimmer of red touched the water, and turning, he saw that Paco and Yaño were in the skiff, holding flaming torches aloft while Raúl rowed.

As the boat advanced, Trin pushed himself up above the water, straining to see the ever-brightening surface. Ten yards beyond him, he thought he glimpsed something afloat, and heart pounding, he swam toward it. When he drew near, he saw the small shape of Pepé's head barely above water, as the animal paddled feebly. In one spurt, he shot through the yards between them and grasped the little dog in his arms. With a weak whimper, Pepé collapsed gratefully into the hollow of his neck.

A moment later, Raúl had brought up the skiff, and Yaño knelt to take the dog. Throwing his arm over the gunwale, Trin swung himself in.

"I never thought you'd find him," said Paco. "I was sure he'd be gone."

"I, too!" gasped Trin, getting his breath. "There must be good spirits here, along with the bad!"

"Sí!" Yaño agreed. Wrapping a blanket around the shivering pet, he probed the small body with gentle hands. "He has had a hard time, but I can feel no broken bones."

"The capitán told you?" asked Trin.

"That Barraza kicked Pepé," said Raúl. "But what about you? What was he trying to do?"

"Get me down into the hold. You were right, Paco—" Trin stopped abruptly. "Wait a minute. We're all here together! That means Fortino is alone with *them!* We'd better get back, pronto!"

"Sí!" agreed Paco. "He is a strong man, but old, and Barraza has the power of a bear. When he comes to, he will go for the capitán, and I wouldn't trust any of them to protect him!"

"Take the dog!" Yaño ordered, handing him to Trin. "And give me an oar!"

Turning the skiff about, Raúl and Yaño pulled with mighty strokes for the schooner. As they came abreast of her, they heard angry voices from the deck above, and saw that Garcia was waiting for them at the rail. Or was he, instead, watching, to warn of their approach?

"They have the dog!" Garcia shouted to the others.

"Next time he'll be shark bait!" Barraza's strident voice came back.

"You touch that dog again, and it will be *you* who goes over the rail!" Fortino predicted, his voice topping Barraza's.

Hastily, Yaño and Raúl climbed aboard, and Trin passed

Pepé up to them while Paco made the boat fast. As he followed them to the deck, Trin had the feeling that they had arrived just in time. The hulking Barraza was on his feet, belligerently confronting the captain, while the two Yaquis watched impassively in the torchlight.

"That sounds like a threat of murder," said Barraza smoothly, "and if anything should happen to me, there are witnesses here who will not forget it!" His eyes darted to the two Indians and Garcia. "The law is on my side, and I say the boy does not leave this ship until I turn him over to the police at Mulegé!"

"You will not turn him over to the police at Mulegé—or any other place!" declared Fortino strongly. "I have told you, he is innocent!"

"You expect me to take your word, and his, against the word of Don Gregorio Velazquez?" demanded Barraza scornfully. "The rico has offered a reward for his capture, and you will not cheat me out of it, Old Man. That gold belongs to me!"

"If it belongs to anybody, it belongs to Yaño!" said Fortino. "It was he who 'captured' the boy, not you!"

"It is true!" asserted Yaño firmly. "It was I who caught him at Turtle Bay, and I who brought him aboard this ship—not once, but twice! The gold belongs to me—and to the capitán and Raúl and Paco. He is our captive, not yours. And when it is time to turn him over to the police, it is *we* who will do it!"

"You had your chance, and you passed it up!" shouted Barraza angrily. "And now *you* are criminals *with* him—all of you guilty of harboring a fugitive. But you will not harbor him long!"

His eyes darted again to Zapo in an almost imperceptible signal, and the Yaqui moved to seize Trin, but Yaño was too swift for him. With an agile leap, he sprang between them and drew his knife. There was a breathless silence.

It was Barraza who broke it. "So you have him," he said smoothly. "It makes no difference. We are four men to four, and I am worth any two of you. The ship is half mine, and I order you, now, to pull up anchor and sail for Mulegé. If you cooperate with me, I'll turn the boy over to the police and say nothing more about it, and you can go on about your pearling. But if you cross me, por Dios, I swear I'll see that every one of you rots in prison—if I don't feed you to the sharks, first!" Behind him, the two Yaquis and Garcia waited tensely, hands on their knives.

"If we carry out your command," said Yaño easily, "you will collect a small reward and lose your chance for a great treasure."

"On that island?" demanded Barraza contemptuously. "You think I am a fool?"

"If you don't believe me," said Yaño, "look into the eyes of your Yaqui friends. They know I speak the truth."

Barraza's eyes sought those of the two Indians and caught the sudden intentness there. It was clear that the divers had heard the old story of the island, handed down among their people for generations, though they had never known where it lay.

"So there *is* something out there!" exclaimed Barraza. "Then we will not need *you* to find it. Zapo, Insa," he commanded, "you will go ashore at daybreak!"

The Yaquis shook their heads in silence.

"No?" cried Barraza, outraged. "You're divers, aren't you? You'll dive in the morning!"

"No!" said Insa. His guttural voice carried a note of finality.

"Why not?" demanded the big Grizzly.

"No man can dive there and live!" asserted Zapo positively. "It is a place of devils!"

"So! It is not exactly four to four, after all!" declared Fortino. "You have shown us that there is nothing but greed in your soul, Ignacio. Now let your greed decide: is it to be a small treasure—or a great one?"

"What do you mean?"

"I mean your men will not dive, but I have a man who will dive in spite of devils, and a boy who is man enough to dive with him!"

"There is no need for the boy to go. Let Yaño dive—and show me the oysters!"

"If Yaño goes ashore, Trinidad goes with him, and he will not come back to be turned over to the police. You make your choice now, Ignacio. Is it Mulegé or the island?"

Torn with indecision, Barraza searched the faces of Zapo and Insa. Their knowledge of the island's treasure was as unmistakable as their fear, and he knew he had to take the gamble.

"All right. You have won again," he conceded. "Let them both go ashore. But we are not through, Capitán Chavarria. There will be a time when *I* win!"

CHAPTER FIFTEEN

Through the remainder of the night, there was no sleeping aboard the schooner. Divided into enemy camps, the men of *La Virazón* waited for daybreak. The time of underground hostility was past; open war had been declared.

Keeping watch from atop the captain's cabin with Fortino and his comrades, Trin knew that he was at the core of it. Because he was aboard the ship, the lives of his friends were threatened; without him, they could pursue their search for pearls in safety. No matter how his mind tried to escape from it, there was only one truth, and he knew he must face it.

"Padrino," he whispered, "I have put you into great trouble."

"No, my son," his godfather answered, "the trouble is not in you, but in Ignacio—in the evil that fills his heart."

"But he directs it toward you because of me," Trin insisted. "He will kill to get gold, padrino, and *I* am the gold he wants."

The captain's searching eyes fixed on the huge shape skulking in the bows, while the Yaquis lay on the deck and Garcia stood watch atop the fo'c'sle. In the wavering shadows cast by the light of a single torch, Barraza looked even more grotesquely bearlike than by day.

"If you find oysters, in the morning," said Fortino, "he will forget the gold."

"Sí. His greed will fasten on the pearls that lie hidden inside them," echoed Paco, and Trin realized that the others had been listening.

"No, amigos," he said firmly, "whatever treasure we find, it will not be enough when there is more to be had. I will dive with you, Yaño, when the light comes, and if I find pearls, I will give them to you, padrino, to take to my family, but I won't trade your lives for their freedom. When the diving is ended, I will give myself up to Barraza!"

"No! No! You will not!" protested his friends.

"There will be no giving up!" declared Fortino. "If the police should deliver you, now, into the hands of Don Gregorio, you would pay with your life for the crime of your brother. The Don is very angry over the theft of the great pearl, and he will be even more angry when he has paid gold to get you back. Against the rage of a powerful rico, a penniless peon has no chance."

"Sí," agreed Paco. "He will say you are guilty, and you can't prove you are *not!*"

"No, my son!" said Fortino, with finality. "When you can pay the debt, you will go back to Cinco Ríos—and I with you! But not before!"

"That is what I wanted, too, padrino, but now it is no good. Please. You must let me surrender, amigos. It is the only way you will be safe."

"While there is one piece of gold to be had," said Yaño, "or one pearl in the pocket of any of us, there will be no safety from Barraza."

"Except in the strength of all of us—together!" declared Fortino. "We will not speak of surrender, Trinidad. We will stand as one."

There was a rush of wings, as seabirds skimmed over the mast on their first morning flight from their roosting place on the crags. Dawn was not far away. The stars paled and the island emerged from the darkness. Brightened by the glow in the eastern sky, it was no longer black and forbidding, and as the sun rose, its cliffs seemed to take on a reddish hue.

For Trin, the living color of blue sea and red rock dissipated the dark aura of evil, and he dismissed from his mind the fear of menacing spirits as one dismisses a frightening nightmare in the bright light of morning. He could not as readily dismiss the giant in the bows and the three men he had gathered around him. Their menace was as real by day as by night. But for the next hours, there would be a truce while he and Yaño probed for the island's secret treasure.

Paco was already making breakfast in the galley, and the odor of burning mesquite wood filled the air. Trin stopped to look in on Pepé, sleeping comfortably in the captain's bunk, and then joined the young cook. Coffee was coming to a boil in a large earthen olla, while Paco added salt and water to corn flour to make dough for tortillas.

"Paco, I've been thinking," Trin began. "Why don't you dive?"

"*Me!*" Paco stopped his mixing to stare at Trin in astonishment. "You must be loco!"

"You swim well. I remember, from Turtle Bay."

"Sí. In Turtle Bay I swim fine. I dive. I am very good. But in the Sea of Cortez—no! Gracias, amigo—but no!"

"Why not?" demanded Trin.

"Why not?" He took a handful of dough and shaped it into a round ball. "It is very simple. I am a coward!"

"You're making a joke, and I'm serious." The coffee was

boiling, and Trin poured himself a bowlful. "If we find pearl oysters, and those two Yaquis refuse to dive for them, it will take Yaño and me all summer to bring them up. But if you dive with us, we can lessen the time by a third—and you'll have an equal chance of finding a great pearl!"

"I was making no joke, chico!" Paco began to pat and revolve the dough on his forearm. "In the whole sea, there is not a pearl big enough to make me dive for it!"

Trin sipped the hot coffee carefully. "If you mean you're afraid, so am I, but—"

"But you have the courage to dive anyway," Paco cut in. "You are a brave one, amigo, but me—I am all fear and no courage, and this makes me a coward!"

"I don't believe you!"

"It's true," insisted Paco. "When I think of diving, I remember the jaws of the *tinterero,* hanging in the captain's cabin."

Trin had seen the trophy—the jaws of a gigantic shark with four rows of teeth, two hundred and forty-two in all.

"When I think of diving, I try *not* to think of the tinterero," he said.

The dough was nearly two feet in diameter, now, and thin as a piece of cloth. Paco threw it into the flat earthen bowl heating over the fire. "If I don't think of tintereros," he said, "I think of *cornudas* and great barracudas and killer whales—and, worst of all, the great white shark!" He shivered as he turned the tortilla over with his fingers.

Standing in the open passageway, Trin looked out to sea. "You forgot to mention *marrayos!*" he said. Less than fifty yards away, several giant manta rays were cruising just below the surface, the upturned tips of their wings showing above the water.

"Marrayos!" Paco's eyes bulged. "Do you know that they have a mouth a *yard* wide?"

"But they don't use it to eat a man."

"If you think not, ask Zapo and Insa. They have seen it happen!" Paco had been turning the tortilla at intervals of a few seconds, and now he pitched it to Trin, and began to roll out another. "They were diving with another Yaqui in Bahia Concepción when the monster came over them. He swam past them to hover above the third diver—"

"I have heard that they hover and sometimes follow a diver wherever he moves," said Trin, as he munched on the warm tortilla, "but it is because they are curious."

"And are they just "curious' when they stay over him until his lungs are bursting, and do not let him come up for air?"

"I think men may have died that way," Trin agreed, "but it was an accident."

"What Zapo and Insa saw was no accident! When the other diver tried to fight his way up to the surface, the monster seized him with his great flaps and hugged him until he suffocated. And then the beast opened his huge mouth and swallowed him!" Paco flipped the second tortilla into the hot cooking bowl.

"Do you believe that?" asked Trin.

"I believe that I will not give them a chance to swallow *me!*" He turned the tortilla expertly. "No, amigo. To dive is to risk death in the jaws of the killers. I admire your courage, but for me, I am very happy to be a coward, and stay alive."

When the men had been fed, the sun was high enough to reveal any pinnacles of rock that might lie below the surface, and with Fortino at the helm and Yaño in the crow's nest, the schooner crept in toward the island. The water was quite clear, and yet from his perch on the bowsprit Trin could look down into the descending fathoms without glimpsing bottom. It was as if the sheer cliffs were the peak of a mountain that dropped steeply to unimaginable depths below the sea, and the hidden lagoon—if it was there—was the throat of a long-dead volcano. Perhaps, eons ago, blazing hot lava had poured through the crack in its side.

The island appeared to be somewhat less than three miles long, with a craggy spur that projected out to the northeast and plunged abruptly into the sea. There would be shelter from the northerly winds in the lee of that promontory, and the captain pointed his ship toward it. As *La Virazón* moved in from the southeast, a sunken reef appeared like a dark shadow beneath the bowsprit, and Trin shouted a warning, but from his superior position on the masthead, Yaño had already given the signal, and Fortino swung clear of it to edge carefully northward.

The schooner was close under the dark red face of the cliffs, now, and Trin saw that they rose a stark one hundred and fifty feet and more above the fringe of surf at their base. The higher crags to the north were white with guano, and the hundreds of seabirds who roosted there scudded overhead like a great cloud, filling the air with their cries.

The water was still very deep, and even in the lee of the point there was danger in the strength of the tidal current. It took time to get a firm anchorage, and during the slow, careful process, Trin felt as if every nerve in his body was red hot.

Less than two hundred yards away, the island held

within its bleak circumference the power to change his life. If the great crack in its side was still open, then the tidal current would still be pouring into the lagoon to nourish the submarine garden beneath its surface. The waters would be teeming with living things: plants, fishes, all manner of sea creatures. There would be oysters, and the chance for pearls—and a whole new world of freedom from bondage.

But if, as the Old One had hinted, an earthquake had closed the gap, then the lagoon would be a parched and empty void, its creatures dead—and with them, his hopes.

At length, the schooner was securely anchored, with slip-ropes on her cables and all other preparations made so that she could slip and go to sea at the first sign of a storm and escape being hurled against the rock face of the cliffs. The men had worked together at these duties because the safety of the vessel—and their own lives—depended upon them, but now they separated again into enemy camps.

In the bows, Barraza and his cohorts watched warily as Raúl and Yaño lowered a skiff.

"Paco, you will be boatman," Fortino ordered.

"But Capitán, you will need him more than we!" protested Yaño.

"Sí, padrino," Trin whispered urgently. "Without Paco, you and Raúl will be only two against four!"

"You will not leave this ship without a boatman," insisted Fortino. "To dive is enough. Ignacio will not give us trouble until he has learned what is inside the island. You go, Paco. Follow them closely, and keep a sharp eye out!"

"Sí, Capitán!"

"And you, Trinidad—obey Yaño in all that he tells you. This sea is not like the water tank or the bay of your childhood. Here there is danger in every fathom. And remember, my son: to find the crack would be good, but to *live*—that is the big thing!"

"Sí, padrino. I will remember."

"Then go, my friends!" Fortino raised his hands in a gesture of blessing. "May the Mother of God protect you!"

As they cast off, Yaño ordered, "Pull for the reef, Paco!"

From the deck above, the harsh voice of Barraza commanded the Yaquis to lower a dinghy and follow them. The low-spoken reply of the Indians was not audible, but it was soon evident that again they had refused, for the Grizzly's outraged shouts filled the air as Paco pulled away from the schooner.

"They are even greater cowards than I!" exclaimed Paco.

"They believe that the devil-spirits will bring death to all who seek the island's treasure," said Yaño.

"Do *you* believe that, Yaño?" asked Trin. "Do you really think we are marked for death?"

Yaño was silent for a long moment. "I think it may be that some of us are," he said finally. "It is the risk we took in coming here."

"Then you *do* believe the island is haunted!"

"It is the belief of my people, Trinidad. I cannot say whether or not it is true. I can only tell you that for three summers the pearlers came here—three ships, and on them more than seventy men. And of them all, *two* men survived!"

"Two?"

"Sí. The Old One returned to the island just once, in the first summer. Of that crew, only he and the cabin boy lived to tell the story."

"Don't tell it to us!" warned Paco. "I am already one scared hombre!"

"You are right!" Yaño agreed. "It is not a story to hear on this morning."

"Though I think it can't be any worse than what I am imagining!" added Paco, shuddering.

"I think it may be," declared Yaño.

Trin was silent. Above them, the island rose like a fortress, immense and impregnable. Staring up at its stone ramparts, he felt infinitely small and weak. Deliberately, he shut out all frightening thoughts, and with an act of will, drew his forces inward until the total energy of his being was concentrated in one center. Yaño was right, he thought; it was no time to dwell on horrors of the past.

The skiff had been moving along the eastern face of the island, where for most of its length the cliffs pitched steeply into the blue depths, but just north of the reef and inside the stretch of its sheltering arm, there was a shallow curve of beach.

"It must have been there that the Old One built his raft," said Yaño, as they approached it. "There is no other place where a man could stand safe above the sea."

Trin's pulse quickened at the thought. This, then, was the actual setting of the old man's story. The drama of eighty-six years ago came alive in his mind: the hurricane blowing out of the southeast, driving the ship through terrible seas—the reef, clearly visible now under the calm surface, but hidden then beneath the wild waters—the helpless vessel grinding onto the sunken pinnacles of rock.

Yaño was seeing it, too. "The ship must have foundered here," he said, as Paco carefully maneuvered the boat around the reef.

They were facing the southern wall of the island now, where again the rugged slopes plunged directly into the sea. If Yaño was right, the wind and waves would have smashed the ship against these cliffs. Trin knelt on the floorboards of the skiff and peered down into the depths. Perhaps somewhere beneath him there would be remnants of the old wreck.

"The storms of eighty years will have beaten the wooden hulk to a pulp," said Yaño, guessing his thought. "But there may be some clue to tell us where she went down. I will dive first, Trinidad, and you wait here in the skiff till I come up." He sat on the edge of the boat, sucking in air till his lungs were full, then slipped into the water and jack-knifed toward the bottom.

Trin strained his eyes to follow the Indian's bronze body as it glided on a long downward slant, while a stream of bubbles floated to the surface. The Old One had said the crack appeared at six fathoms, but Yaño was soon below that depth; yet he continued to swim down into the bottomless mist until he was no more than a vague shadow—a shadow blotted out entirely when a school of small, striped fish drifted into view and hung there, motionless.

The seconds stretched out unbearably. Trin knew that Yaño was one of those rare divers who could remain under water for three minutes, but he could no longer endure the waiting. Taking a deep breath, he plunged in while Paco shouted after him in protest.

Swimming down on a slant, as Yaño had done, he saw the undersea face of the island looming ahead of him and was caught in the sudden grip of fear. The vertical cliffs, dropping into the obscurity below, were split into fissures and caverns whose gloomy recesses were lost in darkness. Any one of them might well house some carnivorous monster who was, even now, lying in wait for his prey.

The heaving sea lifted Trin's body and carried him into the mouth of the cave. Fighting against its pull, he grasped a slender pinnacle of rock and clung to it, lest he be sucked into a trap.

All around him the lush foliage of sea plants swayed and floated in the active water, and the sloping rock was sheathed in the living color of flowerlike anemones and sea urchins, orange starfish and purple fans, and sponges of blue and yellow and reddish-pink. Vivid crabs scurried into hiding, and a trio of black-nosed butterfly fish darted in and out. Everywhere there was brilliant, pulsing life, but Trin had an eerie feeling that behind the façade of beauty, some deadly creature lay concealed.

Pulling himself away from the cave, he moved downward along the wall of the cliff. His ears began to give him pain and he cleared them, then descended deeper, placing his hands carefully lest he press onto the poisonous spines of some rock dweller. In the diffused light, seeing became more difficult, and he peered nervously through the blue mist hoping for a glimpse of Yaño, but fearing that he might see, instead, the long gray shape of a killer.

His breath was nearly spent when suddenly the wall down which he was groping divided, and the swirling water rolled him into a deep fissure. His instant thought was that this might be the crack for which he was searching, but to be swept into it with his lungs almost empty could only mean his death. Frantically he reached out to grab onto some knob of rock. His hand grazed along the jagged edge of a crevice and caught hold.

Hanging suspended in the restless waters while he sought a foothold, he felt something slimy brush his fingers. Looking up to investigate the cause, he froze in horror. Inadvertently, he had placed his hand in the hide-out of one of the most ferocious creatures in the sea—a huge moray eel. Should the animal decide to clamp its powerful jaws shut on the intruding hand and then draw back into its hole, it would be impossible for him to break free. Holding his arm rigid, he waited while the ugly creature slithered its nine-foot length out of the crevice.

His need for air was becoming critical, but not until the rattlesnake of the deep had squirmed into the dark recesses of the fissure did he dare move. Then bracing his feet against the serried rock, he pushed off and shot up to the surface.

Bursting into the open air, he filled his lungs gratefully. A few yards away, Paco was holding the skiff against the current with skillful strokes, and Trin saw, with relief, that Yaño was clinging to the stern. The Indian lanced through the water to give him support, and together they swam back to the boat and climbed in. Still shaken and short of breath from his narrow escape, Trin told the story of his encounter with the eel and the fissure into which the animal had disappeared.

"You think it might be the crack?" asked Yaño, when he had finished.

"It was nearly six fathoms down, and it went far into the side of the island—so far that I couldn't see the end of it," explained Trin. "And the water pulled at me to suck me in, just as the Old One said."

"It could be," Yaño agreed. "I dove to eleven fathoms, and below me on the bottom there was an anchor lying half buried in the sand."

"Then this is where the ship went down!" Trin exclaimed, his heart pounding with excitement. "That proves it!"

"It only proves that *some* ship went down," Yaño reminded him. "There may have been many wrecks here. But I saw only one anchor, and it had been there a long time. It was so encrusted I could barely make out its shape."

"It's the one! I know it! And that's the crack! I'm going down again." Sitting on the edge of the boat, Trin began to inhale deeply.

"You will stay here and rest, while I go down!" commanded Yaño. "If it is the crack, you will do us no good by drowning in it."

He filled his lungs and swam down toward the fissure, and Trin watched until he had disappeared into the shadows. Again the seconds crawled by interminably: one minute—two minutes—three—

"He must have gone through," Trin said hopefully.

"I am thinking of the moray," said Paco.

Their eyes met, and without a word, Trin drew his knife from its sheath; but at that moment the Yaqui broke through the surface.

"It is not the crack," he told them, when he had the breath to speak. "It is a deep cleft, and I followed it all the way in—maybe forty feet. But there the two sides of it came together, and there was nothing but solid rock."

Trin could hardly bear to voice the fear in his mind, but he had to ask Yaño. "Do you think it went all the way through, before the earthquake, and then the quake closed it up?"

"We will not know the answer to that, Trinidad, until we have covered every inch of the cliff," said Yaño quietly. "We will begin here, and move west along the face of it."

Trin's need to know the answer was urgent, and without speaking he moved to the edge of the boat to prepare for his dive.

"Wait!" said Yaño. "You will search to a depth of four fathoms, and I, below that—"

"But the Old One said the crack was at six!" Trin cut in.

"What was six then may be four today," Yaño explained.

"This far north, the tides are large and they change greatly with the moon."

"I can dive easily to five!" insisted Trin.

"Five, then," Yaño agreed, "but remember to watch for sharks, and don't draw your knife unless your life depends on it. The glint of it in the water might bring them to you."

Trin had already begun to fill his lungs, and he merely nodded.

"If you find anything that looks like the crack," Yaño went on, "don't go into it alone. Come up for me, and we will go in together."

Acknowledging the order with a nod, Trin slipped into the water and swam down against the current, moving west along the wall of the island. Here, too, there were crevices and caves, and again he felt drawn into the aura of something mysterious and sinister. Sea snakes oozed out of cracks, and an indolent zebra fish swam past, hiding beneath its lacy fins a venom deadly enough to kill a man. The long arm of a giant octopus writhed out of its hole, and Trin knew that back in the dark recess the ugly creature was staring out of its huge glittering eyes like a watchdog of the devil-spirits. But he was too intent upon his quest to be deterred.

Four times he and the Yaqui dove, zigzagging up and down the cliff, only to find nothing.

"Just once more!" warned Yaño, as Trin inhaled for the fifth dive. "Then we will rest."

The thought of stopping the search, even briefly, was unbearable to Trin, but already his body was tiring from the battle against the current. Jackknifing down to five fathoms, he determined to swim west at that level until his breath gave out. But still he found no fissure big enough to invite further investigation, and he was about to push up to the surface when something golden streaked past his eyes. Instantly the thought of the Old One's spirit-serpent flashed through his mind, and he struck out after it. Peering through the blue water, he saw that it was a large fish whose body of pure gold was as long as his own—the beautiful dolphinfish.

Pursuing it, he wondered if, like the golden serpent, it was a guardian spirit come to lead him into the island. But if so, it had appeared at the wrong time, for though he swam frantically to keep pace with it, his breath was soon spent, and he was forced to go up while the golden fish shimmered away out of sight.

As he broke water, he saw a second skiff riding the swell alongside of Paco. In it were Garcia—and Barraza. In a panic lest they try to seize him, he gulped in air hastily and went down again, seeking the depth at which he had seen the dolphin. The brilliant fish had disappeared, but he stroked rapidly westward, straining his eyes for a glimpse of it.

He was swimming parallel to the cliff when he saw that just ahead of him the rock opened in another great cleft. As he approached it, he was caught up in a whirling eddy and spun into its depths. For an instant he tried to fight the powerful current, but as it swept him into the darkness, he surrendered, knowing with a strange certainty that his search had ended. Whether the dolphin had been a guardian angel or merely a golden fish, it had led him into the island's secret portal.

It was too late to go back for Yaño, and even if he could have, Barraza was there, waiting. Reaching out with long strokes, he swam with the surging water into an ever-deepening blackness, aware that whatever hostile creature might lie hidden in the passage, his greatest peril was in his lack of breath. Alarmed at the sight of Barraza, he had gone under without wholly filling his lungs, and now if the channel was a long one, that haste could cost him his life.

The sound of the sea, sucking and swirling within the narrow confines of the rock, seemed to pour into his ears until he felt the roar of it would split his head open. A large body, cold and slippery, touched along his length, and recoiling in horror, he drew his knife. If the creature was a man-eating shark, it could bite him in half before he could raise his weapon against it, but at least he would try to defend himself. With heart pounding, he waited like a blind man in the violent darkness, while the current pulled him deeper into the black core of the island.

Suddenly he crashed against something hard. Half stunned, he reached out to touch the barrier, and his hand took hold of solid rock. All fear of the unseen creature dropped out of his mind as a greater fear took its place: had he reached a dead end? If this rock was a closed wall, he could never make it out again. Already his lungs were bursting with the need for air.

Pushing the knife inside his waistband, he groped along the rugged stone, feeling for some break in it, some reopening of the channel, but everywhere his hands touched there was a wall blocking him. The pain in his chest was agonizing now, and he knew he was only seconds away from death. To turn back was useless; he would drown before he was halfway out of the crack. If there was any means of escape, it had to be somewhere around him. He stretched out his hands again, probing the darkness, but his strength was gone and the churning waters took hold of him and spun him in a whirlpool.

Helpless in the powerful current, he could no longer fight the awful torment in his lungs. He was drowning. In

Turtle Bay, Yaño had been there to save him, but here in this black trap there was no one.

Nuestro Señor Jesucristo, help me! he prayed in silence, but his mind told him it was too late for help, and he added, Señor Padre, forgive me for my sins.

He tried to make the gesture of the cross, but the swirling waters swept his body around a long curve of rock, and yielding to them, he became vaguely aware that the blackness was paling to a luminous blue mist. He clung desperately to consciousness, instinctively fighting his way upward toward the source of light. Breaking the surface, he sucked in air in painful, sobbing gasps.

Around him, blue and brilliant in the sunlight, stretched the waters of the secret lagoon. He was *inside* the island!

CHAPTER SIXTEEN

One thought filled Trin's mind as he floated on the warm surface of the lagoon: somehow, his cry for help had been answered. He was alive—inside the island.

He had come up out of the depths bleeding from eyes, ears and mouth, but though he knew that the scent of blood in the water spelled danger, he could do nothing about it. His limp body was too spent to move toward the safety of the shore. Lying on his back, he breathed in the life-giving air, grateful, after the smothering darkness, for the blaze of light that penetrated his closed eyelids. The comforting heat of the noonday sun burned into his cold flesh, and he felt as if his body, weighted down with exhaustion, was sinking deeper and deeper into the cradling waters. He tried to open his eyes, but his lids, too, were weighted, and he abandoned the effort.

Drifting into sleep, he felt a cold touch on his cheek. Was he dreaming? Or was something smooth and slimy moving from his throat to shoulder and along his length? As he tried to draw his mind back from oblivion, the same cold sliminess moved along the other side of his body until he was completely encircled by it. He struggled to open his eyes, but they seemed to be sealed shut. Minutes passed, while he lay helpless on the buoyant water, and the strange cold touch slithered around him in ceaseless motion.

The thought of the devil-spirits floated into his consciousness, and with a supreme effort he lifted his heavy lids—to be blinded by the dazzle of the sun. Turning his head slightly to one side, he saw an undulating mass of colors. His lids closed again, and he rested, remembering the strange moving bands of red and green and yellow, like striped ribbons—and then it seemed to him that he turned his head to the other side, and opening his eyes, saw again the bright, undulating stripes. They were all around him, covering the water until there was no blueness. And suddenly he knew they were not real, but a dream, because the brilliant twisting ribbons took on the shape of snakes—scores of snakes with blunt heads and flat tails.

He tried to rouse up from the nightmare, but he was powerless to move. The horrible vision of the snakes filled his eyes, and when he shut them out, their cold slithering touch was even more terrifying.

Then the dream changed. His eyes were still closed against the evil sight, when the slimy touching ceased, and there was only the gentle swell of the water and the hot burning of the sun. After an interval, another cold creature seemed to come up from beneath him, and touching his shoulder and breast, it began to pull him through the water.

Once more he strove to wake, but his mind could not overcome the deep fatigue of his body, and he was forced to remain within the fantasy that seemed so strangely real. Submitting to the will of the unseen creature as it drew him across the surface of the lagoon, he lost all awareness of place and motion and drifted into unconsciousness.

When he awoke, he was lying on a sandy beach with a man leaning over him. As the man's face came into focus he saw that it was Yaño.

"You have had a long sleep," said the Yaqui.

Trin stared up at him in confusion, trying to sort out the images that crowded his mind. "I was dreaming," he said, "and I couldn't wake up."

"And now you are wondering what was dream and what was real," declared Yaño.

"It wasn't real! It couldn't have been!" exclaimed Trin, with a shudder.

"If it was a dream of coming through the crack—" the Yaqui began.

"The crack!" Trin sat up with a jerk. Surely that hadn't been a dream! His eyes took in the clear green waters beyond the narrow curve of sand and the ring of cliffs that contained them, as the bowl had contained the water from the olla, in the Old One's hut.

"The depth of your sleep has told me you had a bad time coming through the crack," said Yaño, "a time that was like a nightmare. But you see now, amigo—it was no dream! We are here on the beach where the Old One slept, even as you have been sleeping."

"It was not the crack, but the snakes!" said Trin. "They were all around me in the water, writhing against my skin, and I couldn't wake to shut them out!"

"It is fortunate you didn't wake, chico, or you'd be lying dead here on the sand, with your body turned black," Yaño asserted. "The snakes, too, were real!"

"No!" protested Trin, in disbelief. "It was a nightmare!"

"You are wrong, amigo!" Yaño insisted. "When I came out of the crack, I saw you floating on the water with the snakes twisting around you like many ropes. If you had made a sudden move, they would have sunk their fangs into you. I know their venom by the color of their stripes, and I have seen a man die within a few minutes from the bite of one of them!"

Trin felt hollow inside. "What made them go away?" he asked.

"In the same instant that I saw them, they saw me," said Yaño, "and they dove under the water. When I had filled my lungs, I went down to look for them, but they were gone."

"Then the creature that came up from under me was you?"

"Sí. I swam with you to the shore."

"And all the time I thought I was asleep and dreaming, I was really *awake?*"

"Sí. Your body was heavy as a rock, but you felt with your skin and saw with your eyes because your *mind* was awake," the Yaqui explained. "It has happened to me when I have been down too long—and come close to death."

Trin was thoughtful. "Yaño—" he began, "perhaps those snakes didn't bite me because they weren't really snakes. The Old One said the serpent he saw was not really a serpent but a guardian spirit. Maybe the snakes we saw were the devil-spirits of the island."

"Then their venom will be no less deadly," warned Yaño, "for all devils have the power to kill."

"It could be they will not kill us unless we take away their pearls," said Trin. "If there *are* pearls!"

"If they were not spirits, but snakes," said Yaño, "then they have already given us the answer to that!"

"The answer?" asked Trin, in puzzlement. "How?"

"The Yaquis believe that snakes feed on oysters, and when a school of sea snakes lies on the surface, there will be an oyster bed beneath them."

Instinctively Trin's eyes sought the bright stripes of color on the water, but there was only the diamond-like glitter of sunlight. "Have you looked?" he demanded.

"No. I, too, needed rest. But now I am ready."

The Indian rose to his feet, and Trin jumped up after him. His legs felt rubbery and he swayed slightly.

"For you, it is still too soon," said Yaño, steadying him. "I will search for the bed, and when I find it—"

"No!" Trin cut in urgently. "To wait is torture. I'll go with you."

"But you are too weak to dive."

"I won't dive," Trin promised, "but I can float above you and watch."

The Yaqui studied him for a moment in silence, and then sensing his determination, surrendered. "Come, amigo," he said, "we will search together."

The water was a light tropical green, deepening to blue as the seabed deepened, and so transparent that the bottom was clearly visible to the swimmers as they stroked toward the center of the lagoon in a lazy crawl. Beneath them lay a submarine garden luxuriant beyond anything they had ever seen. The abundant life in the cave on the outer wall of the island was here multiplied a thousand-fold. Plants and creatures carpeted the sea floor in a rich profusion of shapes and colors, and the scene was animated by swarms of fishes.

Peering anxiously into the depths, Trin searched for the *concha de la perla fina*—the pearl oyster—but he was unable to spot one rough-backed shell. Surely in such a marine paradise there must be an oyster bed. Floating face down, he scrutinized the sea garden foot by foot. Here and there the uneven bottom was split by chasms, some of them barely a foot wide, but several fathoms deep. It was almost impossible to see down into them, yet Trin knew that oysters would be likely to conceal themselves in just such recesses.

With a strong kick, he propelled himself to a position directly over one of the shadowed apertures, but a cloud of bizarrely colored fish drifted in to obstruct his view. As he waited for them to pass, Yaño dove down across his line of vision. The fish darted back and forth in startled agitation, and when finally the scene cleared, Trin saw that the Indian was reaching down into the chasm. At the same moment, he glimpsed the brilliant stripes of one of the poisonous snakes slithering up to meet him.

There was no time to warn the Yaqui, though Trin let out a desperate shout, suspecting even as he did, that the sound would not carry through many fathoms of water. To dive was equally futile, but he found himself jackknifing under, his eyes riveted on Yaño as he lanced down toward him. The man's arms were inserted full length into the narrow fissure, and to Trin's horror he saw that the snake, approaching at an oblique angle, was only inches away.

Yaño, his attention fixed on something within his grasp, seemed entirely unaware of the creature's approach. With a mighty wrench, he pulled the object free and shot upward. Diverted by the sudden movement, the snake writhed back into the shadows, and Trin pushed up after his friend.

As they filled their lungs, the Indian exhibited the object he had ripped from the wall of the chasm. It was some seven inches in diameter and covered with parasitical growth, but Trin realized at once that it was a pearl oyster.

"While you were getting it, a snake almost got you!" gasped Trin. "I saw him from above and went down to warn you, but I couldn't have made it."

"He was one of the striped ones?"

Trin nodded. "The minute you put your hand down to take that oyster, the snake came up to protect it, just as if he were a devil-spirit. And those fish—did you see them?"

"Sí."

"They had stripes of the same colors as the snakes, and when I tried to look down into the chasm, they swarmed in so I couldn't see. Maybe they were devil-spirits, too."

"Then let us see what they were guarding," said Yaño.

Oyster in hand, he streaked for the shore with Trin following him. When they reached the beach, Yaño placed the heel of the shell upon a rock, and with his sheath knife, hacked off the weed and tiny crawling creatures that clung to it. Then inserting the blade between the valves of the oyster, he severed the adductor muscle and broke the hinge. Separating the valves, he cut the animal out of the shell and examined it carefully, probing with his fingers and squeezing the flesh in case there might be a pearl concealed within its organs. But there was nothing. Abandoning it, the Indian took up the shell. Its iridescent mother-of-pearl interior sparkled in the sunlight, and Trin knew that shell of such lustre would bring a good price. Inspecting it with Yaño, he saw that there was no pearl attached to the lining, but his heart skipped a beat at the sight of a blister on the inner wall. Men gambled on blisters, for that little sac of nacre might contain nothing more than a lump of rotten matter—or it might contain a pearl.

"The blister is mine, amigo, but because you tried to warn me of the snake," declared Yaño, "I will give you a chance to win what lies hidden inside. What do you bet?"

"I have nothing," said Trin.

"You have a knife."

"Yes, but it is worth little."

"I say what is inside will be worth nothing. What do you say?"

"I say there will be a pearl!" declared Trin firmly.

"Bueno! Then we are agreed," announced the Yaqui. "If there is nothing, you give me your knife, but if there is a pearl, both knife and pearl are yours."

Working slowly and with great care, Yaño began to cut out the blister, while Trin watched in nervous fascination. The bubble of nacre had some value in itself, as a brooch, and the Indian intended to save it if he could.

Unable to endure the suspense in silence, Trin said, "How often does a blister hold a pearl?"

The Yaqui shrugged his shoulders. "I have seen hundreds of blisters cut out or broken, and maybe twenty held pearls."

"Then there isn't much chance?"

"Who knows?" asked Yaño. "One man may open ten tons of shell and find no pearl, and another may open one ton, and find ten pearls. It is a matter of luck. And now we will see which of us is the lucky one."

He completed the cut in the nacre and lifted out the blister. Beneath it nestled a tiny sphere, the size of a small pea. Trin stared at it in dismay.

"You are right!" exclaimed Yaño. "I have lost, and you have won! It is a good pearl, amigo, smooth and perfectly round."

"But black!" declared Trin gloomily.

"On the other side of the world, black pearls are valued," insisted the Yaqui. "It will bring you many pesos toward your debt."

Trin picked it up between his thumb and forefinger and held it to the sun. The light revealed its lustre, but he could

:173

find no least tinge of blue or green to redeem it. The pearl was unmistakably the dark gunmetal color called "black," and to the Indian tribes on the Sea of Cortez a black pearl was a symbol of the devil. To find it in the first shell taken from the lagoon could only be an omen of evil.

CHAPTER SEVENTEEN

There could no longer be any doubt about the truth of the Old One's story: the unchartered isle with its great crack, six fathoms down; the hidden lagoon; the fabled oyster bed—they were all there. In a succession of exploratory dives, Yaño discovered that the sea floor was rich in treasure beyond any man's dreaming. Oysters were everywhere, lying concealed in weeds and crevices, clustered on rocks and under ledges, clinging to the walls of eerie chasms. The shell would fill the hold of *La Virazón* —*if* they could get it out.

Under normal conditions, Trin and Yaño would work from the dinghy, while Paco sculled back and forth above the bed. Diving to the bottom, they would seize as many oysters as possible and place them in the net-bag which they wore around their waists. Surfacing for air, they would throw their shells into opposite ends of the boat, hang on to the gunwale for a brief rest, and then dive again.

But here, circumstances were anything but normal. Neither dinghy nor boatman could be brought in through a crack six fathoms beneath the sea, nor could a diver go in and out with each load of shell. He would do well to survive the hazardous swim into the lagoon and out again once a day.

On the other hand, the cliffs that ringed the island offered no easy access, for they dropped almost as sheerly to the inner waters as to the sea outside. There was only one possible place of ascent, and Yaño had climbed it while Trin was asleep to signal Paco that they had come safely through the crack.

"It must have been there that they carried up the sacks of shell, in the Old One's time," he told Trin, indicating the steep and rugged trail. "Then they let them down by rope to the dugouts below."

"But in his time there were many men," said Trin, "and we are only two."

"Sí, amigo, you are right," declared Yaño. "And two who must give their strength to diving cannot also carry the shell to the top of the cliff. But there may be another way."

"How?"

"Have you noticed the current—how it enters the lagoon from the south, through the crack, and flows to the north? We have crossed from the east side to the west, and nowhere in the lagoon does the current flow south."

Trin stared at Yaño thoughtfully. "You mean that if it comes *in* from the south—and flows *only* to the north—"

"Then it must go *out* at the north!" exclaimed Yaño. "You have the idea, amigo. Somewhere there must be another crack."

"If it's another like this one, what good will it do us?" asked Trin, puzzled at the Yaqui's obvious excitement.

"It may not be like this one," said Yaño. "From here, we cannot see all of the north end, beyond the jutting cliffs. In that corner, to the west, there may be a channel open not only beneath the water, but at the surface—and above it."

"But if there was such a channel, surely the Old One and

his compadres would have found it, instead of carrying their shell up the cliff," protested Trin.

"If it had been there, they would have found it," the Indian agreed, "but that was eighty years ago. You are forgetting, chico, that since then there has been a mighty earthquake."

"That's right! The Old One thought it might have closed the crack."

"Sí, but instead, it may have opened another. Come, amigo," urged Yaño, "let us see where the current will take us."

As the Yaqui had anticipated, the current carried them toward the northwest, and swimming over the deepening bottom, they saw that the opulent garden growth extended the full length of the lagoon. Delicately patterned sea plants of muted hue swayed gently beneath thousands of brilliant fish, as they glided through the liquid blue world. None of them were killers of men, but here and there, down where the oysters lay, Trin glimpsed the vivid slithering stripes of the devil-snakes.

The pull of the current strengthened as the swimmers neared the northwest corner, where the sheer cliffs elbowed out into the water, hiding what lay beyond. Striking their way around the point, Trin and Yaño were startled to find themselves in what looked like the narrow gorge of a mountain river, reaching at an oblique angle to the southwest. It was as if the land, rising abruptly on either side, had been split asunder, and the waters of the lagoon had rushed in to fill the cavity. But though it stretched more than a thousand feet ahead of them, it led nowhere, for it funneled to a dead end.

"There's no opening," declared Trin dejectedly, as they

trod water to study their surroundings. "The current flows straight into the cliff."

"Or *under* it," suggested Yaño. "The tide is going out—and it's going out *there*. Somewhere at the end of this gorge, there is a passage to the sea."

Trin knew he was right. Even as they talked, the current was carrying them toward it, swiftly, dangerously. If there was another crack, fathoms beneath the surface, they could be swept into it and held under longer than their capacity to survive. Yet Yaño struck out toward the dead end.

Following him, Trin had an uneasy feeling that the cliffs, towering up on either side, were closing in on them as they swam. The sun, slanting into the depths, only added to the uncomfortable illusion, for there was no visible bottom, and it seemed as if he and Yaño were hanging suspended between two giant pincers that might at any minute clamp shut. If indeed an earthquake had split the cliffs apart, then another could as instantly bring them back together again, crushing any creatures unfortunate enough to be in the waters that separated them. The thought gave him a sinking feeling in the pit of his stomach, and he increased his pace to catch up with the Yaqui.

They had covered some two-thirds of the channel's length, and the power of the current was increasing alarmingly, when Yaño spotted a ledge extending out from the upper cliff, an arm's reach above the water. Heading for it, he climbed onto it and pulled Trin up after him. From this vantage point, they surveyed the gorge.

At its open end there had been at least forty feet between the cliffs on the north side of the channel and those on the south, but here there were no more than twenty, and the long arm of water narrowed to a width of twelve at the dead end.

"It is as I thought," said Yaño, peering down-channel. "The earthquake did open this gorge. It split the earth apart all the way to the sea, but the shock of it jarred loose a great section of the cliff on the north, and it *slid* across the narrow channel until it was stopped by the cliff on the south. Look closely, and you will see the crack where they meet."

Scrutinizing the rock wall that formed the dead end, Trin saw that there was indeed a crack extending the full height of its juncture with the cliff, and at the top, the rock slanted down from north to south, indicating the angle of its fall. The quake had opened the passage, only to close it —but not all the way.

"Look there—at the water level!" he shouted in sudden excitement.

The tide was falling rapidly, and at the end of the channel an opening was appearing beneath the sloping wall of rock.

"I see it, amigo!" exclaimed Yaño. "Only the *top* part of the cliff slipped. From there down, it held firm. Under that mass of slanting rock, a channel is open. And when the tide is well down, it may be that we can swim, as in a tunnel, all the way out to the sea."

In the interval of waiting, Trin yearned to go back to the lagoon, but this was a day for reconnaissance, not diving, and there was still the long swim back to the dinghy. If they were forced to return by way of the inner waters, they would have to face again the hazards of the great crack; but if the falling tide revealed a passage below the rock, then they would be swimming miles through the dangerous waters of the outer sea. Either way, it would take strength to survive. Resting on the ledge, they watched the descent of the waterline.

"Someday," said Yaño thoughtfully, "another quake will split this island in two, and that will be the end of the pearls."

"Why will it?" asked Trin.

"We are too far north for oysters, here," the Yaqui explained. "It is only the circle of high cliffs that has made the climate warm enough. If the island were split open, there would be no sheltered lagoon, and the cold current from the north would kill the sea garden."

"I wonder when it will happen," said Trin, with a touch of uneasiness.

"Who knows?" Yaño shrugged. "Maybe a day—a year—a hundred years. But it *will* happen. And when it does, the secret island and its treasure will be gone forever. Men may still hear the story, and search for it, but they will never find it."

Fingering the round shape of the black pearl, where he had tied it into the fold of cloth at his waistline, Trin thought of its evil meaning, and wondered whether he or any of the other voyagers would live to tell their story. To find a pearl in the first shell would have been good luck—if it had been white. But a black one! Did it promise death?

His thoughts turned to the Old One and the men who dove with him. Had their first pearl been black? he wondered. Had the island, through its own mysterious symbols, foretold their doom? This morning, he hadn't wanted to hear their story, but now he needed to know.

"Yaño," he said, breaking the silence, "what happened to those men who came before us, with the Old One?"

The Indian stared at him, his face impassive. "Are you sure you want to know?" he asked, at length.

"Yes. I don't know why, unless perhaps it is a way of being ready. If I know the *worst* that can happen—"

Yaño nodded. "Then I will tell you. It is a long time since I have heard the whole story," he began, "and there is much I have forgotten, but the vessel sailed here without trouble and anchored, as we have, in the lee of the point. The Old One went with another diver to search for the crack—"

"And found it."

"Sí. They swam into the lagoon, and there were then, as today, a great many oysters. With twenty divers on the ship, they brought up many pearls—"

"And one fit for the crown of a king," said Trin. "I remember the Old One told me."

"It was that pearl that brought the trouble," declared Yaño. "The men dove until they had nearly filled the hold with shell, and in all that time they had lost only one man—to a shark. Except for him, their bodies were safe, but the death had already entered their hearts."

"You mean the devil-spirits?" asked Trin.

"Sí. The spirits had put the poison of greed in them on the day the great pearl was found, and on the night before they would have sailed for Guaymas, it was stolen. Each man suspected that another had it, and they fought until seven men were dead."

"Seven!"

"That was only the beginning," warned Yaño. "At daybreak a storm began. They managed to slip and go to sea before the worst of it struck, but the pearl had not been found, and the poison in their hearts made them value it above their lives. Even while the hurricane drove them northward, there was fighting and killing over it, and the few who tried, with the Old One, to man the ship, couldn't hold her against the wild wind and terrible seas. At last she was driven onto the rocks of Tiburon."

"Tiburon!" exclaimed Trin, aghast. "But that's where the Seri Indians live!"

"Sí. The ship broke apart quickly, and the men were trapped between the mountainous seas and the cannibal tribe."

"And the Seris captured them?"

"All but those who preferred to die in the sea. Only my grandfather and the cabin boy escaped because they were able to outrun their captors."

"They must have been very fast," said Trin. "I have heard that the Seris capture deer by outrunning them."

"It is true. But this time, *they* were outrun. My grandfather and the boy hid in the hills until they could reach the eastern shore, and there they stole a bamboo canoe and crossed the dangerous waters of El Infiernello Channel."

"And the others—were all eaten?" asked Trin, hesitating to give voice to the thought.

"My bisabuelo did not stay to see it happen," said Yaño, with bitter humor, "but none of the captives was ever seen or heard of again."

"It was a terrible thing," said Trin, after a long pause, "but how do we know they died because of the evil spell of this island? Other men have killed for pearls, without ever coming here."

"Sí—in a summer, perhaps one man—maybe two," admitted Yaño, "but so many—*never!*"

"But this was a pearl for a king."

"It *was* a very rare pearl," the Yaqui agreed, "a rainbow."

"You see!" said Trin. "It could have been the *pearl*, not the island!"

"But the pearl was *of* the island!" insisted Yaño. "Perhaps nowhere else in the whole Sea of Cortez could a rainbow pearl have been found."

"And there must have been other ships," Trin went on, pursuing his argument, "ships that never came near this island, but were wrecked on Tiburon and their crews eaten by cannibals. It could have happened to any pearler from Baja."

"Perhaps it could have," Yaño agreed somberly, "but it *has not!* If on the expeditions to Baja only two men returned out of every seventy, the pearling would have stopped long ago."

"Still it does not *prove* anything," Trin argued tenaciously. "The Old One came here twice, and he has already lived to be one hundred and six."

"You are right, Trinidad," said Yaño. "We will think only of him."

But Trin knew that he was thinking also of Ignacio Barraza and the men who had joined forces with him. The poison was already in them. How swiftly it would lead to killing, if there was a great pearl to covet!

"Look, amigo!" exclaimed Yaño, rising suddenly. "Our tunnel is open! Already there is an air space of two feet between the water and the rock. It is time we looked inside."

Diving from the ledge, they swam down the remaining length of the gorge and into the shadowed interior of the passage. There was barely room for a man's head and shoulders beneath the giant slab of rock, and as the current swept them into increasing darkness, the so-called "tunnel" began to bear an uncomfortable resemblance to the great crack. The violently swirling waters, the narrow confinement between walls of rock, the blackness, were all the same. Only the space for breathing was different, and Trin was well aware that it could end abruptly, and the still-falling tide, seeking its exit at a lower level could suck the swimmers down into the depths.

Fighting the pull of the current, he trod water, searching for some small glimmer of light in the darkness ahead, and when he spotted a tiny pinpoint, his shout of discovery echoed down the passage simultaneously with Yaño's. As they pushed toward it, excitement adding power to their strokes, the pinpoint expanded into a rectangle of light.

"It's open all the way!" shouted Trin jubilantly, when at length they emerged into the sea. "Now we'll never have to go through the crack again!"

"The guardian spirits are good to us!" declared Yaño. "The passage is small, but it is enough. Once a day, at the time of slack water, we shall be able to take the dinghies through."

"Then Paco can come in with us."

"Sí—and bring out the shell!"

"But if *he* can come in—" Trin broke off, appalled at the realization that Barraza, too, could now enter the lagoon—and his henchman, Garcia, as well.

Yaño anticipated his thought. "In this place," he said, "there is no good without also evil."

Ahead of them stretched a swim of some four miles down the western face of the island and along its southern coast—miles made perilous by the ever-present threat of sharks, for the beasts habitually frequented waters near land in preference to the open sea. Trin knew there would be constant danger of an encounter, but it seemed somehow less frightening than the black submersion of the crack, for here one could breathe, and the enemy could be seen.

As he swam abreast of Yaño, nervously watching for the grim silhouette of a killer, he tried to occupy his mind with counting the fish he knew by name, as they lanced through the blue void beneath him: the bonito, fast and beautiful; the big red barco, the snapper; pompano by the hundreds; fat skipjacks and scores of yellowfin; catfish and puerco; guitar fish and mariposas—the butterflies; parrot fish and white-striped angels; a golden sierra with brilliant blue spots.

In the first mile there was a slow period of slack water; then the tide began to flow again, carrying the swimmers southward, and Trin became almost mesmerized by the dazzling parade of fishes that swirled below him in the thousands. But his dreamlike preoccupation ended suddenly when the sinister blue shape of a tinterero spiralled up from the depths.

Jolted into panic, he headed for the cliffs with a frantic thrashing of arms and legs, but the iron grip of Yaño's hand on his shoulder brought him to his senses. Trin had learned something of the nature of sharks from his father, who had been a shark fisherman, but never before had he been confronted with one in the sea, and in that first instant of shock he had acted without thought, instinctively doing the wrong thing. Now, held immobile beneath the water by the strong clasp of the Indian, he realized that his sudden desperate spurt could only serve to attract the monster.

The proof of his folly came swiftly, for the fourteen-foot predator veered out of its indolent spiral to come zooming toward them. Trin froze, only his eyes moving to follow the shark as it passed within five feet of him, and then swung in a semicircle to return for another look. As the brute sculled by for a second time, Trin felt the nudge of Yaño's elbow, and following his gesture, was horrified to see three more tintereros surging up to join the first.

One by one, they glided past like participants in some Neptunian ritual, their immense bodies curving in a silver-blue arc as the sunlight played on their thousands of scales.

Turning back, they cruised in a continuing choreography of rhythmic movements, dropping downward only to rise again and swing around the swimmers in fluent circles.

Trin was badly in need of air, and though he feared to lose sight of the sharks for an instant, he was forced to go up. Breaking the surface beside him, Yaño spoke as soon as he had filled his lungs.

"The guardian-spirits are still with us," he said softly. "The beasts are not hungry. But they are curious, and they may stay with us for a time. Let us try to swim a little, moving as gently as they are moving. It will be better if we can get closer to the dinghy, in case their mood changes."

His heart hammering, Trin ducked under and took Yaño's pace, reaching out with cautious strokes while he watched for any sign of reaction from the sharks. He knew they were completely unpredictable, and just as their leisurely convolutions indicated a certain degree of safety, so would the slightest tremor of agitation indicate grave danger.

But the monsters continued to circle with buoyant grace, undisturbed by Trin and Yaño as they glided through the water in fluid imitation of their movements. The long slow strokes seemed to stretch out endlessly, until finally the sharks melted away into the blue sea-mist.

Wrung out by tension, the swimmers were tempted to rest, but the danger of another hazardous encounter increased with every passing moment, for the sun was already slanting down toward the distant mountains of Baja. Soon the sea would pale to a twilight gray, and the giant hunters would begin their nocturnal prowling.

Aided by the fast-flowing current, Trin and Yaño rounded the southwest corner of the island. The thought of the dinghy, now little more than a mile away, spurred their flagging energies, and they pushed forward until they sighted not one but two small boats.

"The Grizzly's still there!" exclaimed Trin. "Why would he wait all these hours?"

"He trusts no one," said Yaño. "It may be he still suspects that we have come here to meet with men of my tribe, who will help you to escape."

"I wish we had!" Trin confessed.

"I, too!" agreed Yaño. Thrusting himself skyward in a great leap, he hailed the dinghies and received their answering signal. A moment later, both boats were pulling toward them.

"When they get here, he may try to seize me," said Trin anxiously.

"Then he will not succeed," Yaño promised. "I will see to that. I—and the guardian spirits!" he amended, with a smile.

But if the guardian-spirits had been in the ascendant during the brighter hours of the day, the devil-spirits rose to challenge them now. "In this place, there is no good without also evil," Yaño had said, and strangely, the prophetic words were echoing in Trin's mind when the evil appeared in the graying waters. For as they swam to meet the dinghies, the most ferocious of all hunters came streaking toward them. Far bigger than the tintereros, the gigantic beast could only be a great white shark.

CHAPTER EIGHTEEN

The hunger of the great whites for the flesh of man had long been legend on the shores of the Sea of Cortez, and tales of horror had been whispered from generation to generation, for few men had ever come face to face with the monsters and survived. Now, the stories Trin had heard for years came to sudden life, for this was no curious beast approaching in a lazy spiral—this was a ravenous man-eater, eager for the kill.

Its huge dorsal fin barely beneath the surface, the shark rushed toward them, great tooth-studded jaws gaping open. Gripped in the paralysis of terror, Trin waited for the colossal mouth to envelope him, but the creature shot past, an enormous blur twice the length of the tintereros, and he was astounded to find that he was still alive. Instinct forced him to go up for air, and in the brief moment that his head was above water, he saw that the boatmen were racing to the scene and was vaguely aware that Barraza, pulling mightily on the oars, was in the lead.

He ducked under, his mind too numb with fear to take in the significance of what he had seen. Yaño was at his side, waiting with drawn knife as the mammoth gray and white shape whizzed by again to disappear into the twilight blue. There could be no doubt that he would return. Hunger was all too evident in the driving power and incredible speed of his passes. The great white had found his prey and two men alone in the water, armed only with knives, could not hope to fight off the thirty-foot shark.

But for an instant he was gone, and the Yaqui surfaced. Trin followed him up, forcing his rigid hand to draw his knife. The dinghies were still racing toward them, and for the first time he realized that if the unpredictable killer postponed his attack long enough, the men might reach them. Yaño waved a frantic signal, and they went under again, hoping to fight a delaying battle while the boatmen sculled the last hundred yards.

Seconds passed as they scanned the opaque water, and then the shark emerged from the mist to charge straight for them. They gripped their knives, determined to strike out in one final desperate gesture—but unaccountably, the beast braked to a stop less than twenty feet away. His pectorals spread, he hung in space staring out of savage eyes, his long gill-slits pulsating while the terrible mouth slowly opened and closed as if he were already savoring the taste of human flesh.

A full minute they waited, frozen in suspense, for their deliberate antagonist to make his next move, and Trin felt that his whole body would burst from the pounding of his heart and the excruciating need to breathe. The slightest move might precipitate the beast's final assault, but as the seconds slipped by he knew he could hold out no longer. Almost imperceptibly, he broke water.

Sucking in air, he saw that the boats were still speeding toward them, Barraza's powerful strokes keeping him in the lead while Paco rowed frantically to close the gap between them. Garcia was kneeling in the dinghy, leaning out with arms ready to grab him—but in that instant he glimpsed the tip of the dorsal fin.

With a terrified shout, he drew back into the boat, and Trin realized that the race had not been to save them from the shark, but to seize him before Paco could reach him. Cued by the shout, the shark exploded into action, and in a swift confusion of images, Trin saw the monster slicing toward him while Barraza reversed his oars to send his dinghy cutting away across Paco's course.

Instinctively Trin lunged to one side, and a tremendous blow sent him hurtling backwards as the gigantic body of the fish reared out of the water to pass over him. Choking and gasping, he managed to pull himself to the surface. The foaming sea was red with blood, and there was no sign of Yaño.

The impact of a crash cut into his consciousness, and he saw Paco's boat plow into the retreating Barraza. The jolt sent two men plunging into the water, and he heard a horrified scream. At the sound, the tail of the giant white flashed above the surface thirty yards away, as the beast circled to come streaking back right on the surface.

Trin felt a wild impulse to swim for the dinghies, but the distance was too great, and he knew the frantic motion would only seal his doom. In despair, he reached for his knife—but the sheath was empty. Only then did he realize that it had been knocked from his hand by the blow of the shark's body.

Pulling his legs up to his chest, he curled himself into a tight ball and waited, immobile, as the monster came straight for him—to roll on its side and arc down under him at the last second. Shooting past beneath his feet, the beast left a red streak in its wake.

To Trin's amazement and joy, Yaño broke water near him, knife in hand, and he realized that the blood reddening the sea was not his friend's, but the shark's. Rising from somewhere below him, the Yaqui had stabbed into the brute, diverting him from his course.

"Twice, I got my knife into his belly," gasped Yaño, "but fifty slashes will not kill him!"

He looked desperately toward the dinghies. Paco's was empty, but Barraza was pulling away while Garcia swam after him with frenzied strokes, his pleas for help echoing against the cliffs.

Roused by the anguished cries, Paco rose above the gunwale on the far side of his boat, a livid bruise on his forehead. As he struggled to climb in, Yaño and Trin lanced toward him with desperate speed, but before they could reach the dinghy there was a terrible, piercing shriek, and Garcia disappeared beneath the water. The great white had made his kill.

Sickened with horror, they clambered over the stern of the boat and drew Paco in after them. Seizing the oars, Yaño rowed to the spot where the swimmer had vanished. Far below in the shadowed depths, the gigantic silhouette hung motionless while a red mist spread through the water. But the man was gone.

Yaño handed Trin one of the oars. "We are spent," he said, "and it will take the strength of both of us to get away in time. The scent of blood will draw every shark within a quarter of a mile, and no dinghy could protect us from a feeding frenzy."

Summoning the last of his energy, Trin pulled with Yaño for the reef, following in the wake of the fleeing Barraza. When they reached the safety of the shallows, they looked back.

Where minutes ago the monster had hung below the quiet surface, the sea was foaming and turbulent, as fins and tails flashed in the glare of the descending sun. No longer killer, but himself the victim, the great white reared out of the water in his death throes to fall back into the slashing, ripping jaws of the blood-crazed pack. The greedy man-eater had fallen prey to his brothers.

Safely back on the schooner, Trin and Yaño and Paco slept out their exhaustion through all that night and the next day, waking only long enough to eat fresh-caught fish and beans and tortillas before dropping off again. But in the pre-dawn darkness of the following morning, they set off with two dinghies for the submerged tunnel. According to Yaño's calculations, the tide would drop to its lowest point near the time of sunrise.

Haunted by their encounter with the great white, they rowed in silence, dipping their oars quietly lest they attract the attention of another predator. On this first day of diving, they would have no help from Zapo and Insa. The death of Garcia had filled the two Yaquis with a terror that did not lessen when Yaño told them of the fabulous oyster bed within the secret lagoon. Nothing would ever tempt them to dive, except possibly the sight of pearls brought up from the bed. Yet Trin had not dared to show them the black one, for it would only have compounded their fears. But if today he and Yaño could bring up pearls of another color, perhaps then they would dive.

He knew the lure of the gems would be great, for all pearls brought up by a diver belonged to him alone. With the shell, it was different. Half of that would become the property of the owners and the captain. The other half would belong to the divers and their boatmen. The shell was the cargo for which the ships came, but it was the hope of finding a great pearl that made men risk their lives. It might yet tempt Zapo and Insa to pit their strength against the devil-spirits. If they could be persuaded to dive, it would not only help to give the captain his cargo but it would get them off the ship.

"I don't like to think of Zapo and Insa on the schooner while we work," Trin said, speaking his thoughts aloud. "With Barraza, they are still three men against two."

"Sí. And the big Grizzly needs only to seize my brother or the capitán to have us all in his power," declared Paco, as he pulled on the oars.

"It is true," agreed Trin, "for he values no man's life but his own, and he knows we will surrender anything before we will let him kill one of us."

"You have sensed our gravest danger, amigos," Yaño admitted, "but I think the time of it has not yet come. There is much that Barraza wants, and he will wait until he thinks he can get *all* of it."

The seabirds rose from the rocky ledges above them with a great crying and flapping of wings, and they knew that daybreak was near. Gradually the stars paled and the sky brightened with the first color of dawn. Reaching the hidden entrance of the island, they found that Yaño's calculations had been correct: the water was slack, and the tunnel was open. Carefully they moved through the narrow channel, the second dinghy with its load of diving ropes and nets bobbing behind them. In a matter of minutes they were inside the lagoon, and soon the tide would rise again, sealing them in and closing everyone else out.

Diving could not begin until the sun was high enough to illumine the sea floor. In the meantime, Paco built a fire and prepared hot coffee and tortillas while Yaño and Trin gathered heavy stones from the beach, to be used as weights, and placed them in the dinghy with their equipment.

Customarily each diver wore a net attached to his waist

and brought up whatever oysters he had gathered—sometimes only one or two—each time he surfaced. But in so rich a bed the added weight of a netful of oysters would tire a man unnecessarily. For this reason, Yaño had brought, instead, two large nets which would be sent to the bottom at the end of many fathoms of rope. When each diver had filled one of the nets, he would signal the boatman, who would then pull it up. It was for the nets and the diving rope that the weights were needed. Small sticks, nine inches long and sharply pointed at each end, to be used for prying the oysters loose from the rocks, completed their equipment.

Leaving one dinghy beached on the sand, they pushed off as soon as the light permitted, heading for the south end of the lagoon. The surface was smooth as a pond, and the ascending sun brought to life the almost incredibly fertile sea garden beneath them. Everywhere there were lush tones of green and gold, vivid pinks and purples, yellows, blues and reds of plants and creatures, but Trin had eyes only for the *concha de la perla fina*—and the death-dealing snakes who guarded them. Yet nowhere could he spot either one.

They were approaching the southwest corner when Yaño ordered, "Rest on your oars, amigo! We will start here." The little boat glided slowly to a stop, and the Yaqui dropped anchor.

Trin understood that his partner planned to move systematically, working the bottom section by section, so that if Fate permitted them time to gather in the treasure, no patch would be overlooked. But he wished that he might have chosen to begin in some other place, for it was here that he had emerged from the crack and floated exhausted on the surface, to be surrounded by the snakes. The horrible vision was still all too clear in his mind, and the memory of their slimy touch sent a shiver down his spine as he leaned over the stern to peer at the bottom. Directly below him, a little hillock sloped gently to the brink of a chasm that was perhaps ten feet wide.

Yaño was viewing the same scene from the bow. "At its deepest, the slope is no more than eight fathoms down," he said. "You will work there, Trinidad, while I work in the chasm."

Placing one of the heavy stones in the bottom of his net, he swung it out from the boat with a mighty heave. Loop after loop of rope sizzled over the gunwale as it sank to the sea floor at the very brink of the fissure. Taking up the slack, he fastened the rope to a cleat. Following suit, Trin lowered his net over the stern until it settled on the slope below him.

"At first you will not be able to see the oysters," Yaño told him. "They are very hard to spot, but in one way they betray themselves: they lie with their mouths open, and when you approach, they close them. How they are warned, I do not know, for they have no eyes, but it is when they shut their shells against danger that they are revealed. As you swim slowly over the bottom, watch closely, for it happens in an instant."

Paco had been tying the end of a third rope around the heaviest rock, and now he put it over the side and let it sink some three feet below the surface. Yaño picked up one of the short pointed sticks and slipped overboard.

"This first time, I will wait for you on the slope," he told Trin. "If I point out the oysters, it may save you a fruitless dive."

He took hold of the rope and stood with his feet on the rock, his toes gripping the hemp. When he had pumped his lungs full of air, he signaled with a wave of the stick, and Paco let out the line. Rock and diver shot down to the bottom, and as soon as the Yaqui released the rope, Paco began to pull up the weight.

Grasping a stick, Trin lowered himself into the water, and emulating Yaño, seized the rope and put his feet on the rock. Practicing in the water tank at Cinco Ríos, he had dreamed his wild, impossible dream, and now at last it had come true.

Above him, Paco was grinning his encouragement. "You will find a great pearl, amigo!" he announced firmly. "The spirits have told me!"

At the mention of the spirits Trin felt a sharp twinge of apprehension. He gave the signal, and Paco let go. The rock plunged into the depths, carrying Trin with it. When the swirl of bubbles from his descent had cleared, he peered through the twilight blue of the sea bottom in search of the striped snakes, but the only visible creatures were a quartet of brightly colored damselfish that swam past at eye level and slipped between the branches of a perfectly shaped tree, its black coral structure coated in red velvet.

Beyond it, Yaño waited for him, a pair of oysters tucked under his arm. The Yaqui pointed to the sea floor, and moving slowly over it as he swam toward him, Trin tried to spot the gray, ruffled shape of the pearl oyster. All the familiar and beautiful life of a submarine garden was spread out beneath him, but though he strained his eyes, he could not see even one oyster.

Letting the air out of his lungs in small bubbles as he watched, Yaño smiled and tapped with his stick what looked like a dark lump of rubble, barnacle-encrusted and overgrown with weed. Prying it loose with his pointed stick, he moved to place it in Trin's shell-net, along with the two oysters he had already collected, but Trin shook his head and waved him away. Grinning, the Yaqui swam off toward his own net, and Trin again gave his attention to the sea floor. Now that Yaño had pointed out their disguise, he saw that several other oysters had been clustered around the one the Indian had taken up, their frilly exteriors hidden by growing weeds and animated by tiny scuttling crabs.

He tried to dislodge one of them with his stick as Yaño had done, but the shell did not budge. Grasping the rough, lacerating surface in both hands, he pulled and was astounded to discover how firmly the creature was fixed to the rock bottom. With grim determination, he tugged again, exerting his full strength. Suddenly the thing tore loose, and thrown off balance by the intensity of his effort, he found himself tumbling upward, carried toward the surface by the buoyancy of the water.

With his breath half spent, he swam back down, discouraged by the waste of time and energy and his own inadequacy. As he moved toward the net-bag, he glimpsed a flash of motion beside it and realized that he had seen an oyster close its mouth. But though he had spotted it, he could not wrench it free before he had to go up for air.

Grasping the net-rope, he gave a strong pull that sent him shooting to the surface. Clinging to the gunwale, he filled his lungs and told Paco of his failure.

"I have *seen* five oysters," he gasped, "but I have collected only one!"

"For the first dive, one is good," insisted Paco.

"But to cut your hands is not good," declared Yaño, who had come up beside him. A tiny trickle of blood was oozing down onto Trin's wrist, and the Yaqui examined his palms. "You are lucky the cuts are not deep, but even a small cut can become a bad wound if it is infected. You must use your stick to pry the creature loose. When we go down again, I will try to teach you the trick."

After they had rested, they plunged down again in quick succession, and Yaño demonstrated his technique of the stick, but it was a twist of the wrist not easily mastered, and Trin had to persist through a disheartening series of dives before he succeeded in prying an oyster loose. So intent had he been on his own problem that he lost all track of time, and as he pulled on the rope to propel himself to the surface, he was startled to see a bagful of oysters ascending above him. Already Yaño had filled his net, while he had only two!

Breaking water, he clung to the gunwale and watched with the Yaqui as Paco emptied the oysters into the bottom of the dinghy. Then he took up his knife and one by one, cleaned them of debris, cut them open, and examined the fleshy body inside. In the first six there was nothing, though the nacre of the shells was beautiful. In the seventh, he found a small but perfect pearl—and again, it was black.

"It is not strange," said Yaño reassuringly. "In this sea there are many black ones."

"Sí," agreed Paco, "there will be white ones later, and pink and green. All the colors."

His words were cheerful enough, but his eyes betrayed the anxiety behind them, and Trin knew that Paco was as disturbed by this added omen of evil as he was.

Climbing into the dinghy, Yaño swung out his net, and when it had again settled near the edge of the chasm he tied the rope to the cleat and slipped into the water. "Give me the weight, Paco," he said. "I have rested long enough."

Paco let the rock down below the surface, and the Yaqui placed his feet on it. "Go ahead and open the oysters, amigo," Yaño ordered. "I trust you."

"I promise you I will never steal a *black* pearl!" pledged Paco, forcing a grin, but when the Indian had plunged beneath the water his face sobered.

"I don't like it, chico," he confided, as he pulled up the weight. "On the day he found the first one, the great white killed a man. Now there is a second, and I'm afraid to think what could happen to one of us, maybe here in the lagoon or on the way back to the schooner."

"It is only a superstition," said Trin, trying to brush off the fear that nagged at them both. "A pearl is a pearl, and it will bring Yaño a good many pesos." But as he stood on the rock, sucking in air, he felt the same apprehension he had felt on the first dive, and he found it difficult to give the signal that would send him rushing down to the bottom.

"Maybe you should rest a little longer," said Paco, sensing his hesitation.

Summoning his courage, Trin motioned with the stick, and almost regretfully, Paco released the rope.

In the blur of his swift descent, Trin saw nothing, but when the water had cleared he stood on the sea floor gazing intently at the garden around him. There was no motion anywhere: no oyster closed its lips, no crab scuttled across the hidden shells, no lacy leaf or blade of sea grass stirred, no fishes floated across the scene. It was as if the life of the sea garden had suddenly been suspended by some magic spell.

Trin stood alone among the frozen plants and creatures, holding his breath, letting no bubble of air escape, feeling as if he, too, were suspended in time and space, waiting for something to happen. Even his heart seemed to stop beat-ing.

There was no sign of Yaño in the mists beyond him, and he wanted to look upward to see if the dinghy was still there, but he could not move his head. Nothing had touched him, yet he was as frozen as the plants and crea-tures around him. Had the taking of the black pearl set off a spell, and put him into the power of some evil spirit? He was filled with a feeling of terrible desolation—and then, to his amazement, a golden dolphinfish lanced down from above him, hung suspended, its gleaming body less than a yard from his face, and cut away into the blue twilight.

Immediately the lush green and gold leafage around him swayed in response to the vivid motion, a pair of brilliant red crabs scuttled across the rocks at his feet, and a cluster of oysters opened their lips. Once again, the scene was alive, and Trin himself was released.

A golden dolphinfish had led him into the great crack. Could this have been the same one? he wondered. Did his guardian-spirit appear in the form of this beautiful fish, and had it now come to release him from an evil spell? Or had he been frozen by his own fear and imagined that every-thing else was frozen with him?

Through the blue veil of distance, he saw Yaño emerge from the chasm and place an armload of oysters in his net bag. Then with a look toward Trin and a wave of his hand, he descended again into the chasm. Glancing up, Trin saw the bottom of the dinghy some eight fathoms above him. He moved, and the cluster of oysters closed their mouths, but he had spotted them and with his newly acquired skill with the stick, he began to dislodge them.

For another hour Trin continued to dive, resting in the water alongside the dinghy each time he surfaced, and watching as Paco opened the shells and searched for pearls. When they stopped work for the midday break, Paco had found no more, but Trin, gradually becoming more expert at spotting and collecting, had gathered seventeen oysters into his net.

Though the day was hot, the divers were chilled from the coolness of the depths. Leaving the dinghy anchored, with its partially filled net-bags still at the bottom, they swam ashore and Paco made a fire, and prepared a hot gruel to warm them.

Lying on the sandy beach beside Trin while the sun burned down on their cold flesh, Yaño said, "You have done well, Trinidad. In many places, a diver is lucky to bring up twenty oysters in a day. But with a bed as rich as this, you will soon be bringing up one hundred."

Trin knew that Yaño would be bringing up many more than that, for he stayed down two minutes in every dive, and collected seven or eight oysters each time. And though they rested several minutes between dives, both of them went to the bottom six or eight times an hour.

"If Zapo and Insa would dive with us," the Yaqui went on, "the four of us could soon fill the hold of the ship."

"But they won't be tempted unless we find white pearls —or pink," said Trin.

"We still have three hours of diving ahead of us," declared Yaño, "and with every oyster we bring up, there is a chance."

The thought of that chance nagged at Trin, and though he was tired, he found it hard to relax during the time allotted for rest. When at last Yaño allowed him to return to the lagoon, he dove without fear, too driven by his hope of finding a pearl to think of the devil-snakes.

An hour passed—two hours—and three-quarters of the

third. Yaño had sent up another load of oysters and was filling his net again. In the dinghy, Paco was opening them
and stacking the cleaned shells in sacks ready for the trip
back to the schooner. But Trin's bag had not yet been
drawn up, for he was too proud to send it up until he had
filled it, and though he was collecting with increasing
speed, it had not quite reached its capacity.

Gathering a final quartet of oysters in the last dive permitted him, he filled his net and signalled Paco to pull it
up. He had worked his way to the end of the slope, and
now a fissure yawned open at his feet. There were still several seconds' worth of air left in his lungs, and he peered
into its depths in search of one more catch.

At first he saw nothing; then on the opposite side, three
feet down beneath a narrow overhang of rock, he spotted
one lone oyster. It was not one of the ancient ones, rotten
with age, that according to legend often held within their
bodies the greatest of pearls. It was, in fact, a very ordinary
looking oyster of average size; yet he felt extraordinarily
drawn to it, as though, intuitively, he knew he had come on
this day to collect it.

Stepping off into the chasm, he finned down until he was
opposite it, but as he reached toward it with his stick, a
cloud of tiny fishes swept into the space between his eyes
and the barnacle-covered shell, and for a moment he could
see only their brilliant stripes. *Stripes!* With shock, he
realized that these were the same fish that had appeared
before, when Yaño had taken the first oyster with the pearl
in it. And in the same moment, the poisonous striped snake
had been streaking up toward him.

Trin's heart hammered, and he peered down into the
shadowy twilight below him, but if a snake was there it was
invisible. The tiny fish hung between him and the oyster

like the dazzling design of a veil. Did their presence indicate that he had come upon a pearl? There had been one in that first oyster—black, yes, but this one might be white.

He didn't want to touch their bodies, for if there was anything to the superstitions of the Yaquis, they might be spirits, not fish. Yet he could not bear to ignore his hunch. The seconds were going—his breath was running out.

He pressed the stick toward them and they darted away as suddenly as they had come. Inserting the sharp point under the oyster, he tore it loose. Then pushing off from the ledge, he swam to the surface. Paco was pulling his net-bag into the dinghy, with Yaño's help.

"Have you found any pearls?" gasped Trin, when he could speak.

"Since the black one? None," said Paco regretfully.

"Then open this!" Trin insisted, handing him the single oyster. "I know there is no time for opening, but just this one! The striped fish of the color of the devil-snakes appeared when I reached out to take it, and I have a hunch."

While Yaño pulled up his own net-bag, Paco hacked off the barnacles and slipped his knife between the valves of the oyster. Hardly breathing, Trin watched him cut the muscle and break open the hinge.

"It is yours," said Paco. "You should make the search."

Climbing over the gunwale, Trin took the oyster into his hand and lifted the mantle. Nestled in the folds of flesh, he saw not one pearl but two—both *black*.

Paco stared at them in horror. "You and your hunch!" he said. "I wish you had left it at the bottom of the sea!"

Trin could guess what he was thinking: one pearl—and one man dead. Now there were three black pearls—and three of them.

CHAPTER NINETEEN

But if the black pearls were harbingers of disaster, it did not strike on the trip back to the schooner, for
the trio reached *La Virazón* in safety. Standing at the rail
with Barraza, Zapo and Insa watched as Raúl pulled the
cargo aboard, their faces masked with stony indifference,
but no detail escaped them.

"They have not missed the size of Yaño's catch," Paco
whispered to Trin, as his brother pulled up the sacks.
"Never have they seen so many shells brought up in one
day by one diver. And that a boy like you, in his first try,
should fill so big a net-bag—that, too, will make its mark!"

"Look at the eyes of the Grizzly," Trin told him, under
his breath. "Already they have the glitter of the devil!"

"Sí. If there is a white pearl in the oysters when we open
them, they will dive—or he will find a way to make them!"

The suspenseful ceremony of the opening started with
Trin's catch. When his netful of oysters had been dumped
in a heap on the deck, the men gathered around them in a
circle and the work began. Chopping off their camouflage
of marine growths, Raúl and Paco passed the shells to
Fortino, who sat on a low stool, a wooden block in front of
him and a tub alongside.

Wrapped in blankets, their bodies still chilled from

hours in the water, Trin and Yaño squatted beside him while the Grizzly and his henchmen stood over them, their eyes riveted to the captain's hands. Placing the first oyster on the block, he severed the muscle and pressed the shells apart. When his fingers had explored the creature's body and found no lump that might be a pearl, he removed the animal from its shell and squeezed it in his hands. Still finding nothing, he handed it on to Trin who again examined it, before passing it on to Yaño. Searching in vain, the Yaqui tossed the body into the waiting tub, while the shells, their nacred interiors free of blisters, were passed to Paco for final cleaning and packing.

One after another, the oysters were inspected with equal care, while Trin waited in taut suspense, hoping—praying —that beneath each mantle there might lie a pearl, and fearing that it might be black. Gradually the pile diminished, until the last oyster had been opened, but no one of them held a pearl of any color.

When the shell had been sacked and weighed and credited to Trin's account, Yaño's net-bag of oysters was emptied onto the deck, and the whole process began over again. At every cut of Fortino's knife, the tension mounted, for the need to find a pearl was great, and each time he forced a pair of shells apart, there was a new chance.

Stealing a glance at the men standing above him, Trin saw that their eyes were still intently focused on every move of the opening. The iridescent beauty of the mother-of-pearl lining had made its impression, for shells of such quality would bring a good price. Now all that was needed was the added lure of a pearl that was white.

But hope turned to despair as the pile melted down to the last half dozen oysters. Picking up one of them, Fortino placed it on the block. It was an old oyster and large, its black flutes riddled by worms. Cutting it open, the captain lifted its decaying flesh.

For a moment, no one breathed. Then Fortino put the rotten mantle back in place, and handed the oyster in its half shell to Yaño. Their eyes met, and in that meeting telegraphed their message: danger.

Yaño slipped his fingers under the fringe and pressed into his fist what lay beneath. Then handing the oyster to Trin, he rose and went into the captain's cabin. Even after he had disappeared, no one moved or spoke. It was as if lightning had struck them, and indeed they had been electrified in that instant when Fortino lifted the fringe and they saw the pearl lying in its withered bed. For this was no ordinary gem, but an exquisite miracle of beauty—a pearl to grace the crown of a monarch. And suddenly Trin realized that it must have been just such a pearl that the men of the Old One's expedition had found: pear-shaped and of magnificent size, it was a pinkish-white and tinged with every color of the rainbow. Raising his eyes, he saw in the faces of Barraza and the two Yaquis the same lust that had driven those men to murder, eighty years ago.

The silent tension snapped as Paco leapt to his feet and let out a great shout. Spontaneously, Trin and Raúl joined him, releasing their excitement in whoops of elation. But the presence of the Grizzly and his somber companions soon quenched their spirits, and they returned to the job of the oysters. In the remaining five there were no pearls, and while Raúl and Paco completed the sacking and weighing of Yaño's catch, Fortino and Trin followed him to the cabin.

The young Indian was sitting on the edge of the captain's bunk, his fist clenched, and Trin guessed that he had closed his hand around the pearl at the sound of their footsteps on the companionway.

"Where are they?" he asked.

"In the bows, whispering together," Trin told him, knowing that he referred to the three men who were now, more than ever, his enemies.

"They will have much to whisper about," he said bitterly.

"Sí," agreed Fortino. "The sight of so great a pearl stirs evil appetites." It was growing dark in the cabin, and he lighted a lamp.

Yaño moved to it and opened his hand. The jewel lay in his palm like a living thing, its lustrous satin surface glowing with a radiance that seemed to come not from the reflected light of the lamp but from a flame within.

Gazing at it, Yaño forgot for the moment the men whose lust for it would threaten his life from this day forward, and his face shone with the sheer joy of fulfillment.

"I have been diving since I was a boy younger than you," he told Trin, "and always I have dreamed of a rainbow pearl such as the Old One saw here, but even then I did not imagine one of such size and orient."

"For centuries, men have been diving with the same dream," Fortino reminded him, "but not half a dozen of them have found a gem like this one. It must be one hundred grains or more."

"And perfect!" Yaño turned it over in his palm, showing them its full surface. "Nowhere can I see a single flaw!"

"It is a jewel of rare beauty, and worth many thousands of pesos," said the captain. "You will be rich, mi hijo!"

"If I can live to sell it," said Yaño, his thoughts returning to Barraza and his men. "But that will not be easy. It has come too soon."

"We needed it—to get them to dive!" Trin reminded him.

"We needed a white pearl, but not *this* one. Now their

thoughts will be less on the pearls that lie hidden in the lagoon than on the one that lies here in the captain's strongbox!"

There was a rumble of voices on the deck above, with Barraza's topping the others. Startled out of his slumber by the sound of it, the little dog, Pepé, rose from his place under the table, his hackles erect.

"Capitán! I have come to talk to you!" Barraza shouted.

Fortino's strongbox was at the foot of his bunk. Moving to it swiftly, he unlocked it and took out a small wooden box lined with sheep's wool.

"Chavarria! Tell your men to let me pass! I have come as a friend!" the Grizzly boomed, from the top of the companionway.

Yaño dropped the great jewel into the soft bed of wool, and the captain stowed it away and locked the strongbox.

"Now we are ready," he whispered, "but be on your guard!" Moving to the companionway, he called up to Raúl and Paco. "Let him come!"

The hulking figure lumbered down into the cabin, while the three of them watched him in silence. The dog growled low in his throat and bared his teeth.

"Your men don't trust me, Capitán," said Barraza, with a grimace, "but I won't hold it against them. I have not trusted them—or you—and I have been wrong. That's what I have come to tell you."

"If you mean that, Ignacio," said Fortino quietly, "then at last you sound like the son of your father."

"You have been disappointed in me, Capitán, and I have given you reason. I should have known the partner of my father would be an honest man, but in a world full of wolves, who can know which one to trust?"

"To judge the heart of a man is something each one of us must learn for himself," declared Fortino.

"You are right, Capitán, and I have learned it on this ship. When the boy, here, told me you had sailed to this uncharted island in search of pearls, I could not believe him. But today I have learned that he spoke the truth. And if the island and the oyster bed are true, then how can I not believe in the truth of his innocence?"

"You *can* believe in it, Ignacio," said Fortino firmly. "Trinidad is a young man of great honor—and so, also, are Yaño and Raúl and Paco. They are, all of them, men to be trusted."

"And *you*, Capitán—you are a man to be trusted. *This* I have learned."

Barraza said the words with a great show of earnestness, but to Trin they did not ring true; yet it seemed to him that the captain was believing them.

"This is what I have come to tell you," Barraza went on, "that I know now you are an honest man, and wise. You would have been a good partner to my father, and you will be a good partner to me. From this night we will work together, and there will be no need for distrust between us."

"I would like to have it so," admitted the captain. "In the memory of your father, I would like very much to have it so."

"Then it shall be, compadre! We are friends!" His look included Trin and Yaño, and again his loose mouth stretched wide in the grimace that passed for a smile.

Trin's eyes moved from Barraza to Yaño. The face of the Indian was expressionless.

"We are friends!" Barraza reiterated. "Eh, Trinidad?"

Trin made no response, and undaunted, Barraza went on.

"And I shall begin to help you by trying to find a way to make Zapo and Insa dive."

"Was the great pearl not enough?" asked Trin, in surprise.

"Before the great pearl, they refused," said the Grizzly. "Now they *consider*. But how many men find a great pearl? In the whole island, there will be only *one* of them. But if they could be told how many *other* pearls you found—if I could say I have *seen* them . . ."

There was a moment of silence as the eyes of Fortino met those of his divers.

"Come, amigos, surely the rainbow was not the only pearl?"

No one of them had moved since Barraza came down the companionway, but now he ambled casually to the strongbox and kicked it lightly with his toe.

"Come, Capitán," he said, with a sly look at Fortino, "we have said we will trust each other. Am I not to be trusted to see what is in the box?"

"Sí. You may look at what is in the box," said Fortino quietly.

To Trin's horror, he crossed to the strongbox, took the key out of his pocket and unlocked it.

"You are right, Ignacio," he went on, "there were other pearls, and as an act of faith in your friendship, I will show them to you." He picked up the small wooden box and carried it over to the lamp. "But you will be wise not to speak of them to Zapo and Insa."

Barraza followed him, his mind so focused on the box that he barely heard the words. The captain lifted the lid, and the light touched the great pearl. At sight of it, the Grizzly unconsciously sucked in his breath, and Yaño's hand moved to his knife.

"It is no wonder you gasp," said Fortino casually. "It is a pearl to take a man's breath away."

With an effort, Barraza masked the greed that burned in his eyes, as the captain covered the glowing gem with a layer of wool and pressed it aside to reveal the black ones beneath.

"Now you see why we could not show them."

"There were no others?" demanded Barraza suspiciously.

"Only these," insisted Fortino, "and to your Yaqui friends they would be omens of evil."

"You were right not to show them," agreed the Grizzly, his small crafty eyes still intently seeking pearls that might lie hidden in the wool, as the captain smoothed it down over the gems. "But I can say that I have seen them, without speaking of their color. You will find that I can help you, compañero! I will tell the Yaquis of four good pearls, besides the great one. It may even be enough to make them dive." He paused. "Of course, if I could *show* them a white one—" he suggested slyly.

"There are no white ones, Ignacio," declared Fortino. "You have seen them all." He snapped down the lid and crossed to the strongbox. "Tell your friends what you will; we have nothing more to show them!" With a gesture of finality, he locked the strongbox and returned the key to his pocket.

Barraza moved with clumsy haste to the companionway, as if, having achieved his purpose, he couldn't get away quickly enough. Again the hackles rose on Pepé's back, and he bared his teeth.

Halfway up the steps, the man turned back. "You have been honest with me, Capitán," he said, "and now I will prove that I deserve your trust. You will see that I am a good friend."

He swung his big bulk out of the cabin door, and in the

next instant Raúl and Paco appeared at the top of the companionway, their faces clouded with concern.

"He gave you no trouble?" asked Raúl, looking from one to the other.

"No trouble," said Fortino. "He came as a friend."

"It's not true, padrino!" Trin burst out. "He was lying! He is still our enemy!"

Fortino turned his gaze on Trin. "You did not believe him, my son? His words were good."

"They were good, padrino, but they were not true. I could see behind them, in his eyes."

"Bueno, Trinidad. You have judged well."

"But—I thought—" Trin began in confusion.

"You thought I believed him?"

"Sí."

"I *wanted* to. It would be good to be able to trust the son of my friend, and I will give him every chance to make his words the truth. But I am not a fool, and I, too, read his eyes."

"But padrino, you showed him the hiding place of the pearls!"

"The strongbox is no real hiding place," Fortino explained. "It is where any thief would expect to find them. Yaño must hide his pearl in a place more secret than that."

"No place will be secret from Barraza long, if he can seize one of us," Yaño declared. "It will be as we said in the dinghy: he needs only one man to take us all—and with us, the pearl. It is ourselves we must guard."

"You are right," Fortino agreed. "To each of us, life is a treasure greater than ten thousand rainbows, but to the man who would steal it, our lives are no more than the dying oyster from which we took it. From now on, there will be no moment when any one of us will be safe."

Throughout the night, Raúl and Fortino stood watch while Trin and Yaño and Paco tried to sleep before the work of the morning, but each in his own way was haunted by the beauty of the great pearl and the danger that came with it. Tossing restlessly on his pallet of canvas on the starlit deck, Trin was tormented by the memory of Barraza's words: ". . . how many men find a great pearl? In the whole island, there will be only *one* of them." Could it be that he was right?

Yaño was his friend, and he had no wish to take the great rainbow from him. For the Yaqui it was the just reward of many long and hazardous seasons of diving. Now he would never have to risk his life in the sea again. The pearl would bring him many thousands of pesos. He could travel to the great city of Mexico, or even beyond it to the far countries across the oceans. Or he could buy land—perhaps even a hacienda. He could buy anything, but he did not *need* to buy his freedom: he was already free.

Trin's mind ranged out to his loved ones, tied by their bonds of debt to Cinco Ríos, and the thought cut into him like a knife. If *he* had found the pearl, they could be free. The big Grizzly had to be wrong. Surely it must be true that when there was one rainbow, there *could* be another— a great pearl, worthy of the Madonna.

In memory, he saw the hand-carved figure of the Blessed Virgin, robed in blue satin, her jeweled diadem sparkling in the light of the altar candles. As he held her image in his mind, the chiseled wooden face seemed to take on the texture and color of living flesh, and the Virgin stood before him, her lovely eyes bent on him in sadness and longing. The great pearl she had worn, suspended from its golden chain, was gone, but everything else was as he had seen it on that first morning in the chapel at Cinco Ríos: the gilded altar, the walls draped with crimson velvet, the paintings of saints and virgins . . .

Staring in awe at the haloed vision, he saw a pearl materialize where there had been none—not the pearl the Virgin had worn before but the great rainbow that was Yaño's. Hanging suspended on a shining chain, it glowed as though it contained a holy fire. The longing went out of the Virgin's eyes, and her lovely face was suffused with a joyous radiance.

At her breast, the pearl blazed into a rainbow-colored flame that brightened the sainted faces in the paintings— and then, to Trin's amazement, the faces began to change, their bright holiness darkening into ugliness, and he realized that they were now the faces of Barraza and Zapo and Insa, twisted almost beyond recognition by the intensity of their lust.

As they learned down toward the Virgin, her shining blue robes turned black, and her face was filled with a terrible sorrow. The flame went out of the pearl, leaving it black and dead, and the evil images became larger and larger, until Trin could no longer see the holy figure. Powerful hands seized him, and struggling to escape, he awoke—to find his godfather's hands upon his shoulders.

"You were having a bad dream, my son!"

Trin sat up and stared into the starlit darkness around him, the evil faces and cruel hands still more real than the kindly face and strong but gentle hands of Fortino, who was bending over him, but gradually the mist-wet deck, the towering masts, took on the form of reality, and the nightmare faded. In the bows, Barraza and the Yaquis lay huddled under canvas, apparently asleep, while the captain stood watch.

Sorting out the real from the unreal, Trin told him his

dream. "Do you think it is an omen of evil, padrino, that the great pearl turned black?" he asked, in concern, when he had finished.

"I think it is no omen at all, my son," Fortino assured him. "It was your own fear that spoke to you while you slept. You have learned that the Indians fear a black pearl, and you have let their fear become yours. That is wrong, Trinidad. There is enough to fear that is real: the sea with its tides and currents; the predators, both beasts and man —these are dangers a man must recognize if he is to learn to protect himself. But a pearl that is black is no more to be feared than one that is white. It is an accident of color."

"Was it only an accident that Garcia died the day we found the first black pearl?" asked Trin.

"No, my son, it was no accident," declared Fortino. "Garcia died because he made a choice that was wrong. He chose, with Ignacio, to put his own greed above your need. He would have pulled you out of the sea for gold, but he did not pull you out to save your life, and when his own life was threatened, he found that Ignacio put no more value on it than he had put on yours. No, Trinidad, Garcia did not die because of a black pearl; he died because the partner he chose betrayed him."

"Then, padrino, you do not believe that three more of us will die, because we found three more black pearls?"

"No, my son, if we die, any of us, I can promise you it will not be because three small pearls happen to be black. That is one fear you may put out of your mind."

"There is another," Trin began, "and I would like to put it out of my mind, also, but I don't have the knowledge to give me the answer. The Grizzly said that in the whole island there would be no more than *one* great pearl. Is that true, padrino?"

"I know of no reason why it *should* be true, Trinidad," said his godfather thoughtfully. "Already we know that in this island there *was* another, eighty years ago. Why should there not be two, now—or even three? Who is to say that where there is one rainbow there may not be *many* more?"

His fears allayed by hope, Trin slept until Yaño wakened him in the hour before sunrise. A heavy fog had settled over the schooner, blotting out the island, and if the figures of Barraza and the Yaquis still lay huddled in the bows, they, too, were lost in the dense whiteness.

An eerie chill sent a shiver through Trin's body. There was something uncomfortably menacing about being trapped on a ship with an invisible enemy, and he was glad to retreat from the fog-soaked deck to the warmth of the captain's cabin and the hot breakfast Paco had prepared for them. There had been no word, no move, from Barraza, but while they ate, it came with startling suddenness. Raúl lunged down the companionway.

"They're coming now—all three of them!" he warned in a hoarse whisper. "I saw them moving toward me out of the fog!"

"Then go up and welcome them!" commanded Fortino.

Trin watched apprehensively as the heavy figure of Barraza again descended the companion stairs, followed by the compact figures of the two Indians. At the captain's feet, the dog snarled, and Fortino put a gently restraining hand on his head.

"Pepé has not yet understood your change of heart," he said, "but in time he will know his own truth."

"The truth is here before you," asserted Barraza expansively. "I told you I would help you, and I have done it! Ask them!"

The Yaquis seemed to have flowed into the cabin while the big Grizzly drew attention to himself, and now, standing in deceptive repose, their narrowed eyes staring out of impassive faces, they were acting out a tableau of complete indifference; yet unobtrusively they had assumed a strong position of attack, and Trin realized that the mere flicker of an eyelash might be the signal to close in.

If Fortino was aware of any danger, he betrayed no sign of it. Turning his steady gaze on Zapo, he asked easily, "Will you dive, amigo?"

For a long moment, the black slitted eyes stared back at him as if they sought the secret content of his mind, and then the Indian parried with a question of his own. "You keep the pearls there?" he asked, indicating the strongbox.

"Sí," nodded the captain.

Zapo moved toward it, and Trin saw that his body was taut as a cat's before it springs. Yaño's hand inched toward his knife, and in the same instant, Zapo and Insa drew theirs. Trin's nerves tightened with strain, and his throat ached from the sudden pounding of his heart. There was a breathless silence.

Surprisingly, it was Zapo who broke it with a question. "If we dive, will our pearls be kept in this box?" he demanded.

"Sí. If you choose, I will keep them for you until we reach port," said Fortino. "But I cannot buy them. I will have no money until I have sold my share of the cargo."

Trin knew that it was customary for the captain or owners of the ship to buy pearls from the divers for a small price, after which they were given shore leave to spend it for aguardiente in the nearest camp. But here there were no shore camps where the Indians could spend their pesos on spirits and revelry. Here there would be no buying or sell-ing; each diver would be obliged to keep his pearls until he reached a buyer in Guaymas or Mulegé—keep them, and guard them.

"It is settled!" declared Zapo, with finality. "We will dive, Capitán, and you will keep our pearls in your box."

"You see?" insisted Barraza. "It is as I told you: not only have I persuaded them to dive, but to trust you with their pearls! In what better way could I prove that I am your good partner—and friend?"

"It is a beginning, Ignacio," said Fortino quietly.

Their faces still void of expression, the Yaquis moved silently up the companionway with the lumbering Barraza. When they had disappeared, Paco voiced his confusion.

"If they are not *really* our friends, why would they want to leave their pearls with you, Capitán? Is it another trick?"

"It is part of the *same* trick," declared Yaño, "but it is also something more: it tells us that they trust the capitán more than Barraza."

The sun rose, and the fog lifted. Taking the schooner's six dinghies, three for each team, the men raced to reach the tunnel before the rising tide could close it for the day. Arriving barely in time, they pulled through the narrow passage against treacherous currents and into the safety of the quiet lagoon. If the Yaquis felt any fear of the devil-spirits, their inscrutable faces gave no hint of it, and under the guise of friendship the diving began.

As on the day before, Paco was boatman for Trin and Yaño, but the two Yaquis chose to work alone, each man taking his turn as diver, though the hulking Barraza, floating alongside in a cargo dinghy, watched every move. Raúl was committed to staying with Fortino on *La Virazón*, for the lives of all of them depended on the safety of the ship, and no one man could hope to get her out to sea if a sudden squall or the swift, fierce cordonazo should strike.

Throughout the day, the diving proceeded without incident, the big Grizzly giving his unwelcome attention, alternately, to the two teams. When the falling tide opened the tunnel in the late afternoon, the men returned to *La Virazón*, the dinghies loaded with their catch, and a great many sacks of oysters were opened on deck. For Trin and Yaño the day's work had yielded no gems, but luck was with Zapo and Insa: each of them had brought up a pearl, not large—but white.

For the next four days the men returned to the lagoon, the hours of their coming and going changing with the changing tide, but on the fifth morning the Yaquis refused to leave the ship. The tunnel would not be open for their return until after dark, and no lure of pearls could persuade them to enter the narrow passage or stay inside the haunted island in the blackness of night.

"It is not that I blame them," Yaño told his companions, as they huddled in the captain's cabin to discuss the problem. "The island is not a place I would choose to be in, at night, in the dark of the moon."

"Santo Dios, no!" agreed Paco. "This time I am with *them!*"

"But it will be seven days—maybe eight—before the low tide of the morning and the low tide of the night come again by daylight. If we wait, we will lose a week of diving."

"And in two or three days beyond *that*," said Fortino, "our water will be gone. Already we have used nearly half of what we brought with us. Unless there is rain, we will have to sail for Mulegé in eight or nine days."

"Mulegé!" exclaimed Trin, in alarm.

"Sí. It is there we must go to refill our casks."

"But, padrino, if we go there, I will never get back!"

"I think *none* of us will get back," predicted Paco.

"We must not sail with the hold half empty," declared Yaño. "Unless the capitán has a good cargo of shells, he will lose his ship."

"You believe," asked Raúl, "that if you three stay inside the island tonight and come out safely in the low tide of the morning, they will be tempted to go?"

"It is something we must try," insisted Yaño. "But I will not leave you with those three on board, and the great pearl on your hands. There is too much danger in it. I will take it with me, and if they should come to rob the strongbox, you must tell them that only I know where it is hidden."

Carrying supplies for an overnight camp on the beach, Trin, Yaño and Paco went into the island. The day was perfect: the hot sun blazed down through the liquid green space of the lagoon, while the divers floated over the teeming sea floor, gathering in their living treasure. Freed of the discordant presence of Barraza, they worked in complete tranquility, filling net-bag after net-bag and delivering them up to Paco. Neither above the surface nor below it was there anything to suggest that hostile spirits surrounded them—until the last hour of diving.

It was then then Trin, clinging to the gunwale of the dinghy for five minutes of rest, saw Yaño lower himself into a narrow fissure that split the sea botton like a deep crack. The opening was little more than a foot wide, yet it seemed to extend down into the rock bowels of the island. In the jagged crevices of its two walls there were hundreds of small cavities in which oysters might conceal themselves.

Slipping down cautiously between the lacerating surfaces, the Indian discovered a colony of them. Ripping several from their hiding places, he rose to put them in a small heap on the level sea floor, then descended again, moving deeper into the crack.

Watching from above, Trin saw him fill his arms a second time. He had reached out for one more oyster when there was a sudden dazzle of color as two striped snakes streaked up from the depths toward his hand. Yaño must have spotted them, too, for he shot out of the fissure with one great push and seizing the rope, hoisted himself to the surface.

"Poison snakes!" he gasped in warning, and the two of them tumbled over the gunwale into the safety of the dinghy. Only then did they see that some sharp point of rock had gouged into Yaño's right thigh, tearing open the flesh so that blood was streaming down his leg.

Hastily drawing up the net-bags, Paco stroked for shore while Trin tried to staunch the bleeding. When they reached the beach, Yaño walked thigh-deep into the cool, clear water, and let it wash the wound.

"Now we can know they are devil-spirits!" announced Paco, in an awed whisper. "The first time you saw them, Garcia died, and the second time, you are hurt!"

Yaño twisted his torso so that he could study the gash, which was slightly to the back of his thigh, near his haunch bone. "If they were devil-spirits," he said, "they have done me a favor."

"A favor!" Trin and Paco stared at him in amazement.

"Sí! Since the night I first held the great rainbow in my hand, I have tried to think of a secret place for it. On the sea bottom, in the dinghy, on the schooner—all the time, I have been working my brain to think of a hiding place—and I have thought of nothing good enough. But now the sharp rock of the island itself has given me the answer."

Bewildered, his friends waited for him to explain.

"You are beginning to understand," he went on, with a hint of a smile, "but you cannot believe you are right. It is true, what you are guessing, amigos—I will hide the pearl in the wound!"

"But how can you?" asked Trin. "Will it not show?"

"This is an ugly cut, torn and gaping, and here where the flesh of my thigh is fullest, the roundness of the pearl will seem to be the swelling, for even though it has been cleansed, it will swell much, and perhaps even fester. But it will not press the pearl out, for you, Trinidad, will *stitch* it in!"

He walked to the camp and took from the folds of his blanket the primitive medical kit that he carried with him. Threading a strand of tendon fibre through the eye of a needle, he handed it to Trin; then from inside his breech-clout, he drew a small deerskin pouch. Untying the tightly knotted drawstring, he turned the pouch upside down and let the jewel roll out into the palm of his hand. The late sun cast its golden light on the pearl, and for a moment the three of them stood in silent wonder, hypnotized by the play of colors in its opalescent "skin."

It was Yaño who broke the spell. "It is well we take a good look," he said, "for we will not see it again before we reach port, unless someone cuts open my leg to steal it." He slipped the pearl into the gaping wound, pressing it deep into the tissues that had been punctured by the point of rock. Then drawing the lacerated edges together, he covered it.

"Paco," he commanded, "you will hold the flesh in place, while Trin puts in the stitches."

Trin had made no protest; he knew the deed must be done, and he proceeded to carry out Yaño's orders in silence, but he cringed each time he had to stab the needle into his friend's body, and his hand trembled as with each stitch he was forced to pull the strand of tendon fibre through the torn flesh. When at length the gash was closed, his own body was wet with sweat, but the stoic Indian had not flinched.

"Gracias, amigos," he said, calmly surveying the wound. "You have done a good job. Even a Yaqui could not have done it better."

Paco, slightly green from his part in the ordeal, made no response, but Trin studied his handiwork carefully.

"The stiches will hold," he promised, "and you are right—no one could guess what is hidden inside."

"Only we three will know that secret," said Yaño, "but I do not ask you to keep it. Any day or night the life of one of you may be threatened: Barraza or Zapo or Insa may put a knife to your throat and demand to know the hiding place—and *you must tell them!* The pearl is mine, and if any man is to die for it, *I* will be that one."

CHAPTER TWENTY

Twilight deepened into night, and the island was shrouded in darkness. A cool wind swept down from the distant mountains of Baja, and in the little camp on the shore of the lagoon, Trin and his companions drew their blankets around them. For the first time there was no need of a night watch; the rising tide had sealed off all intruders. Yet no one slept.

Was it mere superstition that peopled the blackness with alien beings, Trin wondered, or were they surrounded by an invisible horde? He felt an aura of evil that was like a physical presence, as though a thousand devil-spirits were pressing in on him.

A hand gripped his arm, jolting his heart with fear, until he realized it was Paco's.

"I can hear them!" the young boatman whispered.

"Who?" asked Trin, knowing the answer.

"The demons! Hold your breath and listen!"

Trin held his breath and heard the hissing whispers.

"It is the little waves lapping the stones beyond the stretch of sand," said Yaño calmly, out of the silence. "Go to sleep, or you will not have the strength to work tomorrow. I will stand watch."

A far-off planet cast a faint star path across the lagoon,

and Trin fixed his eyes upon the shimmering streak of light in the great bowl of darkness. At length his heavy lids closed, and he slipped into sleep.

A jabbing elbow startled him awake, and he heard one choked word from Paco. "Look!"

Staring straight ahead, he saw them: two pale ghostly figures moving toward him across the water. As he gazed at them, transfixed, another figure joined them, and then another and another, their nebulous bodies wavering toward the shore in a filmy column until they seemed to merge and become a solid wall of white. The first gray light of day outlined the circling cliffs, and Trin saw that Paco's ghosts had been wisps of fog, now consolidating into a dense white mass that swirled in over the camp and covered it.

"So it *was* the fog I saw, and the waves I heard," said Paco defensively. "But there was something else! I *felt* it —and so did you! It was *here!*"

It *had* been here, Trin thought. Even in the pale chill of daybreak, it lingered on—something brooding and intangible, beyond his power of words to describe.

"Sí, amigo," admitted Yaño, a strange look in his black eyes. "It *was* here!"

Again the sun burned off the fog, and the Yaqui, his wound sealed by a film of lymph, made one dive to bring up the oysters he had left in a small heap on the sea floor at the edge of the fissure. Yesterday's catch, opened in the hours before dark, had yielded three small pearls, all of them Yaño's. For Trin there had been none since the black twins, though each day had brought a small harvest for the other divers.

Now there was barely time to open the added armful of oysters before making the trip back to the schooner with the loaded dinghies, for the morning's low tide was already uncovering the hidden channel. While Paco chopped off the debris and broke the hinges, Yaño searched the folds of flesh and found one more pearl. Close to gunmetal in color, it was not black but a rare silver-blue of some fifteen grains.

"If anything can make them spend the night inside the island, that will do it!" predicted Yaño.

The passage opened, and they struck out for *La Virazón*, pulling strongly to make speed, for they had to get back before the tide turned and rising, closed them out. When they reached the ship, the Yaquis viewed Yaño's bruised and swollen thigh with some alarm—but true to his prediction, the silver-blue gem turned the trick. Hastily stocking their boats, they raced with Yaño and Trin and Paco for the tunnel, leaving Barraza aboard. Beating the tide, they entered the lagoon and set up their camp at the opposite end of the sandy cove.

From that day on, both teams remained inside the island, retreating to their separate camps when the diving was done, and going out only with the low tide of morning to take their catch back to the schooner. If Zapo and Insa sensed the presence of spirits in the black hours of the night, they spoke no word of it. Perhaps they were not disturbed, thought Trin, because their own spirits were in league with the devils, but for him, the ominous atmosphere intensified with each passing night.

Yet by day, all was serene: the striped snakes did not appear again, and there were no accidents or injuries to mar their peaceful progress. The sacks of shells piled up in the hold, and the store of gems in Fortino's strongbox increased with every catch. Only Trin seemed touched by misfortune, for still he had found no pearls since the black ones.

Lying beside the dying embers of the campfire, while Paco stood watch in the shadows, Trin brooded on their meaning. "If black pearls are no more evil than white," he whispered to Yaño, who lay near him, "why is it that only I am unlucky? Soon the ship will sail, and I will have no way to pay the debt!"

"There is yet time," said Yaño reassuringly.

"How much? There has been no rain, and each day there is less water."

"I think two days more—maybe three."

"Madre de Dios!" whispered Trin in anguish. "It is not enough!"

In the morning he dove desperately, staying down longer and resting for shorter periods than ever before. Ripping oyster after oyster from the rocks, he filled his net-bag again and again, keeping pace with his Yaqui partner. In the last minutes before the low tide of midday, he found himself over the narrow fissure from which Yaño's silver-blue pearl had come.

The devil-snakes had risen out of its depths, but so great was his need of a pearl that he decided to risk their venom. Directly under him, the crack was no more than ten inches wide, but he eased his body down into it and felt the sharp rock scraping his chest and back, his knees and heels. Still he pushed down lower and lower, searching the cavities that pitted its rough walls.

A pocket a foot deep opened up under his hands, and peering into its shadows, he saw a clump of oysters, all of them very large and old. Trembling with excitement, he tore them loose, piling one upon another into the circle of his arms. Then pushing up carefully, blood seeping from a dozen lacerations, he swam with them to his net-bag. Placing them inside, he shot to the surface.

There was no time to search for more. Already, the Yaquis had shoved off, and Yaño and Paco were drawing up the nets. But surely in those ancient oysters there had to be a pearl—perhaps a rare one.

Piling the precious bag on top of the heaped up sacks of shells, Paco struck out for the tunnel, while Yaño and Trin, taking their places at the oars of the other two boats, followed in his wake. Negotiating the narrow passage, they emerged into the outer sea—to face disaster. For as they started down-coast, Paco let out a shrill cry of alarm.

"Marrayos! Santo Dios! They're coming at us!"

Turning, Trin saw them: five giant manta rays, heading straight for the dinghies. Swimming with their peculiar flying motion, the devilfish sped toward them, their immense diamond-shaped bodies just below the surface, the tips of their "wings" projecting above the water. In panic, Paco tried to veer out of their path, but as he swerved the dinghy, he collided with one of the onrushing mantas.

Its stern flipped into the air by the flap of the monster's wing, the little boat stood almost on end, its bows deep in the water; and in that dreadful moment before it righted itself, Trin's net-bag of unopened oysters slipped from its place on top of the sacks and fell into the sea. Trin watched in dismay as it disappeared, while the huge ray swam directly beneath him, its protuberant tips passing on each side of the dinghy.

Still clinging to the thwart, Paco gasped out his relief. "Sainted Virgin! I thought he would upset me!"

The five mantas had cruised by, and Trin stripped off his

shirt. "It's bad enough that he upset my oysters," he said grimly. "I'm going to get them!"

"Wait!" shouted Yaño, from the rear dinghy. "You can't! It's too deep!"

"And you are bleeding!" cried Paco. "Your blood will bring them back!"

But Trin had already plunged in, and if the shrill sound of Paco's fear reached him, he did not heed it, so intent was he on rescuing the oysters. Staying beneath the dinghy from which the net-bag had fallen, he swam down six fathoms—eight—ten, feeling the pressure increase, knowing that he was going deeper than he had ever gone before. And still there was no glimpse of the sea floor. His breath almost spent, he pushed on down desperately—another fathom—and another—but the murky depths were bottomless, and he knew he would have to go up.

Straining once more to see through the blue-gray mists, he spotted the dim silhouette of a large fish moving toward him. Lunging toward the surface, he swam frantically, unaware that the big fish had arced away, as alarmed as he. In his blind rush, his shoulder grazed against a pinnacle of rock that rose like a spire from the invisible sea floor, fathoms below. Pressing away from it, his hand encountered a heavy rope.

Could it be? Hope snapped him out of his panic instantly, and he followed the hanging length of hemp upward until it led him to the net-bag. Stopped in its fall by a jagged upthrust of rock, it hung perilously on the side of the pinnacle. Grasping the rope, he hauled it up swiftly until he held the end of it in his hand. Then thrusting toward the surface, he met Yaño lancing down to meet him. Together, they broke water.

:229

"You have found it?" asked the Yaqui, staring incredulously at the rope.

Trin nodded and waved it triumphantly at Paco. "It caught on a spire of rock!" he gasped, at length.

"Then black pearls cannot be bad!" declared Yaño. "You have had the luck of an angel. The bottom here is fifty fathoms down—maybe more!" Taking the rope from Trin, he swam toward his dinghy.

"Be careful!" warned Trin, following him. "If we make one wrong move, it may slip off the rock and be gone for good."

Climbing aboard, Trin steadied the boat while Yaño took in the rope until it was taut. Then bracing himself, the Indian tried to lift the bag—but it did not budge. Again, he pulled, and again. It was useless.

"For the love of God, hurry, before the marrayos return!" shouted Paco.

"It must be caught," said Trin. "I'll go down and loosen it."

Sucking in air, he jackknifed down to the pinnacle. One little section of the net was caught under a jagged outcropping, but as he struggled to free it, the bag was ripped loose and its weight thrown against his body, pressing him onto the rock. For one excruciating instant, he was pinned between them while shafts of pain stabbed through his back and chest; and then the great bag with its precious cargo swung out like a pendulum, hung for a perilous moment in space, and sank into the depths. Looking up, he was horrified to see the vast spreading body of a manta between him and the surface.

Gliding through the water, the enormous creature had swept away rope and net-bag, and now it hovered over him, a full twenty feet from wing-tip to wing-tip, its heavy, hornlike arms extending out on each side of its cavernous mouth. Paco's frightful story invaded his mind, and staring up at the great flaps of the ray, he saw himself being suffocated in their grip and devoured by that huge mouth, as the diver had been.

Half of his supply of breath had been knocked out of him, and fighting panic, he tried swimming away very slowly as he and Yaño had done with the tintereros, but with one slight stroke of its flippers, the beast was over him again. His body was shaking with the familiar heartbeat of fear, but he forced his mind to dismiss the terrifying image and think back to what he, himself, had told Paco that morning in the galley.

"I have heard that they hover and sometimes follow a diver wherever he moves, but it is because they are curious," he had said.

Now, trapped under the stare of the big cold eyes, he wasn't so sure. What was back of their gaze? Was it simple curiosity—or hunger? Seconds more without air, and one would be as fatal as the other.

Desperately his brain sought a means of escape. There could be no help from Paco or Yaño. If they shouted or slapped the water they might draw the other four mantas back to the scene; and the stab of a knife would only enrage the monster.

The thought of the knife sparked an idea. If the devilfish was merely curious perhaps it would work. He drew his knife from its sheathe and holding it at arm's length, swam slowly on an upward slant. The fish followed, slanting up with him, its immense expanse of white belly spreading out like a great smothering canopy.

As they sloped toward the surface, the blade caught the glint of sunlight, and Trin saw the eyes of the monster focus on it. Treading water, he held it above him, turning it back and forth to make a dazzle of dancing light. The huge calf eyes stared at it in fascination. But would they stay with it, apart from him?

Trin could no longer wait to find out. Bending his arm, he heaved the gleaming knife out and away from his body. It fell through the clear blue water, and still hovering over him, the manta watched it. In another moment, it would sink beyond the reach of sunlight, and the creature would lose interest. His chest cramping painfully, Trin waited—and then with one beat of its powerful wings, the ray swooped down after the glittering blade, its long tail trailing behind it.

Trin lunged to the surface, and Yaño, already in the water, caught him in strong supporting arms. Drawing him to his boat, he lifted him inboard.

"You are hurt, amigo," he said with concern, as he climbed in after him.

"It was the bag," gasped Trin, letting himself down carefully on the sacks of shells. "It swung against me and threw me onto the pinnacle."

"It may be you have a cracked rib—or a broken one—but even so, chico, you are lucky to be alive!"

"Not lucky enough," Trin groaned. "The oysters went down."

"But for the knife, you, too, would have gone down. It was a good trick."

The inquisitive manta came back again, the blade of the knife having lost its dazzle as it sank into the depths. For a while, he followed in friendly curiosity as Paco and Yaño rowed southward, pulling the third dinghy at the end of a towline, but finally he dropped away to join his fellows. Resting from his ordeal, Trin saw them in the distance, leaping high out of the water in their play to fall back with thundering belly-flops.

The harrowing incident had disproved Paco's story, but if Trin had escaped the legendary "death-embrace" of the great ray, nothing had happened to change his luck with the pearls. Whatever treasure the old oysters had held had gone to the bottom with them.

The encounter with the manta had taken time they could ill afford, and towing the extra dinghy had slowed their pace. When they reached the schooner, Zapo and Insa had already unloaded their cargo and were taking on supplies for another night inside the island.

Working quickly, Raúl helped Yaño and Paco get their shell aboard, while in his cabin, Fortino poured out a small glassful of brandy for Trin.

"Sip it slowly," he said. "It will warm you and ease the pain."

The smooth liquid, burning as it went down, was comforting, and sipping it, Trin told the captain of the unfortunate skirmish with the manta and the loss of the oysters.

"There may have been nothing in them," said Fortino consolingly. "Sometimes the old ones get tired of the pearls within their flesh and push them out. You may have lost nothing more than the shells."

"What of Zapo and Insa?" asked Trin. "Did they bring up pearls today?"

"No. Today they had no more luck than you."

"But they still bring them to you when they do get them?"

"Yesterday each man brought one," said Fortino. "In the small box inside the strongbox, I keep the two deerskin pouches that belong to them. When they come, I open the box and hand to each man his own pouch. He, himself, puts into it his pearls, and then, while they watch, I put the leather pouches back and lock them up."

"Do they look to see Yaño's pearls when you open it?"

"They *look*, though they pretend not to, but they see nothing. Their pearls are on one side of the box, and on the other side, hidden under the sheep's wool, would be yours and Yaño's—*if* they were there. But they are not!"

"They're not!" exclaimed Trin, in surprise. "Then where?"

"In this cabin there is a secret place—not so secret that it cannot be found by a clever thief, but more secret than the box," Fortino told him. "To find it would take time, and if the thieves trapped one of us here, alone, *time* might give the others a chance to come to his aid."

"They must have a plan, between them," said Trin, "and I have been trying to guess what it may be."

"Sí, I, too," said Fortino. "I have thought much about it, and I believe they will move against us, at night, here on the ship."

"But the Yaquis fear the blackness of the tunnel," Trin protested. "They will not come through it at night."

"And for that reason," said Fortino, "they will wait until the night tides are over, and they are all three here, together."

"That could be tomorrow night!"

"There is something else. While we still have water, I think they will wait to bring up more shell and pearls. But when the water is down to where we must sail . . ."

"How long will that be, padrino?"

"Sooner than I had thought. But we will have tomorrow here, and the next day."

"And after that we must sail?"

"Unless there is rain."

"I will pray for it," promised Trin. "Even a chubasco!"

"The thought of a chubasco may be in the back of their minds, too," said Fortino, "for in such a storm, they could not sail the ship without us. Because of that, I think they will wait until we are close to the shores of Baja."

"Then until we leave the island, we are safe."

"*If* that is their plan," said Fortino, "but who is to know?"

"Paco and Yaño will be ready with the dinghies," said Trin, rising, "and I am better now, for going back. The brandy has warmed me. Muchas gracias, padrino!"

Springing up the companion steps before the captain could stop him, he ran to the rail, but to his amazement, Yaño and Paco had pulled away without him and were already some one hundred yards downcoast.

"Amigos!" he shouted. "Wait!" And climbing onto the rail, he prepared to dive, but Raúl caught him and pulled him back.

"Let me go!" he stormed, struggling to break away from the grip of his friend.

"You must not go, Trinidad," insisted Fortino, hurrying across the deck toward them. "It is on my orders that they went without you. You are hurt, my son, and diving will be too painful. Today you must stay on the ship and rest."

"But I must dive!" Trin protested.

"You will dive better tomorrow. Today, you are not only hurt, but over-tired. Yaño has told me you have been pushing beyond your strength."

"But padrino, after this, there is only one more day! In one day, how can I hope to pay the debt?"

"Already, you have three pearls," Fortino reminded him. "That they are black is not important. They are *good*. The first is small, but the other two are maybe twenty grains, each one, and perfectly matched. A fine pair will bring many more pesos than two single pearls. And besides them, you have now to your credit a great many sacks of shells. When I have paid you for your share of the cargo and you have sold the pearls, I think you will have the pesos you need to pay your mother's debt."

"But to pay that debt is not enough!" insisted Trin. "I must also replace the great pearl of the Virgin."

"And to find a great pearl, chico, it is not how *many* oysters you bring up, but which ones," suggested Raúl. "All you need is *one*, if it is the right one."

Yaño and Paco were beyond his catching, and Trin surrendered. Fortino was right, he knew. His body was not only hurt, inside and out, but he was exhausted. Climbing into the captain's bunk, the little dog, Pepé, stretched out beside him, he sank into sleep.

In the late afternoon, he was wakened by a shout.

"El dorado!" The dolphinfish! And the voice had been Barraza's. All week he had been passing his time in sleeping and in fishing—not with hook and line but with an iron harpoon.

Whether it was true or not, Trin had the feeling that the magnificent dolphinfish was his guardian angel. Certainly it had led him into the island, and now the thought that Barraza might harpoon it filled him with horror. Leaping out of the bunk, he rushed up on deck. The Grizzly was at the rail, taking aim.

"Stop!" yelled Trin. "Not the dolphin!"

But the huge arm had already swung back to its full reach, and with a tremendous heave, Barraza sent the harpoon toward its target.

In the clear blue water, the golden fish had at that moment slipped under a mass of floating seaweed, and the harpoon missed its mark. Before Barraza could try again, the dolphin streaked away and disappeared.

On the far horizon, the setting sun burst through a thin veil of clouds, bringing back to Trin the memory of his night alone in the great barranca, his strange dream of oysters floating on the sea, and the rain that fell into them. In the dream, the sun had burst through the clouds, lighting the drops of water until they glowed with the colors of the rainbow. Could the dream have been a promise, he wondered? Could it have meant that he would, even yet, find a rainbow pearl for the Holy Virgin?

The evening was soft and warm, and Trin lay under the stars on his pallet of sailcloth while Barraza kept to the fo'c'sle and Raúl and the captain took their turns standing watch. An infant moon disappeared behind the dark mass of the island, and Trin drifted into a fitful sleep.

In the last dark hour before daybreak, he dreamed again of the statue of the Virgin, and was vaguely aware, even as he gazed at the blessed figure, that he had seen it all before: the exquisite Madonna, radiant with joy, the rainbow pearl glowing at her breast, the sainted faces in the paintings. Staring in fascination at the scene, he waited in dreadful suspense, not knowing what he waited for—and then it began, and he knew that it, too, was horribly familiar: the slow, strange transformation, as the wicked faces of Barraza and Insa and Zapo were superimposed upon the holy faces of the saints. Once more the shining robes of the Virgin turned black. The light went out of the pearl, and it became a death's-head.

A cry rose in his throat, but again, brutal hands seized him, and the sound was choked back before it could issue from his lips. Struggling to escape from the crushing grip, he began to waken—but the nightmare persisted. The dark bulk of a giant bent over him, and he fought to open his eyes and shut it out. It seemed to him that he *was* awake, that his eyes were open but still the huge figure remained, and he felt himself being lifted bodily from his canvas pallet. His arms were pinned behind him, and sharp pain stabbed through his chest—pain agonizingly real.

The yellow light of the lantern slanted grotesquely across the face of the giant, and it was as ugly as the face in the nightmare, but this was no longer a dream. The face, the hands, the crushing grip, *were* real. The giant was Barraza.

CHAPTER TWENTY-ONE

Trin was fully awake, his mind shocked into total awareness, but his body was bent backward in the constrictive embrace of Barraza's arms, and he could see nothing but the ugly face above him. The man was trying to clamp his wrists together behind him, and for that moment had taken his smothering hand from Trin's mouth. Sucking in air, Trin tried to shout a warning, but the bear-like arms crushed inward, and pain strangled the sound.

Before he could cry out a second time, the Grizzly had locked his wrists within the grip of one immense hand, and spinning his body in a half-turn, had again pressed the other over his mouth. Now the captain's cabin was within Trin's view, and he saw why there had been no warning. Raúl lay motionless upon the deck, his hands and feet tied.

Had his assailant been Barraza, Trin wondered, or had the Yaquis come out through the tunnel, in spite of their fear? And what of the captain? A hoarse cry rose from within the cabin and instantly the Grizzly lifted him off his feet, carried him to the top of the companionway, and flung him down the stairs. His body crashed to the floor, and involuntarily, he let out a moan as pain knifed through him.

"Are you an animal, that you treat the boy without feeling when you know he has been hurt?" Fortino demanded, from somewhere behind him.

Relief flooded through Trin at the sound of his voice. At least his padrino was still alive! He tried to scramble to his feet, but Barraza, coming down the steps, kicked him back to the floor.

"If I *am* an animal," he retorted arrogantly, "it is better that he learns it before he gives me trouble!"

The yellow beams filtering down the companion from the deck had been the only light, but now the Grizzly struck his flint, and a flame flickered along the wick of the kerosene lamp and took hold. In the center of the room, Trin saw Fortino seated in a chair, his arms bound to it with a heavy hemp, while Zapo stood over him, the edge of his knife blade touching the captain's throat. In the darkness, the sharp metal had nicked the flesh, and a tiny stream of blood had trickled down onto his shirt. Kneeling beside them, Insa was tying the old man's leg to the legs of the chair.

So the greed of the Yaquis *had* been stronger than their fear, Trin thought; or perhaps their refusing to come through the tunnel at night had been part of their plan all along. They had managed to climb aboard and surprise Raúl from behind, as he stood watch; then they had crept down into the cabin, overpowered the captain in his sleep, and forced him into the chair. They had done it all so stealthily that even the little dog had not been wakened until Trin's body thudded to the floor, and the captain spoke out.

But Pepé was aroused now, and snarling his hatred, he edged toward Barraza. Fearing for the animal's life, Trin rolled against him, and grasping his small, tense body in his arms, held him back forcibly.

"So this is how you show your 'friendship'!" Fortino was saying.

"It is friendship enough that you are still alive!" Barraza snorted. "Now tie up the boy," he told Insa, as the Yaqui tightened the rope around the captain's legs and knotted it.

His face stony, the Indian moved to carry out his command. The little dog snarled and lunged out at him, and struggling to hold him back, Trin did not see the Grizzly's hand go into the captain's pocket.

"Where is the key?" he roared suddenly.

"You are too late," declared Fortino. "It is already in the hands of your partners. My pocket was not hard to find, even in the dark."

Barraza's eyes blazed as he looked from Zapo to Insa. "Give it to me!" he commanded.

Insa rose to his feet, but he made no further move, and knife still in hand, Zapo stood staring back at Barraza, his face inscrutable. The silence stretched out between them, sharp as drawn swords, and boy and dog seemed forgotten.

"I will open the box!" said Zapo finally, his voice tight.

Barraza stared at him, mingled rage and astonishment in his eyes. For a taut moment, he seemed to measure his own brute power against the strength of the two Yaquis, and then he muttered, "Open it!"

Zapo moved to the strongbox at the foot of the captain's bunk and inserted the key in the lock. Turning it, he lifted the heavy lid, while Barraza stood over him, his body rigid with anger and distrust. Inside and clearly visible was the small wooden box. The Yaqui reached out to pick it up, and Insa moved toward them warily, his hand on his knife.

Trin's mouth was dry as paper, and his eyes sought Fortino's. Helpless in his chair, the captain was watching the three men, his face inscrutable, and Trin knew that he was bracing himself for the moment when they would open the box.

Suddenly it occurred to him that this was also the one moment when he might be able to make a getaway. In his arms, the dog was silent now, but if he were to release him, the little animal would rush at Barraza, and the man would kill him. Yet he could hardly hope to escape up the steps with the dog in his arms. For a fraction of a second, he considered his chances. Here in the cabin, pitted against three men, he would be as helpless as Fortino, but if he could reach Raúl and free him . . .

He felt for his knife. It was missing! Barraza must have stripped him of it. Without a knife, he could hardly hope to work quickly enough to liberate Raúl before they caught up with him. Obviously the Yaquis had knocked him out before they tied him; they could have killed him with a single blow. Trin had seen it happen once, on the hacienda.

Zapo was opening the little box, and the attention of the three men was on it. It was now—or never.

Silently, he crept toward the companionway. The Yaqui's fingers were already exploring the sheep's wool inside the box. Still clutching the dog, he rose to his feet and started up the steps. He was halfway up when with the speed of lightning, Insa whirled and leapt after him. Seizing his ankles, the Indian threw him back to the floor. Frightened by the crashing fall, Pepé struggled to break free, and half-stunned by pain, Trin clung to him frantically.

"Try that again, and I'll cut out your gizzard!" the Yaqui

hissed, as he bent to loop a rope around Trin's ankles.

"Where are they?" Barraza was thundering.

Insa sprang to his feet, more intent on the gems than on the knotting of the rope, and Trin saw that Zapo was shoving two small deerskin pouches into his pants pocket.

"The pearls of Zapo and Insa are there, exactly as they have been—each man's gems in his own pouch," Fortino was saying.

"I have seen them," said Barraza, confronting the captain menacingly. "Now you will tell us what you have done with the others."

Flinging aside the little container that held the pearls, Zapo began to ransack the strongbox.

"The others do not concern you," said Fortino.

"They concern me so much," said Barraza, "that I will kill you before I leave this cabin without them. Insa! Let the capitán feel the blade of your knife, so he may know this is no game we play!"

Trin's heart contracted, and he held his breath as the Indian drew his knife and pressed it against Fortino's throat.

"Only I know where the pearls are," said Fortino, "and cutting my throat will not lead you to them."

Zapo had scattered the contents of the strongbox on the floor, in his search, and now he rose, empty-handed. "There is nothing," he muttered.

"You already have what is yours," Fortino argued, speaking with difficulty against the pressure of the blade. "In your pouches there are many good pearls, and in the hold, many sacks of shells that will bring you more pesos than you have ever had before. You have no need to rob Yaño and Trin of what they have earned by hard labor."

Was the captain playing for time? Trin wondered. Did he hope that Yaño and Paco might come to their aid? Perhaps they did not even know that the Yaquis had slipped out through the tunnel. Had the Indians attacked them first? The thought of what might already have happened inside the island hit Trin with the impact of a physical blow.

"We're wasting time!" snapped Barraza. "Which is it to be, Capitán, the pearls—or the knife?"

"It will not be the pearls," declared Fortino flatly. "I have no more right to surrender them than you have to steal them."

"We're not speaking of rights!" said Barraza. "One more minute, old man, and then I will give the signal!" He drew his fingers across his throat. "After that, we will find them without you!"

"Tell him, padrino!" Trin cried. "For the love of God, let him have the pearls! Mine are nothing, and Yaño has said no man must die for his!"

"To die of a knife at the throat is easy," said Zapo evenly. "One cut and it is over. But for a man as stubborn as the capitán, there is a better way!"

"Sí," agreed Insa, taking his knife from the captain's throat, "a way that takes as many hours as there are pearls —until a man begs for death."

"Until a man *must* die," Zapo added, "because he is not fit to live."

"Please, padrino, I beg you!" pleaded Trin desperately. "They are savage men, and once they begin . . . Please! Don't let them begin!"

"The boy understands the minds of Indians," said Barraza, "but you, Capitán—you are a stupid old man who will not believe until you *see!*"

He swung around suddenly, and seizing Trin by the arm, jerked him to his feet. In the same instant, the dog sprang free and with a wild lunge, sank his teeth into Barraza's leg. The man let out a yell of rage and pain and tried to fling him off, but Pepé clung tenaciously, his teeth sinking deeper into the flesh.

"Get him off!" Barraza shrieked. "Get him off and kill him!"

Swiftly, Zapo leaned down and pressed his hands around the animal's neck.

"No! You're choking him!" yelled Trin, and heard the protesting voice of the captain rise with his own. Breaking away from Barraza's grip, he tore at the Yaqui's hands, but they only tightened.

The rope that Insa had slipped around his ankles had loosened in the struggle, and yanking it off, Trin swung back his leg and kicked the Indian full in the face. Staggered by the unexpected blow, the Yaqui fell back, and Trin scooped up the gasping dog, dropped him into the strongbox, and pushed down the lid.

Cursing in his native tongue, Zapo rose to his feet and lunged at Trin, his powerful hands going for his throat, but Barraza pulled the boy out of his reach.

"Wait!" he commanded. "We have a better use for him! Draw your knife and we will show the capitán how we mean to get the pearls!"

"Sí!" agreed Zapo. "It will be better!"

"Then begin!" Barraza snapped.

The two Yaquis sprang at Trin and flattened him against the cabin wall, their knives ready.

"Now, Capitán," said Barraza, "you will see how it is done!"

"If you harm that boy," roared Fortino, straining against his bonds, "I swear by the sword of St. Michael that you will never get one pearl!"

"To wait was your idea," sneered the Grizzly, "and now I am not sure that I can stop it!"

"You'll stop it if you want the gems!" snapped the captain.

"So at last you are ready, old man."

"I am ready! Let the boy go!"

"Where are the pearls?" demanded Barraza.

"Not while the boy is in the hands of your savages."

"Let him go!" Barraza commanded.

Reluctantly, the Yaquis released Trin and he moved to the captain's side.

"Now, order your men to bring the strongbox to me."

"The strongbox!" exclaimed Barraza suspiciously.

"It's a trick!" Zapo growled. "There is nothing in it!"

"But the dog," Insa reminded him.

"If you want the pearls," said Fortino, "you will do as I tell you!"

"Bring it!"ordered the Grizzly, "but if this *is* a trick, Capitán, I warn you . . ."

"It is no trick!"

Lifting the box, the Yaquis carried it to Fortino and placed it on the floor beside him.

"Now—step back!" Fortino ordered.

Eyeing him distrustfully, they moved back.

"In a moment, I will tell the boy how to find the pearls," said the captain, "but first, Trinidad, you will take the tooth of the sperm whale from my desk."

Zapo growled in protest, but Barraza silenced him, and Trin crossed to the desk and picked up the petrified tooth.

"Now, lift the lid of the strongbox and put the tooth between it and the box, that Pepe may have more air to breathe."

"Caramba!" bellowed the Grizzly, as Trin complied.

: 246

"We will not wait for dogs to breathe! Give me the pearls, or I will give your boy to the Yaquis!"

"The pearls are next," said Fortino, "but until the box was moved, he could not get to them."

Instantly the three men moved to the spot where the box had stood, at the foot of the captain's bunk, their eyes searching the floor for some sign of the place of hiding, but there was nothing visible.

"I have told you to stand back!" commanded Fortino.

"I give the orders!" declared Barraza angrily. "You will tell *me* how to find them!"

"If you choose," said Fortino, "but it will be interesting to see who gets them, you—or your friends. The pearls are not hidden under the floor, but in the end of the bunk."

Barraza sprang forward, his great bulk edging out the smaller Yaquis, and kneeling, he felt along the teak paneling. At the bottom, a section of the panel slid away from his massive hand, and instantly he thrust his fist into the opening, blocking the hands of the Indians.

He rose to his feet with a tin box in his hand. The Yaquis rose with him, their bodies tense and their eyes watchful, as he lifted the lid and pushed away the sheep's wool covering. Underneath it lay Trin's black pearls and Yaño's. Only the rainbow was missing.

"Now you have them all, except the great one," declared Fortino. "That is not on the ship."

Barraza stared at him, his face contorting with fury. "You cheater!" he bellowed. "By all that is holy, you'll pay for this!" Closing the box, he rammed it into his pocket and lunged toward the captain, but the Yaquis were there ahead of him.

"We have waited too long," said Zapo. He raised his knife, pointing it toward the captain's body.

"Wait!" screamed Trin in terror, throwing himself against the Yaqui. "He's told you the truth. The rainbow isn't here. It's in the island!"

"You lie!" growled Barraza, seizing him.

"No! It's true! The pearl is with Yaño!"

"It is *not* with Yaño," said Zapo. "We have searched."

"You didn't find it, but he has it on him," insisted Trin, "and he will trade it for the capitán's life. You have only to ask him!"

"Yaño will trade nothing," said Insa. "He is dead!"

"Dead!" Trin's heart sank.

"And you lie!" the Indian went on. "The pearl is not on his body. It is here on the ship. Paco has told us!"

"Paco doesn't know," lied Trin, fearing for the life of his friend—if indeed Paco was still alive. "But *I* know! The pearl is in Yaño's body. It was I who sewed it into the wound on his hip."

"The wound!" breathed Zapo, in amazement.

The Yaquis stared at each other.

"The wound!" Barraza murmured after them, taking the idea in slowly.

The eyes of the Indians held for a fraction of a second, and then as one man, they seized the Grizzly and threw him to his knees. With a deadly chopping blow, Insa smashed his clenched fists down on the back of Barraza's neck, and as the big man swayed forward, Zapo reached into his pocket and drew out the tin box of pearls.

While the Yaqui stuffed it into his own pocket, Insa raised his knife to plunge it into the Grizzly's back, but the huge bearlike body was not so easily felled. Twisting onto his side, Barraza yanked at the Indian's leg, and the knife missed its mark.

With the fury of an enraged beast, Barraza was struggling to his feet, and Zapo fled up the stairs. Insa broke away from the big man's grasp to follow him, and powered by his greed, Barraza staggered after them.

Swiftly, Trin found a knife and cut Fortino's bonds; then he crept up the companionway, hoping to free Raúl before their attackers might return. By the light from the lantern, he saw Barraza at the rail, harpoon in hand. His arm swung back, and with a mighty heave, he flung the harpoon seaward. There was a sickening scream of pain—and then silence. Swinging over the rail, Barraza dropped into the water.

Trin knelt and cut the ropes from Raúl's hands and feet. The young seaman was beginning to revive and Fortino, coming up the companionway steps, would take care of him.

"They've gone over the rail!" he told the captain, as he ran toward it.

Faint beams from the lantern reached out beyond the deck to the water below, and in the dim light he saw the three dinghies of the Yaquis. In one of them, Zapo was cutting the towline that linked him with the second boat; then grabbing the oars, he began to row away from the schooner. In the dinghy he had cut loose, the body of Insa lay slumped over the gunwale, his head submerged in the sea. The harpoon had entered his back, between the shoulder blades.

Barraza was swimming toward the little boat, and as Trin watched, he reached it, climbed inboard, and pushed the body of the Yaqui into the water. The dinghy was loaded, not with sacks of shells, but with what looked like provisions. Taking up the oars, the Grizzly struck out after Zapo, pulling the third dinghy behind him. As it passed through the beam of light, Trin saw what looked like the body of a man, tied and gagged, lying in the bottom.

"*Paco!*" he whispered to the captain, who had come to

the rail. "I'll try to cut him loose!" He ran down the deck until he was beyond reach of the lantern's glow, and dropped into the water. Barraza could not have seen him, nor heard him over the sound of his oars, and he swam with frantic strokes for the little boat. Overtaking it in the darkness, he hauled himself up over the stern and slid down beside Paco.

"Lie low and don't make a sound," he whispered. "Barraza is towing the dinghy so that we can't follow him."

Removing the gag, he began to cut the ropes that bound his friend's hands and feet.

"Santo Dios, but I am glad to see you!" breathed Paco. "Raúl—and the capitán—are they safe, too?"

"Both safe," Trin told him.

"May the saints be praised! I thought you would be dead, all three!"

"And I, you!" whispered Trin. "But Yaño . . ."

"I'm not sure."

"You mean there's a chance that he's still alive?"

"Sí. They got their knives into him, but he broke away, and in the darkness they lost him."

"But if he is there—and wounded!"

Barraza was pulling powerfully in the race to reach the tunnel before the rising tide could close it, and still Trin had not severed the towline.

"Are you not going to cut us free?" asked Paco.

"Not yet. It will be better if he does it himself. The weight of the boat is slowing him down, and when he gets beyond sight of the schooner, I think he will leave us behind. Then we'll pull for the crack."

"The crack!" gasped Paco. "Now? In the *dark?*"

"It's our only chance to help Yaño. If he's still alive, they'll kill him. Zapo and Barraza are racing to get the pearl, and I've got to get to Yaño first!"

"But amigo," protested Paco, "even in the *day*, you risk death if you go into the crack. In the blackness of night, it will be impossible!"

"Not for me!"

As Trin had predicted, the dinghy slowed to a stop, and he moved to take up the oars.

"I will take them!" insisted Paco. "But it's loco. You won't reach Yaño. You'll only die yourself!"

"Row, amigo, row!" Trin commanded.

"Did they get the pearls?" Paco asked, as he dipped the oars quietly.

"Sí. They have all but the rainbow."

"And now they will get that!"

"Let them have it!" said Trin. "It's Yaño's life that matters. But unless I get to him first, they will have *both!*"

The first gray light of day paled the stars, and a fresh breeze sprang up from the south. Pulling safely around the reef, Paco brought the dinghy to the base of the cliffs where, on the first morning, they had searched for the crack.

"It was a little farther to the west," said Trin. "I swam many yards before I found it."

"How will you find it now, without the sunlight to guide you?"

"Now I know where to look, and the tide is rising. The pull of the current will tell me. Wait! Go slow. I think it was somewhere here."

Paco rested on his oars, and the boat glided forward. "Chico," he said, "for one minute, listen to me. I want to help Yaño as much as you. It is because of me that he is hurt. I was standing watch while he slept, and I saw them coming at me out of the water. But it was the same as on the first night, when the gray shapes came, and it was only the fog. Tonight, I thought it was the fog again."

Scanning the base of the cliff for some clue that might lead him to the crack, Trin barely took in the words.

"I will be sick in my heart if he dies," Paco went on, "but if you die, too, it will be worse. The sea is dark, and the predators are still on the prowl."

"*You* listen, amigo," said Trin, cutting in. "There is no time to be afraid. I made it before, and I'm a better diver, now. You wait here, in the dinghy. I'll go through and try to reach Yaño ahead of them. If I make it, I'll try to bring him out through the crack."

He slid over the gunwale, and clinging to it, he sucked in air. The pain of his injured ribs stabbed sharply, but in successive gasps, he filled his lungs and pushed under. Jackknifing down into the gloomy waters, he swam blindly, probing the depths in search of the swirling eddy that would sweep him into the crack.

CHAPTER TWENTY-TWO

Luck was with him, for almost immediately Trin was caught up in the powerful current, and pulling with it, he swam into the turbulent blackness. As before, the roar of the sea was like thunder in his head, and the smothering seconds stretched out interminably, but the thought of Yaño filled his mind, and he pushed forward, reaching out with each stroke for the rock wall against which he had crashed on that first morning.

His lungs were nearly empty when at last he was slammed against it, and surrendering to the racing waters, he let himself be swept around the long curve of the passage and into the lagoon. Lunging upward, he broke the surface and gasped in air.

Overhead, seabirds in the hundreds were winging out from the cliffs, their cries piercing the silent air, and to the east, the sky was brightening. Trin scanned the gray waters for the dinghies of Zapo and Barraza, but they were nowhere insight. He had beaten them! He struck out for the beach, and realized that it was strangely bare. The three boats of Yaño and Paco were missing. Apparently the Yaquis had towed them out through the tunnel, so that if Yaño had survived their attack, he would have no means of escape. Certainly if he was badly knifed, he could not swim out.

Keeping a watchful eye to the north, where the enemy must emerge from the tunnel, Trin searched the narrow curve of sand and the rocky rubble that backed it, but he could find no sign of Yaño. Fleeing his attackers, in the darkness, had he taken refuge in the waters of the lagoon and drowned there? Trin stared across their gray surface to the ring of high, sheer cliffs that encircled them. In all the island, there was no other hiding place, unless . . .

He spun around to face the trail that climbed steeply up from the south end of the beach to the crags above. If Yaño was still alive, he *had* to be there.

Zapo and Barraza had not yet appeared, and Trin sped down the strand, keeping to the shallow water at its edge so that he would leave no revealing footprints. At the approach to the trail, he saw blood on the stone, and ripping off his shirt, he dipped it in the water, and sponged the spot clean.

The path rose sharply, slanting up the face of the cliff, with a sheer drop to the lagoon below. Along its length, as it cut to the south, there was nothing to hide a fugitive from view, but halfway up, it switched back to the north, and on its upper reaches an occasional thorn bush or cactus had found enough soil in the hollows of the volcanic rock to take root. Perhaps Yaño had found shelter beneath one of those.

Trin climbed quickly, and again saw blood on the stone, but the water had dripped out of his shirt and there was little he could do to wash it away. Once Yaño's pursuers started up the path, they would know they were on the trail of their quarry. Panting, Trin reached the switchback and turned north. A dinghy had come out of the tunnel and was heading south toward the cove! At that distance, it was impossible to identify the man at the oars, and Trin could only hope that the boatman hadn't spotted his figure outlined against the exposed face of the cliff. He dropped to his knees and crawled up the rough ascent. Unless he could overtake Yaño immediately and get him down into the lagoon, there would be no chance of escaping through the crack.

The path turned, following a deep cleft in the rock, and a clump of thorn bushes gave him hope, but though bloodstains revealed that Yaño had rested there, he had moved on.

The man in the dinghy was pulling southward with powerful strokes, and the bulk of him suggested that it was Barraza. Why wasn't Zapo close behind? Trin wondered. Had he and the Grizzly come to grips enroute to the tunnel, or perhaps within the dark passage itself, and Barraza come out the victor?

The trail twisted out again to continue its sharp ascent for more than one hundred yards up the face of the cliff, with only one giant cactus plant to offer shelter between Trin and the top. Carefully, he inched upward, ready to freeze if the boatman should turn his head and raise his eyes, but the man was intent on reaching the cove, and he did not look up.

Trin had climbed to within twenty yards of the cactus when he thought he saw a figure at its base. Rising to his feet, he ran up the trail in one wild spurt, to find Yaño sprawled face down on the rock. Trin's heart turned over, but kneeling beside him, he saw that his friend was still breathing. Struggling to reach the shelter of the cactus, he had collapsed in the shadow of its many tall spires.

At Trin's touch, the Yaqui started up in an instinctive

effort to defend himself, but Trin pressed him back. "Don't move, amigo. I've come to help you!"

"Trin?" breathed Yaño, staring at him in dazed unbelief. "But—how?"

"There's no time to talk," said Trin hastily. "We are safe, all of us, but they took the pearls, and now—" He peered down at the lagoon, through the ribs of the cactus, and identified the boatman. "Now Barraza has come to find you."

"Only Barraza?"

"Sí. He speared Insa with the harpoon, and somewhere between here and the ship I think he has killed Zapo. He knows the pearl is in your wound. I had to tell them, to save the capitán."

"It was what I ordered you to do," said Yaño. "But how is it that *you* are here?"

"I came in through the crack. I thought if I could get here ahead of them, I might be able to take you out, but now it's too late."

"Even with more time, amigo, we could not have made it against the current." Yaño pulled himself up to look through the screen of spires, and Trin saw that his shirt was torn and soaked with blood at shoulder and waist. "But there is still time for you to get away," Yaño went on. "Take your knife, Trinidad, and cut out the pearl."

"Are you loco?" demanded Trin.

"Do as I tell you!" commanded the Yaqui. "Cut out the pearl, and while Barraza is searching among the rocks behind the beach, run down the trail to the switchback. From there, it is a forty foot drop into the lagoon, and you can jump."

"I will not cut out the pearl—or jump!" Trin told him, almost angrily. "I came to help you, not to run!"

"Listen to me, amigo!" Yaño pleaded. "To stay is useless! He will only kill us both. But if you take the pearl and go into the lagoon, then I will let him see me, here on the trail, and while he is climbing up to reach me, you can swim to the dinghy and head for the tunnel. I will hold him off—"

"How?" Trin cut in sharply.

"There's no time to tell you, but there is a way!" insisted Yaño. He was reaching painfully for his knife, and knowing he meant to cut out the pearl, Trin snatched it from him.

"Tell me the way, and we'll do it together!"

Below them, Barraza had beached the boat and was cautiously moving up the sandy slope toward the rocks.

"Chico!" pleaded Yaño. "I have no strength to argue!"

"Then it's settled! If we can hold him off just a little while, it may be enough. He has to get out before the tide closes the tunnel, and it's the day of new moon."

"Sí," agreed Yaño. "The tide will be higher."

"There are provisions in the boats of Zapo and Insa," said Trin. "I think they planned to cut out Barraza and head in the darkness for Baja, and now he must follow their plan before Raúl and Paco and the capitán can catch up with him."

"To find a dinghy in an infinity of sea would not be easy," admitted Yaño, "but here, he would be trapped. You are right, amigo. If we can hold him off, we may yet get out alive."

Barraza had abandoned his search of the beach, and now he stood at the water's edge, studying it thoughtfully.

"He is gaging the level of the tide in the tunnel," said Trin, watching him through the spires. "Maybe he will think you have drowned and go."

Raising himself up with an effort, Yaño again scanned

the shore. "No. There is still time to come up the trail. In a minute he will start, and we must be ready."

"How?" demanded Trin.

"Look there, where the rock juts out," said the Yaqui, indicating a point some ten feet beyond them, up the path.

Following his glance, Trin saw a great slab of stone jutting out from the trail like a platform, and on it was piled a rubble of rock that had broken off from the cliff above it, eroded by the battering of many storms.

"A man lying on that ledge," Yaño went on, "will be directly over Barraza as he comes up."

Looking down, Trin realized it was true; the trail doubled back on itself all the way down to the beach. A man on that ledge with stones for ammunition . . .

"He's coming!" said Yaño, struggling to his knees.

"Get down!" Trin ordered him.

"It doesn't matter if he sees us," said Yaño, gasping from the exertion. "He will know soon enough that we are here." Painfully, he began to crawl up the trail.

"Stay, amigo!" Trin pleaded. "I can hurl down the rock!"

"I will tell you when!" insisted Yaño. "But go—and be ready!"

In a crouching run, Trin covered the distance to the ledge, and saw that Barraza, approaching the foot of the trail, had already spotted him. In the gray light of this hour before sunrise, he would think the running figure was Yaño.

Crawling onto the stone platform, Trin pulled the larger chunks of split rock out of the rubble and pushed them toward the edge. The effort sent a stab of pain through his chest, but he knew it was nothing to the agony Yaño was suffering as he crept up the trail.

Inching out to the rim, he peered down to the lower trail. Unaware of the danger from above, Barraza was running up the steep incline in his haste to reach Yaño and the pearl. Soon he would be beneath the ledge. Trin's heart pounded violently, and he gripped the stone nearest him.

"Wait!" warned Yaño, from behind him. "It is too soon! It must come down in front of him!"

Or *on* him, Trin thought. Already Barraza had brought death to three men, and if he got safely past the barrage of rocks, he might add two more. Trin's hands were wet with sweat as he waited for the Yaqui's signal. If it came too late, the Grizzly would soon be upon them.

"Lie flat," breathed Yaño, "and when you push, just ease the stone over, or it will miss the trail and bounce into the lagoon."

Barraza was climbing higher, and still Yaño waited.

"*Now!*" he commanded suddenly.

Trin pushed, and the heavy chunk dropped over the edge, while unknowing, Barraza continued to run toward it. Trin stopped breathing. It seemed as if the man was going to get safely *past* it! Barely in time, the falling rock crashed onto the trail no more than four feet in front of him, and Barraza sprang back. Immediately, Trin grasped another stone.

Flattening himself against the face of the cliff, Barraza looked up toward them, and seeing the out-jutting ledge, recognized the point of danger. His eyes went back to the place where the rock had crashed, and Trin guessed that he was measuring his chances, wondering whether he could get past the spot before another could fall.

"Again!" commanded Yaño.

Trin pushed the second one over and seized a third. The hurtling rock struck against the cliff and glanced toward the man, and he fled back down the trail, stopping only when he was well out of reach. Hugging the cliff, he stared upward, studying the distance from overhanging ledge to trail. After a moment, he began to edge up slowly.

"Now it will be tricky!" warned Yaño. "He will try to get us to spend our stones while he can still spring back to safety. We must wait!"

"But if he comes too close, he can get past while the rock is falling!"

"Sí, that is the danger," the Yaqui admitted. "If he had dared, he could have made it while the second one went down."

Yaño pulled himself toward one of the stones that lay poised on the rim. "I will be ready with this one, if it should be that two are needed."

Together they watched as Barraza moved up the trail foot by foot, his eyes on the ledge, and again Yaño let him come almost directly beneath them before he gave the command. The deadly missile dropped, and the man sprang back.

Twice more, the three of them played the tricky game of timing until Trin and Yaño had only the two stones they gripped in their hands. Below them, Barraza was creeping dangerously near to the spot where the rocks had been falling. Another yard, and he might be able to make it, even as the stone hurtled toward him. For an instant, he took his eyes from the ledge to check the mark of the tide upon the sand, and they knew he was growing desperate. Craftily, he began to inch forward, daring the final margin of safety, and Trin's body stiffened with tension.

"*Now!*" barked Yaño, and as Trin pushed the rock over, he saw Barraza run beneath it and knew he would pass safely before it crashed. But in the same second that he had given the command, Yaño had risen to his knees and heaved the second rock to the south, ahead of the man. Crashing into it, Barraza staggered over the edge of the trail and plunged into the lagoon.

Yaño sagged forward, his strength spent, and swiftly Trin reached out to catch him and draw him back from the edge. The seconds passed, and he watched with held breath the spot where Barraza had gone down. One minute— two—three. It was over.

"We are safe, amigo!" he told the Yaqui, and crossing himself, he murmured, "Gracias, Señor Padre!"

Masses of black clouds, boiling up from the south, warned that a storm was imminent, and Trin knew that he must somehow get Yaño down the trail and back to the schooner before she would have to slip out to sea.

From far below, he heard a cry, and his heart stopped. It couldn't be! Once more, he searched the place where Barraza had disappeared, but there was only the empty, breeze-ruffled water.

The cry came again, and he caught the word "chico." Scanning the width of the lagoon, he spotted Paco, treading water. Minutes later, they came together on the beach.

"Today, I am a very brave man—braver than a matador!" gasped Paco, as he came out of the water. "For the first time in my life, I have committed an act of great courage. And what good is it?" He shrugged his shoulders. "I am too late. I have risked my life in the black hell of the crack for nothing!"

"You came through the crack?" asked Trin, astounded.

"I came—and I saw!" said Paco. "It was a close thing!"

"Sí!" admitted Trin. "Until the second stone of Yaño, we

were finished! But you did not risk your life for nothing, amigo. You have come just in time to help me bring him down from the ledge."

With stakes and a blanket from their camp, they fashioned a stretcher, while Trin told Paco all that had happened.

"But if Barraza killed Zapo, then he must have the pearls in the dinghy—or *on* him." Paco's eyes met Trin's.

"We will look in the dinghy," said Trin, "after we bring Yaño down."

As they hurried up the trail, the threatening clouds rolled out in all directions, filling the sky over their heads. Staring up at them, Paco said, "Have you thought, chico, that it was the same, eighty years ago? The men killed for the pearl, and then a storm drove them to sea, and after that—" He paused, remembering with horror the fate of the men who had died on the cannibal island. "If those clouds should bring a chubasco—or a cordonazo—"

"They will bring us only the rain we need to fill our casks," Trin said hopefully.

Reaching Yaño, they lifted him gently onto the stretcher, and moving with great caution, carried him down the trail to the shore. The mark of the tide on the sand was high; that meant the tunnel was filling rapidly. Eyeing the dinghy with its load of provisions, Paco said, "I think there is no time to search here for the pearls. It will be quicker if—" He looked meaningfully toward the lagoon.

"Sí," agreed Trin somberly. "I will go."

He walked into the water and swam toward the spot where the Grizzly had gone down.

After a moment, Paco shouted, "Wait!" and plunging in, he caught up with Trin. "If a man is brave as a bull, then he has no choice!" he declared. "I will go with you!"

In the roughened waters, they did not see Barraza until they were almost directly over him. His pant leg had snagged on a small pinnacle of rock, and he floated face down, like some strange, ungainly mammal.

"We will go together, one on each side!" said Paco.

Sucking in air, they jackknifed down. The sea garden was gloomy and menacing under the sullen sky, and Trin felt a shiver of apprehension as he approached the body. Reaching into a pocket, he found the tin box of pearls, while on the other side Paco drew out the two deerskin pouches of the Yaquis. There was a small movement inside the collar of the man's shirt, and in horror, they shot upward and raced for the shore.

"What was it?" asked Paco, as they came out on the sand.

"A devil-serpent!" said Trin. "I saw the stripes of it wound around his neck!"

Easing Yaño into the boat, they rowed full speed for the tunnel. As they headed down the channel, they came upon the dinghy of Zapo and took it in tow. In the narrow passage, the swirling waters were a bare eighteen inches from the top, and lying on their backs, they pressed with their hands against the overhanging stone to push their way through.

When at last they emerged, they saw *La Virazón* bearing around the northwest corner of the island. The breeze had freshened and they pulled for her through rising seas. The vessel hove to, and with Raúl's help, they hoisted Yaño aboard, and climbing up after him, hauled up the dinghies.

The schooner was clear of the island and well under way when the storm struck. Lightning streaked across the livid sky, there was a great clap of thunder, and the clouds opened. Rain poured down in torrents, filling the empty water casks, and the ship lay under easy sail waiting for the calm that would herald the end of the southeaster.

Standing at the rail in the downpour, Trin stared out over the wind-whipped waves and knew that he could never go back to the island. Not even for a great pearl would he enter the secret lagoon, with its mysterious aura of evil.

The captain put his head out of the companionway and called him into the cabin. Yaño was lying in the bunk, his wounds bound with clean strips of white cambric, while Pepé slept contentedly at his feet.

"The rainbow was giving Yaño pain," said Fortino, "and I have cut it out for him." He held the precious gem between his thumb and forefinger, and even in the subdued light, Trin could see its extraordinary lustre.

"Hold out your palm," the captain ordered, and as Trin complied, he dropped the pearl into it.

The jewel felt warm to his hand, as if there were, indeed, a glowing spark within its layers of iridescent nacre, and gazing in wonder at its lovely shape and orient, he thought it must be the most magnificent pearl that had ever come out of the sea.

"It is yours," said Yaño.

Trin turned to him in puzzlement, sure he had misunderstood the words he had heard.

"You will take it back to Cinco Ríos for the statue of the Holy Virgin."

"But you're not going to die!" protested Trin, in confusion. "Soon you will be well, to go wherever you want to go, or buy whatever—"

"Sí, soon I will be well," Yaño cut in, "and I will have no need of a pearl that weighs more than one hundred grains. In the capitán's secret place, I have many others—pearls to buy more than I will ever need; but this one—it is too rare for buying. It is only for *giving*. I will give it to you, and you will give it to the Virgin, and with such a gift, Don Gregorio cannot fail to make your family free."

"But I have no right to such a gift!" Trin told him. "It is too big."

"If it were ten times as big, amigo," Yaño insisted, "it would not be as big as the gift you have given me. Because of you, I have my life."

"Take the pearl, my son," Fortino said. "You have earned it! And when we have sold the cargo, we will sail across the sea to Altata and ride inland together, the three of us, to Cinco Ríos. You will pay the debt of your mother —and of your brother—and when we ride back, your family will ride with us."

The calm came before daybreak. The rain stopped, the wind changed, and when the sun rose, the little schooner was running before a light, steady breeze, her course set for the great pearling port of La Paz, to the south.

A month later, on the other side of the sea, *La Virazón* was once more sailing northward. Taking his turn at the helm, Trin marveled that it had all happened exactly as Fortino had said it would. In La Paz, the cargo of shells and pearls had brought a good price, and they had sailed on to Altata, and together had ridden inland to the vast hacienda. With his own pesos, he had paid the debt that had for so long held his family in bondage, and then with the great rainbow, he had replaced the pearl that Cesar and Gonzalo had stolen. Doña Leona, herself, had taken him into the chapel so that he might present it to the Holy Virgin.

Later, he would keep his promise to his sister, Taresa,

but now, with his family on board, he was steering for Turtle Bay and a life that would be free.

As the little ship pushed through the swells, a school of dolphinfish leapt from the deep blue water to rise in a golden arch across her course, their brilliant rainbow colors shimmering in the sunlight; and to the east, Trin saw the land of mangrove-fringed lagoons and glistening white beaches—the land that was home.